BEN ARCHER

and

THE TOREQ SON

The Realm of Stars.

Rae Knightly

For information, go to :
www.raeknightly.com

ISBN 978-1-989605-21-9 (paperback)
ISBN 978-1-989605-20-2 (hardcover)
ISBN 978-1-989605-22-6 (ebook)
ISBN 978-1-989605-38-7 (audiobook)

Published by PoCo Publishers

Cover design by Pintado
Book formatting by Derek Murphy (CreativIndie)

Second edition: March 2021

For the stars
we can no longer see.

CONTENTS

CHAPTER 1 *New York City*

An unprecedented downpour battered the City of New York. Citizens hunkered in their homes; their sleep disturbed as they wondered how they would get to work the next morning. Lightning and thunder rattled windows and illuminated a sky as black as swirling coffee.

Secretary-General Adhira Prabhakar turned her chair away from the window of her thirty-second-floor office and listened to the persisting storm. Her eyes fell on the pile of documents stacked on her desk. She sighed and lifted the first folder. It held one of a dozen urgent reports that had come in during the past week, with unnerving reports of sudden, catastrophic droughts in Central Africa, abnormal flooding in Europe and the forming of a category five hurricane—called

Hurricane Zeta—that was projected to flatten Cuba and Florida.

The head of the United Nations placed her glasses over her nose and had just begun reading the newest report when a piercing sound cut through the noise of the rain.

Sirens!

Startled, Adhira let the pen slip out of her hand. She listened, tense as an arrow. Was this a drill? No, she would have known beforehand. *But, then...*

A United Nations Police Officer erupted into her office. "Code red!" he barked, saluting with the tips of his fingers touching the blue beret on his head. "Ma'am! Follow me, please!"

Adhira jumped to her feet.

Code red!

Code red meant imminent danger. Something major was happening. Get to safety first, then ask questions.

Forcing herself to act calmly, she headed for a safe on her back wall, pressed a code to open it, and pulled out highly classified documents that needed to stay by her side at all costs.

"Ma'am!" the Officer repeated, the urgency in his voice palpable.

Adhira would not succumb to panic. She

ignored him and finished what she was doing. Stuffing the documents into her briefcase, she headed out of her office without addressing the Officer. There was no time for chit-chat.

Her heart skipped a beat as the shrill siren increased in volume as she walked down the hall. A dozen UN Police Officers with the customary blue headwear rushed to accompany her. She gritted her teeth and headed for the emergency stairs. Procedures required her to head to the roof, where a helicopter would be waiting.

Another Officer barred her path. "Downstairs, Ma'am!"

She faltered for a fraction of a second. 'Downstairs' meant she was headed for the Emergency Operations Bunker located below the UN headquarters.

Plan B, then.

The threat was closer than she'd expected. What could be impeding her from leaving the building skyward? It couldn't be the storm, could it?

Flanked by the Police Officers, she began the long descent, secretly thanking the stars that she was in good shape despite her advanced years. Her morning jogs, which she had continued to practice even after being appointed Secretary-General two years ago, came as a blessing in this precise moment of urgency.

A superintendent joined them as they passed the door to the twelfth floor. "Secretary-General," he said in a manner of greeting, falling in step behind her.

"Talk to me," she said.

"Ma'am, an unidentified craft has landed on the Garden Court. It's some kind of stealth craft that doesn't show up on any radars. Security observed it on visual alone. The U.S. military is sending in F-16 fighter planes and is waiting for word that you are safe before engaging to destroy."

"Engaging to destroy?" Adhira started. "How long has this craft been there?"

The superintendent glanced at his watch. "Nine minutes and twelve seconds since it was first detected."

Adhira slowed, forcing the other Officers to do the same. "If this craft were hostile, wouldn't it have already attacked us?"

The superintendent shifted nervously. "Ma'am, we'll figure that out once you're in the Bunker."

They headed down the stairs again, Adhira deep in thought. She spoke to the superintendent, "It doesn't make sense. Why are they here? Who are they? Terrorists? A secret operative? Who?"

She turned and saw the superintendent hesitate. "None of them, Ma'am," he said.

By now, everyone stood still on the stairs. She stopped when he wouldn't meet her gaze.

The superintendent said, almost apologetically, "We determined the craft's trajectory. It…" he cleared his throat, "…it came from space."

She stared at him.

"It is an unidentified flying object," he said, his voice thick. "We don't know who it belongs to or what it is, and communications aren't getting through. But one thing is certain. It is not from Earth, Ma'am."

Not from Earth…

"Are you pulling my leg, superintendent?"

He blinked, sweat beading on his forehead. "I have seen it myself, ma'am. I am not pulling your leg."

Adhira felt an almost tangible ripple of fear wash over them. She continued her descent in silence, weighed down by the news. Thoughts crashed into her head as she tried to grasp the facts without giving in to panic. She didn't question the superintendent's sincerity. Whatever he thought he had seen out there, she had to accept his position without flinching, and act accordingly.

They had reached the fifth floor. Instead of continuing down the stairs, Adhira rushed to the exit and barged through it.

"Ma'am!" the superintendent shouted behind her.

"I need to see for myself," she said without slowing.

Police Officers spilled into the office area after her.

"Ma'am!" the superintendent repeated, catching up with her.

She ignored him and strode purposefully towards the northern windows overlooking the Garden Court and East River. She glanced around and spotted binoculars in the hands of one of the Officers standing nearby.

"Secretary-General! We need to go!" the superintendent insisted, but she knew he wouldn't dare drag her away by force.

She flicked her hand at the Officer, and he reluctantly gave up the binoculars, which she promptly aimed out the window. And she saw it. The craft. The unidentified flying object. The words flashed through her mind like a warning.

It was larger than she had expected, sleek and dark. *Hovering...* She adjusted the binoculars. Yes, the UFO seemed to be floating on thin air. A helicopter whizzed by, its floodlight piercing through the torrential rains, and Adhira was surprised to detect a thin filter of blue light around the craft as if it were stationed within a bubble.

The lack of a sign of life from the UFO made her skin crawl because it was clear this celestial object had not landed here on its own.

Who—or what—piloted it?

A commotion made her turn.

A pale Police Officer ran up to her and saluted. "Secretary-General," he said, out of breath, holding up a wireless red phone. "The President of the United States."

She had already recognized the phone. She grasped it and held it up to her ear, staring through the binoculars again. "Mr. President," she said.

"Secretary-General," the deep voice replied. "Are you safe?"

"I'm looking at the intruding craft as we speak," she said.

"Adhira!" the President scolded. "This is not a drill. I don't know who they are or where they came from. If the craft doesn't identify itself within the next minute, I'm giving the order to destroy it. We can't afford to wait until it attacks the UN or New York."

"Mr. President," she said. "I'm informed that

this unidentified craft is an *alien* spaceship—as in: *not from this planet.* I don't have time for jokes. Are you confirming this information?"

There was a pause on the other end, then the President said, "I am."

Adhira pursed her lips, pushing down waves of wonder and fear. "Peter," she said into the phone, addressing the President by his first name. "Hold off on the strike."

"What...?"

"I've got to go." She hung up and handed the phone back to the Officer. "Superintendent," she said. "You may get yourself and your men to safety if you wish. I'm going to stay. Whoever is in that craft landed at the foot of the United Nations headquarters for a reason. This is not a random decision. If they had destructive intentions, they would have already acted." She shook her head, determined. "No, if we are indeed looking at an extraterrestrial vessel, I won't be labelled as the one who turned down humanity's first peaceful contact."

"Target in sight!" an Officer shouted, pressing on his earpiece to relay information he was getting from the ground.

"Take position!" the superintendent barked into his mouthpiece, thrusting his own binoculars before his eyes.

Adhira did the same.

An opening appeared in the spacecraft, spilling light from inside onto the lawn. A single form filled the doorway.

Adhira leaned forward. She gasped. "Wait a minute! Is that...?" she began.

The superintendent—voice astounded—finished the sentence for her. "...a *boy*?"

CHAPTER 2 *First Contact*

An hour had passed since the UFO had landed at the foot of the United Nations' building.

Even as Adhira grasped her umbrella and stepped into the battering rain, she could feel the unnerving fear of the men she was leaving behind in the building. She tapped at her in-ear communication device to shut off the superintendent's voice, who continued to insist she not expose herself.

She took a deep breath and walked over the muddy lawn, focusing on the facts: the mysterious craft had—so far—shown no sign of hostility, and, thirty minutes ago, she had learned that the boy had specifically asked to speak to the Head of the United Nations. A computer-search of his face had come up with a missing person's file. The boy had disappeared several weeks ago.

That had stirred something within Adhira. What if this boy needed help? His parents must be sick with worry... And so, not as the Head of the UN, but rather as a mother herself, Adhira knew she needed to speak to him. The superintendent had begged her to wait until they had more intel, but Adhira couldn't afford to linger. The President of the United States had reiterated his inclination to blast the craft into oblivion.

That didn't give Adhira much of a window to operate. She needed to find out what this craft was doing here before things went haywire. She clutched at the umbrella as a gust of wind overturned its canopy. Cold raindrops drenched her hair. She struggled to straighten her umbrella and turned on her communication device again.

"...in place," the superintendent said in her ear.

Adhira shivered. Snipers were in place. Ready to strike if needed.

By now, she was a few feet from the boy. He sat cross-legged on the ground, bathed in the floodlights. He stood as she approached, and she was surprised to find him untouched by the storm. Standing within the mysterious semi-transparent bubble, he seemed affected neither by rain nor wind: his clothes and hair were dry.

Adhira stopped and stared at the teen who could have come straight out of her grandson's school. He wore jeans, a light-grey hoodie and black sneakers. He gave a small nudge of the head to remove a strand of brown hair from his forehead and stared at her with eyes that did not hold a hint of mischief. The muscles in his neck tensed, yet at the same time, he stood with his feet firm on the ground, waiting. She wondered why his cheeks looked so sunburnt and tried to decipher any clue that would clear up this situation. Finding none, she said, "I am Secretary-General Adhira Prabhakar, Head of the United Nations. You may call me Adhira."

The boy nodded, his shoulders relaxing. He seemed relieved.

"And who might you be?" she asked.

The boy locked eyes with hers. "I was hoping you'd know already."

She frowned. He had not spoken in a haughty voice. Rather, his eyes searched hers as if he was desperate to find out how much she knew.

She lowered the umbrella over her head, trying to ignore the rivulets of water entering her shoes. Fine, she would play his game for now. "You are Benjamin Archer, thirteen-year-old son of Laura Archer and Robert Manfield. You live in Chilliwack, British Columbia, Canada. You were reported missing three weeks ago after you became a bit of a media sensation as the *animal whisperer...*" She broke off. "Am I right so far?"

The tenseness in his neck slackened, and he nodded.

What on Earth is this missing child doing out here, so far from home?

"Child," she said. "Do you realize the danger you are in? Snipers are positioned on the rooftops. F-16 fighter jets are a blink away, ready to attack. If this is a prank, you could end up in jail for a very long time..."

"It's not a prank," he cut in. "And I'm sorry to put you in this situation. But I didn't know where else to take them."

Adhira caught her breath. "Them?"

The boy glanced back at the spacecraft as if he were afraid to say more.

"You brought *them* here?" Adhira asked, nudging her head towards the craft. She wondered why the hoodie of the boy's sweater bulged behind his back as if he'd stuffed something heavy into it.

He turned around to face her and nodded, eyebrows creased.

Adhira wiped away a strand of wet hair from her cheek, listening to the Superintendent who was instructing her to remove the subject from the field.

"Look," she said. "This is not a very good place to chat. Why don't we go inside, away from the storm?"

The boy stared at her. He glanced at the spaceship again, then stepped forward, seeming to want to tell her something. She approached also, and when they were close enough to the force field, he whispered, "I don't think they want me to." His tense eyes went from hers to the transparent barrier that separated them.

Adhira stared at blue filaments that travelled around the mysterious force field of the bubble.

The boy raised his hand and placed it against the transparent wall.

Adhira—ignoring the superintendent who was barking warnings in her ear—raised her hand and pressed against the barrier, mirroring the boy's gesture. Yet, they did not touch. The field resisted between them, feeling like compressed air, yet no matter how hard she pressed, she could not get through.

Neither could he.

Their eyes locked again.

"What's going on, child?" she said in a low voice, sensing his fear. "Who's in there?" She nudged towards the spaceship.

"The Toreq," he said, never letting go of her eyes as if he wanted to make sure she was listening.

"The Toreq?"

He nodded. "They come from another galaxy. They told me to take them to the *leader of all humans*. I didn't know what to do. There is no single leader of all humans. But then I remembered learning about the United Nations at school. So I told them to come here..." His eyes looked apologetic.

Adhira set her jaw, feeling like she was being pranked again, but decided to go along with whatever the boy said, to gather information. "And... are these Toreq friendly?" she asked.

His answer surprised her. "Look around you," he said. "Do you think this storm is natural?"

Adhira's mind did a double-flip as she thought of the weather-related files lying on her desk. She shook her head. "Stop fooling around, child. Answer me! Who is in that craft? Who are you? What are you doing here? What do you want?"

Shadows spilled out of the spaceship.

The boy noticed and, with great urgency, said, "Listen! The Toreq have a final message for the human race. They've come to wipe us out! Nothing will stop them. This storm is just the beginning. Tell everyone to hide!" Sweat pearled his forehead, and his eyes darted as he searched for what to say. Five tall beings made their way from the spaceship towards them. The words tumbled out of his mouth. "Find Mesmo! Only he can save us. Find my mom. She'll tell you and... and..." He blinked rapidly. "Come to *The Great Gathering*!"

In a few strides, the beings had caught up with the boy. They pulled him away from the force field, and he disappeared from her view.

Adhira released her hand from the barrier, stepping back as if she had just been stung. The appearance of these intimidating beings stupefied her.

Before she could react, one of them raised a glowing hand into the force field, which expanded to swallow her up. Now she was standing inside the bubble, protected from the pounding rain. The sudden silence within caught her by surprise. She pressed at her communication device. It crackled in her ear, useless.

The being lowered its glowing hand and stepped back, giving way to a tall humanoid with white hair combed back and attached in a thin, waist-length braid.

Adhira noted he would have been easy on the eyes had his gaze not been so cold. She forgot she was still grasping the umbrella, even though the rain no longer reached her.

The caped humanoid stepped forward, lifted his left hand and placed his three middle fingers in the middle of his forehead in what she took to be a gesture of greeting. "I am General Zoltar, also known as the Challenger. I am the leader of the Toreq military force sent by the Arch Council to take control of this planet." His honey-brown eyes bore into hers from above his high cheekbones. "Are you the A'hmun leader?"

A'hmun? Adhira's face went blank.

Ben peeked at her from behind one of the beings. "He means *leader of humans*," he said before being pushed back.

Adhira tightened her grip on the umbrella. "I am Secretary-General Adhira Prabhakar, Head of the United Nations. There is no single leader of all humans. However, world leaders will listen to me, yes."

"Good," Zoltar said. There was a glint in his eyes that she did not like. "Thousands of generations ago, a great war was waged between our people in a distant galaxy. You lost this war. As punishment for inciting *The Great War of the Kins*, we banished you to this isolated planet in the hopes that you would redeem yourselves; that you would prove your worth by acting as custodians of a biosphere teeming with life. Yet, you have not lived up to the task. You are a destructive force, as you have always been. Therefore, the Toreq Arch Council has judged that you must be stopped before you master space flight. You are a threat to interstellar civilizations. Go, and spread this message to your leaders so that they may reflect on their actions before the end."

He spoke each word with an intensity that made her step back. It was as if he had waited a long time to say them, and they carried a weight that stifled her own voice.

He glared at her for a timeless moment, then saluted again, his cape flowing over his silver outfit as he turned to leave.

"No," she said.

He stopped in his tracks. A slight frown appeared over his right brow as he half-turned to glance back at her.

Adhira had never been more petrified in her life. The umbrella slipped from her hand, knocking off her hairpin and releasing her long, grey-white hair. Her feet were wet and cold, and a mesh of hair stuck to her cheek again. *Damn!* She must look a mess. *Nothing like a respectable leader at all...*

But Adhira was long accustomed to bullies. Instead of causing her to crouch in a corner, whimpering, they ignited fires of justice within her. This was no different. Her voice found its strength again.

"No," she repeated. She had his full attention. "I will do no such thing. You can tell the world leaders yourself, instead of cowering in your bubble and hiding behind a storm in the middle of the night."

Zoltar's eyebrow raised higher.

"Also," she continued, unwavering. "I will not negotiate with hostages. Release that child to me at once!"

Zoltar froze for a terrifying heartbeat before the tiniest of smiles appeared at the corner of his mouth. Perhaps this encounter was turning out more enjoyable than he had expected. It didn't last, however, and his face became grim again. "The A'hmun child is not your concern," Zoltar said. "He has his own trial to face."

Adhira saw the boy's face turn ashen.

Zoltar waved his hand, and the other beings turned on their heels, taking the boy with them.

"W... wait! What trial?" Ben stuttered, his voice thick with fear. "What trial?" he yelled, struggling to keep up with the beings' fast strides as they pulled him towards the spaceship.

Adhira reached out as if to hold him back, opening her mouth to protest.

"I... I'll be fine," he shouted at her. "Tell my mom I'll be f-fine!" Then he was gone, and she was left with the imposing General.

She remained tongue-tied—for real this time. She could sense his satisfaction. His control.

"I shall send word within thirty star-rises," Zoltar said. "Should any of your world leaders still be alive, it will be my pleasure to speak to them at that time and watch them beg for mercy."

Adhira remained poised but speechless.

A glint in the alien's eye sent a shiver down her spine as he whirled and left her standing there. The unnatural bubble narrowed as he approached the spaceship, and she felt a tingle in her body as the force field passed through her again, leaving her exposed to the elements. Rain battered on her head.

"Ma'am, are you all right?" a Police Officer shouted over the storm, rushing to her side.

She nodded, stupefied.

"Move away, Ma'am! The F-16s have a clear shot." He pulled at her arm.

Adhira tensed like an ice-pick. She watched

the alien General reach the craft's opening.

"No!" she shouted, clicking frantically at her in-ear device. "Abort! Abort!" The device crackled. "SUPERINTENDENT," she yelled.

The spaceship rose into the air and was joined by four other similar crafts that had been lurking in the darkness.

"We have a clear shot, Ma'am!" the superintendent's voice burst into her ear.

"ABORT!" Adhira yelled. "Do you hear me? They have a hostage! I repeat: they have a hostage!"

CHAPTER 3 *Spacebound*

What do you do when you are the victim of an alien abduction?

Ben Archer asked himself this question for the hundredth time as the aliens whisked him away into space. One minute he had been recovering in a hospital in Dubai after having survived harrowing adventures in the desert; the next, he had found himself on a Toreq spaceship led by General Zoltar, heading for a mysterious Toreq base located far away from Earth. Mesmo had not picked him up in Dubai as he had promised. In fact, there was no news of his alien friend. What had happened to him? Why had he not come? Was Mesmo alive?

Ben barely avoided passing out from fear

half-a-dozen times. He was struggling to keep it together, knowing that he was leaving Earth with hostile extraterrestrials headed towards a secret alien base.

They whizzed through space at an astonishing speed, Ben working to control his breathing by focusing on General Zoltar's cape. The cape had an unusual silver sheen to it that rippled with the General's movements. Ben stared at it fixedly, lacing his hands together before him and squeezing them hard. His hands wouldn't stop glowing as his alien ability picked up the quiet and controlled back-and-forth conversations of the humanoids that piloted the ship. His alien translation skill allowed him to understand every word of the Toreq speech.

Raw fear stopped him from making his power invisible within his skin, despite the possibility that it could lash out, as it had with Sadalbari, King of Horses. What if he gave it free rein now? Would the skill consume him? Would it consume all on board the ship? This was no longer a mere translation power—this was much more than that.

Ben could almost see it in his mind's eye. He imagined giving in to the skill. He'd free that almighty force from within. He'd take over the minds of these aliens, and he'd bend them to his will. He'd make them suffer...

NO!

Ben squeezed his hands tighter together.

How can I even think that?

More frightening than being abducted by extraterrestrials was the idea that he could lose control of the alien skill, that he could lose himself in its hunger for power—a level of power he did not understand. He wondered if Mesmo had known what his daughter's power was capable of, and if he had ever imagined it would act like that after Ben had inherited it from her.

He turned his focus to the cape again, except it was the General's boots he was looking at now. Zoltar had turned and was staring at him. Ben tensed. Not a single emotion showed on the General's face, except for a passing gleam in his honey-coloured eyes.

A cold sweat broke out on Ben's brow. It was as if the General could see right through him. Did he know what Ben was capable of?

The General turned to face the front again, and Ben let out the breath he had been holding. Why did he feel a strange connection to this alien? He set his jaw. As if that mattered.

He had just told the Head of the United

Nations that aliens were coming to wipe out the human race. Would she take him seriously? He was just a kid! Would she listen and contact his mother? Would she look for Mesmo? Would she even know how to look for his alien friend?

And *The Great Gathering*... Whatever had spurred him to tell the Secretary-General about that? As if she would travel to the mouth of the Amazon River on solstice day. As if she would ever figure out what *The Great Gathering* was in the first place.

As if I could ever go...

Ben swallowed.

He had promised. He had promised all living creatures that he would be there at *The Great Gathering*. He had promised he'd bring humans and animals together so they could take the first steps towards healing Earth.

Zoltar moved aside, a glossy wave travelling down his cape. It pulled Ben out of his jumbled thoughts.

A Toreq said something that made Ben look out the cockpit window, and his mouth dropped.

The five small spaceships that had left Earth in formation not too long ago, were now skimming by the Moon, giving Ben a close-up view of its surface. Impact craters from meteorites that had hit its surface eons ago zoomed by below him in a game of light and dark pockets of grey dust. Then they entered the dark side of the satellite—the side that neither Earth-light nor sunlight could reach. Thousands of stars and space spread out before them.

Empty? Perhaps not.

What seemed like dark space vanished in a blink as the ships entered a force field that had served as camouflage. No sooner had they flown through the invisible barrier when the real power of the Toreq came into view. Five colossal warships sprawled before them like lurking monsters.

Ben's heart sank to the bottom of his feet as they approached one of them. The thing was massive. It never seemed to end.

The small spaceship he was in headed straight for the side of the warship, and for a second, Ben thought they were going to crash into it. But then a bluish glimmer caused a hole to appear in the warship's wall, big enough for them to slip through.

Now they were inside, and Ben felt woozy again. It was as if he'd been shoved into the belly of a giant whale, with no way out.

The spaceship landed, and the Toreq filed out of it with Ben at their center. All he could do was follow mechanically, willing his feet to hurry after the aliens' long strides. He glimpsed row upon row of similar spaceships, ready for use, but then everything changed. A wide door slid open before them, and they entered the strangest place Ben had ever seen.

Light streamed down on them from a massive ceiling. Not just any light, but orange sunlight, and Ben pinpointed its source to his right, through a jumble of leaves.

Leaves?

Ben peeked between the Toreq that surrounded him. Yes, that was vegetation covering the inside of the ship. Weird, unnatural vegetation. It was as if the warship was so ancient that plants and trees had taken over its carcass. But that couldn't be it, of course. No, this was intentional.

Bluish clouds rolled across the ceiling, away from the deep orange sun.

Make that... three suns.

He counted them again. Yes, one big orange one, one tiny blue spot, and one white sun. Together, they formed a triangle.

For a second, the hairs at the back of his neck rose. Had he just been whisked away to another galaxy? He breathed hard. *No, of course not!* This setup was to give the Toreq a sense of home. He'd bet the sky was artificial. Maybe it was some sort of projection.

As they continued, the hall widened to show several floors of the ship, and more Toreq men and women appeared—some of them on higher levels. But where he had just been the one gawking at everything, suddenly Toreq aliens spotted him, and now it was their turn to stare.

A whisper spread through the crowds. The Toreq stopped and turned. They pointed... at him!

Fire rose to Ben's cheeks. Suddenly the floor seemed a lot more interesting than the rest of the warship. His heart pounded in his ears. It dawned on him that these aliens had not laid eyes on a human in countless millennia. What did the Toreq think of him? Would he meet accusing glares? Or terrified eyes?

He was a human, or, as the Toreq would say: an *A'hmun*. He belonged to the loathed enemies of the Toreq. For the A'hmun had almost obliterated Toreq civilization during *The Great War of the Kins*, some tens of thousands of years ago.

A long, long time ago.

Ben raised his head and forced himself to meet the stares. He had nothing to do with *The Great War of the Kins*. He had no reason to feel guilty.

Time seemed to stand still, and a crushing

silence fell over the hall. Ben stumbled over his own feet and only avoided falling flat on his face when the Toreq to his left caught him, just in time. It was the one with hair plastered backwards—the one who had called Ben a thief in the Dubai hospital.

The Toreq man helped him straighten up without any of them having to slow down, avoiding Ben a catastrophic embarrassment.

His legs had turned to jelly. He wasn't going to be able to do this for much longer—this parading in front of a whole alien crew, as if he were the one and unique symbol of human terror that they had come to eliminate.

Just then, General Zoltar, who had been leading the group, stepped away while the rest continued towards a corridor to the left.

Ben watched Zoltar's shimmering cape recede as he headed towards Toreq men and women on another level. And that's when Ben saw him.

Einar!

Ben tensed. What was the cunning Wise One doing here? Where were the other six? The last time Ben had seen Einar was when the Norseman had rejected Mesmo's appeal to have the seven Wise Ones teach humans how to be a more respectful species towards all living things. His being here, then—while the other Wise Ones were not—was not a good sign.

Zoltar joined Einar, and both turned and glanced Ben's way just as the guards led him into an empty corridor.

This time, Ben tripped and fell flat on his face.

CHAPTER 4 *The Cell*

The rest of the warship was closer to what Ben had expected it to look like: long, grey corridors with artificial lighting. Less and less Toreq wandered this part of the ship until only he and his four guards remained. They stopped all of a sudden, and Ben stared at the smooth wall before them. A door slid open where there had been none seconds ago.

They shoved him inside.

Ben whirled in time to watch metal bars materialize in the middle of the room, shutting him away on the far side. The door closed, and he was alone.

He began hyperventilating. He stood in the middle of the cell, hands and legs shaking. His ears rang from the tumult of thoughts that clashed in his mind. A nervous wreck, Ben must have stood the better part of an hour before he relaxed just enough to sit down, crossed-legged. Except even from this position, his eyes never left the other side of the room and the smooth wall where the door had been. He kept expecting someone to burst in and whisk him away into another forced adventure.

When nothing happened, the ringing in his ears died down, his breathing slowed, and his erratic thoughts were replaced by a flurry of sharp, agonizing ones.

Where's Mesmo? Why didn't he come? What's up with Zoltar and Einar? Why am I on trial? What's the punishment if I lose? What if I win, but Earth is in ruins? MOM!

A single sob left his mouth, and he shut his eyes tight.

Mom! Does she know? Will she find shelter before the Toreq attack?

The distance between him and home opened up like a gaping hole, and he'd never felt more alone.

Alone...

But I'm not alone!

He straightened, the realization jolting him to attention. He brought forth his skill, handling it like porcelain in his mind. His hands glowed as he connected with the animal in his hoodie.

Echis?

He listened.

Something heavy slithered in the folds of his hoodie. A long mass slid up his shoulder, and a slit tongue tickled his ear, then a voice whispered, *Iss it ssafe?*

Ben relaxed a bit. *I think so, Echis. For now, at least.*

The venomous snake appeared in full, sliding down Ben's arm and onto the floor.

Aah! Finally! Mucch noise. I not like. I hide for long, long time. Long trip to your housse, Benjamin. I get bored. The snake—which had decided to accompany Ben after their encounter in the deserts of the Middle-East—observed its surroundings. *You sspeak of much ssnow in your country. Where iss ssnow?*

Ben slumped. *Oh, Echis...*

It was strange, but watching the reptile with its crimson spots and black rings slithering around him made him feel slightly relieved. Maybe it was because the snake was the only recognizable thing he'd laid eyes on since he'd left Earth. At least he knew what to expect from Echis. The reptile was predictable. Not like the Toreq, who he had no control over and whose actions tripped him up at every corner. Echis was easy to handle. All he had to remember was not to stare.

Staring makes you edgy...

Yess. I glad you remember. The snake slid away happily, exploring the cell. *Your housse comfy. Nicce and warm.*

Ben snorted. *Comfy? You're kidding, right?*

For the first time, he turned to take in his surroundings, having been too distraught before to take notice.

Echis slid under a thin layer of dry yellow grass. *Ssee? Warm hay...*

Hay? Ben blinked and stood, now truly curious about his cell. He stared at the red bricks that made up the floor. Three walls and part of the ceiling were made of red bricks. There wasn't a single window. A thin layer of hay covered the floor. Ben picked up a strand and bent it. It snapped in two. Yes, that was hay, alright, though it didn't smell like hay. In fact, it had no smell at all.

Weird.

In the corner lay a thin mattress with a couple of bedsheets. There was a bucket and a wooden stool with a fruit bowl on top. In it, orange grapes and a blue apple. Ben studied the strange fruit, poking at them with his finger. Right fruit. Wrong colour. No smell.

Weeeird...

He straightened.

Housse ssmall. Echis's voice sounded distant. *What elsse to ssee? Time to sstrecch my legss.* Echis giggled at its own joke.

Ben shivered. Hearing a snake giggle was not the most heartwarming experience. *Echis? Where are you?*

Here...

Ben whirled and stared out of the metal bars of his cell—to the other side! While his side of the cell looked like an old abandoned brick shack, the other side, beyond the bars, had the clean, smooth walls he'd seen in the warship's corridors. "What?" Ben burst. "Echis! How did you get through?" He rushed to the bars and crouched down to be level with the snake.

Ben reached his hand out where Echis would have slipped to the other side, but instead of touching cold, metal bars, he found only compact air.

Like at the United Nations!

He felt the whole barred section. It was made from a wall of air or some kind of transparent barrier.

Ben scanned the cell again, and it hit him.

Maybe the whole thing was some kind of three-dimensional virtual set. And the reason why the cell felt so familiar and yet out-of-place was because it looked like a prison cell from the olden days, one he could picture existed some hundred or more years ago in the Wild West. And the last time the Toreq had come to Earth was exactly two hundred years ago...

Echis! Ben scanned the area behind the fake bars. *How did you get to the other side?*

I sslide on belly. Look, like thhiss... Echis slid in an S-form along the other wall.

Echis, you're not helpful at all. Ben bent on all fours and searched every inch of the virtual wall but found no opening anywhere. So how had Echis gotten through?

An uncomfortable thought entered his mind. This cell was designed to keep him in. Not anyone else. Just him. Maybe the force field recognized his DNA. In any case, his cowboy-inspired prison was far more high-tech than it appeared.

Shoot!

Now he was back at square one.

Echis, I think you should come back.

Not yet. I vissit firsst.

What do you mea...?

The door slid open, startling Ben. He jumped

to his feet and watched the Toreq man with the plastered hair enter the area occupied by the snake.

Ben stiffened. *Echis! Watch out!*

The Toreq man didn't see the snake.

One of the Toreq women who had picked up Ben in Dubai peeked inside, eyes stern. *"I'll stand guard. Make it quick!"* she said to the Toreq man. She pulled back, and Echis slipped out between her legs, unnoticed.

Echis! Ben called after it with his mind, but the snake was gone. Ben straightened and tried to pull an innocent face. *Now what?* Why did the woman have to stand guard? Goosebumps rose on Ben's arms. This couldn't be good...

The Toreq man stared at him with hard eyes. *"I am Torka,"* he spoke in the Toreq language. *"Mesmo is my friend. Tell me where he is!"*

His friend?

Was there a glimmer of hope?

"I already told you that back in Dubai!" Ben said, awed that he was not only able to use his alien skill to understand Torka, but also that he could reply in the Toreq language. *"You should have waited! Mesmo was going to pick me up there!"*

Torka's eyes darkened. *"I have had my eyes on that place ever since we left it. Mesmo did not come. You lie!"*

Ben's heart sank. It didn't make sense. His mom had urged him to get ready: Mesmo was on his way to Dubai. So if he hadn't come, something must have held him back. But what? Or who? Ben shook his head, his stomach twisting. *"You have to find him, please! It's not like him. Something must have happened."*

"Then tell me where to search since you seem to know so much about him. Time is running out. I want to find Mesmo alive before we attack the planet with full force."

Ben's face drained. They'd have to ask his mother. He almost said it out loud but caught himself. Panic rose in his chest. His mom would know where Mesmo was, but he couldn't very well send her the Toreq, could he?

Torka continued. *"I have searched for Mesmo since our arrival. What have you and your people done to him? Why did he not return to the Mother Planet?"*

Tears built behind Ben's eyes.

Torka took a menacing step forward. *"Answer the question!"*

Ben blurted, *"He stayed to be with me!"*

Torka nodded slowly. *"Ah, I see. He needed to watch over his daughter's skill—the one you stole from her."*

"Why do you say that?" Ben yelled. *"I didn't steal anything from Kaia. And no, Mesmo didn't stay on Earth to watch over his daughter's skill. He stayed... for me!"* A thick tear rolled down his cheek. *"He stayed because he cares for me!"* He caught his breath because he knew it was true. He knew in his heart that Mesmo cared for him like a father would his son.

Torka stared at him, a quizzical look on his face.

The door slid open. *"Torka!"* the woman warned, glancing over her shoulder down the corridor.

Torka spat on the ground, addressing Ben. *"You are all the same. A'hmun scum. Liars and manipulators."* He gestured to the woman. *"Let's go!"*

Ben groaned, then jumped forward. *"Wait!"* he yelled.

The two stopped.

"Ask Einar!" Ben said.

Torka stared at him.

Ben insisted. *"He's up to something, I know it! Of the seven Wise Ones, he's been the most hostile towards Mesmo. He even tried to get the Wise Ones to vote against him and have him removed as their leader on Earth. I bet he knows where Mesmo is!"*

Torka and the woman exchanged a glance.

"*One does not accuse a Wise One lightly,*" Torka retorted. "*I would watch your tongue, thief.*" He glared at Ben, then both were gone, and the door slid shut behind them.

CHAPTER 5 *Comeback*

Laura Archer flung open the front door.

Jeremy Michaels stood before her, grinning. "Hi! I heard the news! Can I come in?"

Laura dropped her arm to her side.

Seeing her face, the reporter's smile vanished. "What's the matter? I heard they found Ben in Dubai…" He frowned. "They found him, right?"

Laura didn't feel like speaking to the reporter. She had hoped it had been someone with news about Ben and Mesmo. She stepped back, not caring whether he followed her into the house or not.

"Laura!" he insisted, swearing as his camera bag slid off his shoulder and thumped to the floor.

He rushed to her side, swinging the bag over his shoulder again. "What's the matter? What happened? Tell me!"

Tell you? Laura thought. *Tell you what? That I lost Ben again? That Mesmo told me the Toreq are here? And that he's been unreachable ever since?* Her breath quickened. Black spots swam before her eyes.

"Hey!" Jeremy yelled, his voice muffled from the ringing in her ears. He sat her down in the living-room and placed something in her palm.

My emergency inhaler!

She sucked medication from the asthma pump, grasping his hand in an attempt to hold on to something solid. Her sight cleared, and her breath evened. She opened her eyes and faced all the questions in his.

Poor Jeremy!

All he knew was that Ben was capable of communicating with animals. He didn't know about the rest, and she didn't have the energy to tell him.

"Laura, where's Ben?" Jeremy asked, his eyes filled with concern.

She didn't have time to answer.

A roar shook the house, rattling walls. A sudden wind picked up the curtains and blew them out into the room.

Laura and Jeremy stared at each other, then rushed outside.

A large military helicopter landed on the lawn, its swinging rotors flinging twigs and leaves from nearby trees into the air. A soldier jumped out of the helicopter and ran to meet them. Without removing his helmet, he shouted over the roar. "Miss Laura Archer?"

She nodded.

"High Inspector James Hao wants you at the Dugout right away."

Laura sheltered her eyes with her hand. "Why?" she asked quickly.

"Miss," he said. "We found him!"

Laura gripped her heart. "Who?"

The soldier lifted his visor. "The alien," he said.

A whirlwind of emotions swept over her. She glanced at Jeremy. He stared back at her, his face clueless. The time to be discreet was over. Making a swift decision, she pointed at the reporter and said to the soldier, "He's coming with me!"

The soldier blinked. "No, I..."

Laura grabbed Jeremy by the arm. "Let's go!" She tugged the young reporter towards the helicopter.

"Uh... wait a minute..." Jeremy protested.

Laura paused and yanked him in close, so they were face to face. "You want to break the headlines, don't you?" she shouted, her hair flying in her face.

He opened his mouth.

She didn't wait for an answer. "Then you're coming with me!"

* * *

Four hours later, they were about to land at a secret government location in Northern Ontario, known to authorized personnel as the Dugout.

Laura shut her eyes. She had not expected to return to the place where the remains of the crashed UFOs had been brought for study a year-and-a-half ago.

The soldier nudged her and handed her an iPad with a video of an erupting volcano. She watched it, horrified. *Erupting* was not quite the right term. Rather—a woman speaking on a European news-channel explained—a fissure had appeared on the side of a mountain called Beerenberg, an active volcano on a little-known island in the Northern Atlantic Ocean. The fissure was not dangerous, and experts did not believe the volcano would erupt, but scientists were keeping a close eye on it for further developments.

Laura checked the soldier, hoping he would somehow tell her a different story than what he'd told her three times already: a helicopter flying close to the fissure had found an unconscious man lying at its edge.

Mesmo!

What had the alien been doing on such a remote island? What had happened to him? Where was his spaceship?

Not long after watching the video, they arrived at the Dugout.

Laura wrung her hands together as a steel elevator descended to one of its last underground floors. She marvelled how quickly the government had set up the facility again after it had been destroyed. The memory of it made her want to bite her nails. Just then, the elevator stopped, and the door slid open. Both she and Jeremy stepped out onto a gigantic concrete floor and froze.

Like a fly trapped in a spider's web, an alien spaceship lay before them, caught within an array of scaffolds.

Jeremy gasped.

Laura shivered.

Men in worker's helmets with white outfits

and black, protective glasses hammered away. Bright blue sparks flew from welding machines, and something metallic groaned within the craft.

Laura's mind did a double flip. Was this Mesmo's spaceship, brought back in pieces? No, this was a different ship—slightly smaller and rounder.

"This way," the soldier instructed, snapping her out of her trance.

She hurried behind him, leaving Jeremy with his camera aimed at the alien craft that took up most of the cavernous hangar constructed below the earth.

High Inspector James Hao met her in the corridor leading to the infirmary.

Feeling relieved at seeing her trustworthy ally, she threw herself forward. "Is he alive?" she burst with anguish.

Hao held her back. "He's alive... but unresponsive."

Laura almost burst into tears. *Mesmo's alive!*

Hao squeezed her arm until she met his eyes. "Laura, we're doing the best we can. Do you understand?"

Laura nodded. *He's alive! That's all that matters!*

He let her go, and she rushed into the room.

Mesmo lay on a hospital bed looking terrible. His face was bruised, and his hair dishevelled. The brown hair-dye she had applied to hide his white hair was almost gone. And his hands...

"Good grief, his hands!" she gasped.

They were wrapped up in bandages. But even where the bandages stopped above his wrists, she could see the burn marks. She turned horrified eyes Hao's way.

He looked at her grimly. "I think he crawled out of the volcano fissure..."

Laura slumped into a chair, shocked. She placed her hand gently over the alien's arm. "Why?" she whispered, half to herself. "Who did this to you?"

"Laura..." Hao said, approaching the bed. "He's not doing too well. We have excellent doctors, but still, we've never had to treat someone like him before. Is there anything you know, anything we could do to help him?"

She blinked, then her eyes widened. "Water!" she said, remembering how he had healed once before by plunging into a lake.

"Water?"

She nodded. "Yes! His alien skill is water. He can manipulate it, and his body responds to it. It feeds his cells; he is one with it. You have to submerge him!"

Hao set his jaw, thinking, then nodded slowly.

"And," she added, "this room won't do. Is there a place at the surface with windows? He needs sunlight. He can't handle closed spaces. Please, James!"

"I'm on it," Hao said, jumping into action. In a second, he was out the door, barking orders into a phone.

Finding herself alone with Mesmo, Laura stood and leaned over him, lowering her face close to his. She noticed the scratch on top of his left eyebrow, the split lower lip, the scar on his high cheekbone. "Mesmo," she breathed, longing for his honey-brown eyes to open. "When you went looking for Ben, you promised I wouldn't lose you, too." She brushed his hair with her fingers. "And you never break promises."

CHAPTER 6 *Clues*

It began with a whimper.

Artificial night descended on the warship. Strange, alien vegetation cast shadows on the walls. All was silent except for a handful of Toreq guards who patrolled the halls, their voices low and muffled. Night birds hooted. A curious potato-shaped moon peeked through the foliage without offering much light.

Another whimper, louder this time. Its sound lingered in the darkness, as if coming from the depths of the warship, and clung to its walls.

Ben twitched in his sleep.

This was a strange dream, one he knew would remain in his mind long after waking. He was at floor-level, sliding across tree-roots, then into a vent that went on and on into darkness.

Echis?

Ben had to concentrate for a minute. Perhaps this was not a dream... Was he using his skill to follow the reptile as it explored the warship?

A heart-wrenching sob echoed into the vent, sending icy chills up-and-down Ben's spine.

Echis froze. Ben froze with the snake. The sob had been so close. An orange glow shone into the vent, coming from an opening not far ahead.

Echis advanced.

Echis! Ben recoiled from the fear that filled the snake's mind.

Soul-wrenching moans came from the room beyond. Something there lay in acute pain and blood-chilling terror.

Echis! Don't go!

Echis slid towards the orange light, towards the source of the danger. Ben struggled. He fought to stop the snake from advancing. He fought to escape being discovered by whoever was inflicting such agony...

Echis... DON'T!

Ben woke with a yell, gasping and sweating. He jolted upright. He was back in the cell. Not that he had ever left. He placed a trembling hand over his chest, feeling his heart pounding painfully within, the whimpers still ringing in his ears.

A nightmare... Just a nightmare... Right?

He glanced at his trembling hands. They glowed.

* * *

Laura scrolled up the blinds. A ray of sunlight entered the stark room as the sun rose over a forest of maple trees. The idyllic view was misleading, as, below the trees, army trucks wove their way on the road leading away from the Dugout. Occasional dark olive helicopters cut through the air, and barbed wire fenced off the area.

Laura sighed and turned towards Mesmo.

This will have to do.

The alien lay unresponsive on the hospital bed, but his vital signs had improved. She approached, touched his cheek and bent to kiss him.

A small clicking sound made her turn.

Jeremy stood in the doorway, his camera raised. "Uh... sorry." He fidgeted and lowered the camera. "It's a habit."

Laura turned her attention back to Mesmo, still caressing his cheek. After a while, the camera clicked again.

"Why did you bring me here?" Jeremy asked.

She kept her eyes on Mesmo. "Because we're going to need someone to record everything that's going to happen next. If we don't survive, then whoever does will need to know the truth."

The clicking sound stopped.

Laura glanced at Jeremy and saw the young man's Adam's apple rising and falling.

Jeremy opened his mouth to say something, but just then, Inspector Hao rushed into the room. "Laura, I need to talk to you." He gestured for her to step out of the room, but his eyes fell on the reporter instead. "Wait a minute! You're that Provincial Times report..."

Jeremy's eyebrow raised. "Hey! Aren't you High Inspector H...?"

Both men gaped, pointing at each other, then simultaneously turned towards Laura.

Hao burst, "*What* in heaven's name is he doing..."

"Laura, you didn't tell m..."

They broke off again.

Hao's face turned red. "Laura, did you bring this nosy-faced creep here?"

Jeremy objected, "I'm not a nosy-faced cree..."

"Guys!" Laura cut in. She was in no mood for

squabbles. She turned her attention to the Inspector. "James, the time for secrecy is over. The Toreq are here. We may not be alive a week from now." She glanced at Jeremy. "So it really doesn't matter what we do anymore."

The two men stood by the door, staring at her: Hao in a business suit, brushing at the streaks of white hair above his ears and looking worn; and Jeremy, a young man looking out-of-place with his curly hair and lanky, fresh-out-of-college face.

Laura pulled them out of their trance. "What did you want to tell me?"

Hao cast an annoyed glance Jeremy's way, then said, "We need to go to New York."

Laura frowned. "New York? I can't go to New York!" She gestured towards Mesmo.

"Laura, it's about Ben. We have a lead, but they want us there in person."

He needn't have said more. Within three hours, Laura, Hao and Jeremy were in the air, approaching New York City. The helicopter rattled. Rain thundered so hard against the windows they could barely hear the rotors above the noise. Jeremy grabbed a plastic bag and held it up to his mouth, retching for the third time since they'd left the Dugout.

Hao eyed him from the paperwork he was

reading, then glanced at Laura and shook his head.

Laura bent over towards the reporter. "Are you okay?" she shouted over the noise.

Jeremy shut his eyes, face pale. "Did I mention I don't like flying?"

Laura smiled sympathetically. "Only half a dozen times." She patted his leg, then turned to look out the window. She had to shade her eyes to cut away reflections from inside the helicopter. Although it was past noon in New York, a heavy downpour had turned the sky ink-black.

She swallowed as she thought of Mesmo lying lifeless in the Dugout. She'd whispered in his ear, told him where she was going and that she'd be back soon. She'd felt torn at leaving his side but knew she had no choice.

Hao hadn't wanted to say more, feigning he had no further information himself, but Laura suspected he still hesitated to speak openly in front of the young reporter.

She grasped the edge of her seat as the helicopter swayed beside a skyscraper, then approached another building next to a river. It took the pilot a full ten minutes to find a break in the gusts of winds, allowing them to land on a lawn bathed in floodlights.

"The weather's been particularly bad this

season," the pilot shouted after he'd slid open the door to let them out.

Laura couldn't have agreed more. She, Hao and Jeremy rushed through the rain, heading for the closest doors to the building. UN Police Officers wearing blue berets surrounded them, scanned them for weapons, then led them down several flights of stairs.

They passed drab concrete corridors, then wide doors leading to some kind of operations room with a large oval table, many chairs, and screens on the walls.

"James," Laura breathed, removing strands of wet hair from her face. "Are you going to tell us where we are?"

Hao didn't have time to answer.

Another door opened, and half-a-dozen people entered. They were led by a woman in her early seventies who was still in excellent shape. The woman was bright-eyed and smart-looking.

She spotted Laura and headed straight for her. "Laura Archer?" She shook Laura's dripping hand. Laura noted her long fingers were wrinkled, yet not lacking strength. "Thank you for coming on such short notice. I am Secretary-General Adhira Prabhakar. Welcome to the United Nations." She paused, then said, "I have a message from your son."

CHAPTER 7 *Tuli*

After what he'd heard in the warship's core—despair, pain and fear—sleep was impossible.

Ben couldn't shake off the emotions. Every time he closed his eyes, the sobbing would echo inside his brain. Who could have a heart so cold they would cause such agony in another living thing? Ben rolled over on his mattress as a thousand terrible things crossed his mind. But his breath quickened, and he had to sit up again.

His hands no longer glowed, he noted as he clasped them together. The skill lay dormant, as if teasing him.

Maybe the whole thing had only been a

nightmare after all. It wouldn't be surprising, considering the precarious situation in which he found himself. But the fact that the alien skill had tingled in his hands and blood had rushed to his ears upon waking told him to be vigilant.

And thus, he couldn't sleep.

He didn't know how much time passed. Days, he suspected, with dread settling ever deeper into his stomach. Had they forgotten about him? Did they no longer care about his trial? Were the Toreq going to leave him there to rot? Was this Zoltar's idea or Einar's? What about his mom? Was she safe at home, worrying about him? Or was she fleeing an onslaught of attacks by the Toreq? More than anything, he ached to communicate with her for a brief moment—if only to let her know he was still alive.

He paced the cell for an eternity. When that became too much, he called out for help. He cried his heart out, but in the end, silence remained his only companion. He wished Echis hadn't left. For all the snake's flaws, at least it was a living being with who he could converse. But Echis was gone, and Ben dared not communicate with the snake again.

Before long, day and night mingled until he couldn't tell the difference. Toreq days lasted longer than on Earth, so Ben's inner clock was thrown on its head, making him doze off at the most awkward times. The only thing that changed in his cell was the fruit bowl, which kept magically refilling every time he tasted its contents. The fruit didn't taste like fruit at all, but their juiciness burst into his mouth at every bite, slid down his throat and filled his queasy stomach, nourishing him instantly. His appetite satisfied, drowsiness settled in before he could help himself.

When Ben awoke again, he became aware of a presence nearby. Without moving, he listened, trying to figure out if this had something to do with the whimpering voice he'd heard before.

No sound came.

He cracked open his eyelids, his vision clearing slowly, and saw a girl. She stood on the other side of the bars that split the cell in two. He opened his eyes wide to make sure he wasn't hallucinating.

The girl remained. She had white hair and a long braid that rested over her shoulder all the way to her hip. The end of it was a bright blue, like the end of a peacock feather, and the same blue reflected in her eyes. Ben had never seen a Toreq with blue eyes before. And another thing was odd: the cell door was shut.

How did she get in?

She stood in the shadow of the wall, looking at him.

Ben shuddered involuntarily. He sat at the edge of the bed, wondering if she would disappear, but she didn't. *"Who are you?"* he asked, almost afraid to speak.

She took a step forward, artificial light bathing her ghostly form. She blinked, her piercing blue eyes disappearing behind her eyelids for an instant. *"You may call us Tuli if you wish,"* she said.

Us? If I wish? What kind of an answer is that?

Ben stared at her. She reminded him of Kaia, the alien girl who had given him the skill. He stood and approached her. For some reason, he was glad bars separated them. *"How did you get in here?"*

The tiniest of smiles crept on her face. *"We have our ways..."* she said. She tilted her head to the side, eyes focused on him. *"You have the translation skill,"* she stated.

Ben frowned. *"How do you know?"*

She didn't answer but rather studied him some more. It was starting to annoy him. *"That's not good,"* she said, continuing her line of thought. *"You must leave."*

"Leave?" Ben squished his face. *"Uh, hello! I'm locked up in a cell if you haven't noticed..."*

That fact didn't seem to move her. *"If you stay,"* she said, *"the translation skill will get you killed."*

Ben's stomach flipped. *"What do you mean?"*

Her blue eyes rested on his for a moment. Then she lifted a finger to her lips, indicating he should be silent, and took a step backward into the shadows. She faded into a nook in the wall where he could barely see her.

The door slid open, and a Toreq man entered, making a lot of noise as he struggled to hold on to a leather briefcase and a handful of other objects. A stack of blank papers slid from under his arm.

Ben turned, mouth agape, unable to make sense of the mysterious girl and even less of the clumsy Toreq who had just made his appearance.

Tuli gave Ben a sly smile, then slipped out the door behind the man's back.

"Wait, don't go!" he shouted.

The Toreq man, who groaned from the effort of bending to pick up his blank papers from the floor, looked up at him, eyebrows raised. *"Who, me? But I just got here!"*

Ben stared out the door, trying to catch a glimpse of the girl, but she had disappeared.

The Toreq man straightened and frowned at

him, so Ben took a step back and tried hard to pull a straight face.

"Ah, this won't do," the man said, looking around. He placed an ink pen between his teeth to free his hand, using his other arm to clutch the rest of his things. He tapped at the wall next to the door, and a screen with Toreq symbols materialized there. After coding in a few orders, a square table and two chairs appeared out of thin air, building from the legs up. The cell bars went straight through its middle, dividing the table into two different settings. It was a bizarre sight. Ben's side was wooden and used. The man's side, however, was white and futuristic. Ben received a rickety, hard stool, while the man's chair looked comfortable and futuristic.

There was no time to study the furniture as the man dumped his belongings on it. Then he opened the briefcase and pulled out a massive pile of documents bound together by a string. The stack of blank papers was set to the side with the ink pen right above it.

Ben followed all this with bewilderment.

Once satisfied, the man straightened, laced his hands before him and gave a big smile.

Ben stared at his dark clothes. They resembled business suits from back on Earth but old-fashioned. Also, his white hair had odd curls in them, like tubes. It made him think of the wigs English lawyers wore.

"Fascinating!" the man beamed, reflecting Ben's own thoughts. He studied Ben, just like Tuli had done not long ago. This was turning into a bad habit.

I'm not a zoo animal!

The man said, "Please state your name for the record."

Ben was still trying to gather his senses. He'd been alone for so long he still couldn't get over the fact he'd had two visitors in less than an hour. Not to mention the man spoke English. "Uh. Ben Archer..."

"Ha, ha, ha. Yes, yes. Benarcher, indeed. I am Lord Crawford, Attorney General. I will represent you in the Toreq State vs. Benarcher case." A slight blush rose to the man's cheeks when Ben didn't react. The Toreq added quickly, "Did I say that right? Is it my name? I figured it would be easier to pronounce than my Toreq name..."

Ben stared. "Huh?"

Lord Crawford waved his hand at him. "Please! Don't think me foolish. Lord Crawford is a name I found in some documents from your planet. I can use another name if you like..."

Ben shrugged. "Uh, no, no. That's fine."

Lord Crawford beamed and stretched out his hand. "Please! Sit!" he said. As they both settled on their respective seats, he continued. "The Toreq pride themselves in offering a judicial system adapted to all intelligent life forms. When a conflict arises between two alien species, the laws from both sides are considered and applied in a fair manner.

"I am the leading expert in judicial matters relating to the A'hmun. I have studied your laws to the tiniest of details for many, many years. Not to mention your language and your ways. All absolutely fascinating! Little did I know I would have the great privilege to represent a real, live A'hmun in a real, live court. Ha, ha, ha."

Spiders crawled up Ben's spine. This was all very confusing. "You studied A'hmun law... on Earth?" he asked.

"Ah, no, no. Of course not. We have an extensive library on the Mother Planet. Quite well stocked in judicial proceedings from a variety of planets, including yours."

Ben's mind swayed. He had a very, very bad feeling about this. "Wait a minute. You have law books from Earth in a library on your planet?"

Lord Crawford nodded vigorously.

"But... how old are these books?"

Lord Crawford pouted. "Oh, roughly a hundred-and-fifty years. The equivalent of two hundred of your Earth years. It is a shame that the Observer was unable to provide us with the most recent information about the A'hmun. I would have liked to complete my library. Most unfortunate..."

Ben's mind whirled. "But those are completely out of date! You do realize we've come a long way since then, don't you?" he exclaimed, only to be met with his attorney's raised eyebrow, as if he were a parent silently scolding a rude child.

Ben couldn't even begin to think what law books looked like two centuries ago, but he suspected they would not be in his favour. But then, had he ever expected this trial to be in his favour?

"So," he said finally. "Will you tell me what I'm accused of?"

CHAPTER 8 *Impossible Charges*

"Unlawful possession of a Toreq skill," the alien attorney said, reading from one of the documents.

"Naturally..." Ben muttered, shoulders slumping. The Toreq would never allow a human to possess a Toreq skill. They'd accuse him of having stolen it from Kaia...

Lord Crawford sat opposite him with his back straight. "...and the second charge," the attorney began, lifting a stack of papers and reading another document through tiny spectacles dangling at the edge of his nose.

Ben tensed. *A second charge?*

"Misuse of the translation skill to the first degree," Lord Crawford read, then glanced at Ben over the edge of the spectacles.

Ben gasped, his arms and legs losing their strength. "What did you say?"

Lord Crawford repeated the words. "Misuse of the translation skill to the first degree." He dropped the paper and straightened his spectacles. "It means you used the skill to submit a creature to your will. An offence of the highest order under Toreq law."

Ben's mouth dropped. "You... you mean Sadalbari?" His mind reeled. How did the Toreq know about his encounter with the Arabian stallion? How did they know he had controlled the horse's mind before it could commit a fatal deed? "But... that's not possible! How would you know about that?"

"So you do not deny the charges?" Lord Crawford said, picking up the ink pen and getting ready to write on his blank paper. His face had become hard.

"No! Wait a minute, that's not what I said... I... I..." Words wouldn't come. Alternating cold and hot flashes rose to Ben's face. What was he supposed to say? Wasn't this all a setup, anyway? Wasn't the end aim to get rid of A'hmun men, women, and children alike—him included? So why waste time with this charade?

Lord Crawford waited for Ben to answer.

Ben was on the verge of tears. "What's the point? What does it matter what I did or didn't do? The Toreq are out to get rid of us anyway, aren't they?"

To his surprise, Lord Crawford leaned back into his chair. He munched on the tip of his spectacles. "You are right," he said after a while. "This is a political move. I am afraid, Benarcher, that you have become the symbol of all that is hated in your species.

"None of us, here, on these warships, have ever laid eyes on the A'hmun. We have come to fight an enemy from the depths of our past. All we know about you is what our ancestors have transmitted to us over thousands of generations.

"Our soldiers need an A'hmun symbol to represent their hated enemy. Showing them an A'hmun face that they can learn to hate and linking that face to unacceptable wrongdoings will help them focus on their task. By putting you on display and exposing your unpardonable deeds in a neutral court, our soldiers will be confident they are on the right side of the law—your actions prove that the A'hmun must be eliminated. It is a wise move by our General but an unfortunate plight for you." He crossed his legs, his eyes drifting into the distance. "A historic moment, without a doubt."

Ben slumped with his forehead in his hands. "It's no use, then. I've lost already."

"Tsk, tsk. You forget your good old Lord Crawford. I am quite a successful lawyer, if I may say so myself. We will fight this political move and treat it as such. We will find a flaw in the proceedings. It's all a matter of perspective. Keep in mind that the Toreq court is impartial and upholds the law, no matter the circumstances."

Ben shut his eyes. *Impartial? Come off it!*

He heard Lord Crawford untie the pile of documents. "So, we will start at the beginning. There is much to do and little time! But I am relieved that, in the meantime, I was able to provide you with a decent A'hmun room, copied to the slightest detail from our records about your jails. I trust you feel at home here?"

Ben gritted his teeth. "You could have added a window, at least," he muttered.

Silence.

Ben opened his eyes a crack and peeked at Lord Crawford.

"A window?" the lawyer said, frowning. "But of course! A window..." He grabbed the ink pen and scribbled something that looked like the word 'window' on it. "Anything else?" he asked.

Ben rolled his eyes. "A key would be good."

"A k-e-y," his alien lawyer repeated slowly, writing down the word with difficulty, then stopping. "A key... Is that not one of those things...? Oh, but, ah. You do understand that that is not possible? What a strange request. Ha, ha, ha. Fascinating!"

* * *

A loud knock on the door startled Laura awake.

She sat up, gathering her bearings. She had fallen fast asleep in a room provided to her by the Secretary-General under the United Nations building. Countless hours bringing the Secretary-General up to date on events dating back to *The Cosmic Fall* had left her drained. Could it only have been eighteen months since this celestial event, when Mesmo's spaceship had crashed near her father's land and Ben had been entrusted with his alien skill? She pondered on their adventures before falling back into a dream-filled sleep in which Ben kept slipping away from her.

The knock came again, so she hurried to open the door.

"Ma'am, the Secretary-General has asked for you," a soldier said.

She nodded, not having shaken the sleep from her eyes completely. She dressed quickly, then tightened her ponytail as she hurried to the meeting room, arriving there at the same time as Jeremy. They found Inspector Hao already inside.

Men and women talked over each other before sitting down when Adhira asked for silence. She raised the sound on a large screen. Bright red words scrolled across the bottom of it: NEW YORK CITY IN EMERGENCY LOCKDOWN.

A reporter spoke in a serious voice. "It has now been confirmed that *Hurricane Zeta*, which destroyed Cuba and Florida two days ago, is projected to hit New York City within the next four hours. The hurricane was expected to be downgraded to a tropical cyclone but has regained strength as it travels up the East Coast of the United States, wreaking havoc in its path.

"The mayor of New York has urged citizens to remain home and not head out of the city at this time as roads are already clogged with people fleeing in their cars.

"It will be the most severe hurricane known in recorded history to hit this far north of the United States. Winds are expected to reach 175mph and..."

Adhira silenced the television.

They all looked at each other.

Goosebumps rose on Laura's arms.

"This storm is not natural," she heard someone comment, echoing her thoughts.

Her hands shook as the meeting room erupted in worried arguments.

So this is it.

Laura wasn't ready. Nothing had prepared her for this. Even though she had known about the Toreq threat for some time, she had not expected things to move so quickly. The Toreq were supposed to return to Earth within two-hundred years, not *four hours*! Two hundred years was supposed to be plenty of time for Ben and Mesmo to fulfil their mission. The plan had been that they would be the voices humans were going to listen to, to bring balance back to the natural world. It was a mission she had expected them to pursue for the rest of their lives.

But *four hours?*

On the screen, she caught images of cracked earth and dead wheat in the Great Plains of the U.S., the Ganges River overflowing in India, forest fires burning in Congo.

Hao leaned forward. He had remained silent beside her, until now. He said in a hush, "We need Mesmo."

CHAPTER 9 *Old and New Enemies*

Lord Crawford droned on with his nose in the documents, analyzing each one with exaggerated detail from a Toreq point-of-view. Then from an A'hmun one. The answer to Ben's release would be in these papers, he said, providing clues as to how they should build up their defence.

Ben tried hard not to fall asleep. He let the attorney do all the talking, and Lord Crawford got so engrossed in his work he barely noticed Ben was no longer listening. Ben was thinking of his mom. She'd be worried sick, especially with Mesmo gone as well.

"Lord Crawford?" he spoke up suddenly, not caring that the attorney raised an eyebrow at his rude interruption.

"Uh, yes, Benarcher?"

Ben took a deep breath. "Is there any news of Mesmo?"

Lord Crawford frowned. "The Observer, you mean?"

Ben nodded.

"I don't see how that concerns you. But to answer your question: we have not had any news of the Observer in many, many star-rises. Word is that he is dead."

Ben wished he hadn't asked. His heart constricted. He no longer cared for this supposed trial. Humans had been cornered, and he along with them. The Toreq were pulling the strings, and there was nothing he could do about it.

It bothered him, not being in control. He had not been in control for a long time now. Everyone wanted his skill for one reason or another. Some wanted him to imprison animals for shows; others wanted him to tame them to be ridden and subjugated. Others, still, wanted to pin Ben's misuse of the skill as an example of human corruption.

I'm tired of being treated this way!

He wanted to be released from these chains. He wanted to be given free rein to use his power the way he wished. He wanted to learn how to use it in a respectful, wholesome way that would be fulfilling and helpful, not harmful or deceitful. He wanted to be the master of his skill, not a tool to be used by others to fulfil their personal goals.

Or become a tool at the mercy of the skill itself...

That was his last thought as he began to drift off, with his forehead on his arm.

Lord Crawford's voice turned into a constant murmur in the background. Ben let it lull him until the voice became something else: something deeper, more edgy.

Ben tried to concentrate on the words. There was something odd about them. It sounded like they no longer came from Lord Crawford's mouth but from somewhere else, deeper down within the warship.

Ben ruffled his feathers and peeked through the branches of a massive tree. He took in his surroundings, vaguely surprised at having gone from his cell to the top of a tree in the blink of an eye. The voice came from below. He hopped to a lower branch, feeling light and confident among the leaves. This tree was special, he realized, but he couldn't remember why.

Stretching his long neck, he peered down his beak at two men standing in the shadow of the branches. The night sky on this strange planet was a dark purple, with a potato-shaped moon glowing through the leaves. Not the virtual potato-shaped moon from the warship, but the real thing.

Both men greeted each other, placing three middle fingers against the middle of their forehead in greeting.

"I am honoured to have your trust in this matter," the first said in a low voice.

Ben reeled. He almost dropped out of the tree, but his wings kept him stable.

That voice! I KNOW THAT VOICE!

His mind transported to the night of *The Cosmic Fall*; to the night Mesmo's spaceship had crashed to Earth because a deadly enemy had shot him down. It was the night Ben's whole adventure had begun. And now he wanted to flee; he wanted to hide from this terrifying old enemy. But he was stuck in a dream. Or was it a memory?

"You accept the terms, then?" the other man said, his silver cape shimmering as a passing breeze rippled through it.

The first man with spiky hair said, *"I have your orders and will fulfil them. I will follow the Observer's crew through the wormhole. I will destroy them once they have approached Earth and are unable to call for help."*

"Good," the other answered. *"I want proof of your success. Bring the crew back to me, in pieces if you must."* He paused. *"They must not be allowed to fulfil their mission, do you understand? The Arch Council is putting together an army. They suspect the Observer's information will confirm our worst fears: that the A'hmun are close to mastering inter-planetary flight. As soon as this is confirmed, the Arch Council will send the army to crush the A'hmun. We can't let that happen."*

The spiky-haired man smirked. *"You are full of surprises, Challenger. I must say I did not see you as a defender of the A'hmun. It will be my pleasure to take care of the Observer and his daughter. I will do your bidding as long as you fulfil our agreement. I want full Toreq citizenship upon my return. I trust you will not forget."*

The taller man grabbed the other by the shirt. *"You are under my orders, Bordock. You are in no position to demand anything of me. I know who you are. A'hmun blood flows in your veins. You crawl under our cities like vermin. One false step and I'll deliver you to the Arch Council myself!"*

Bordock licked his lips. *"Now, now. I'm sure you wouldn't go that far, Challenger,"* he said, his eyes two pools of darkness that turned Ben's blood cold. Images of his grandfather and his dear dog

Tike flashed before his eyes. They were dead because of this monster.

Bordock's face began to tremble at a terrifying speed. The shapeshifter's body lengthened, his face became older. His hair grew into a long braid that fell down his back and, soon, he turned into a spitting image of the man standing before him.

The Challenger released him. *"Stop fooling around, Bordock!"*

The identical men stared at each other.

The corner of Bordock's mouth curled. *"At your command, Challenger."* He gave a mock salute and returned to his natural form. *"Don't look so worried. I will fulfil my part of the deal. But will you?"*

The Challenger's fists tightened at his side, but he nodded. *"We have a deal."*

Bordock gave one nod, then turned to leave, and as he did so, his twisted eyes glanced briefly towards the tree.

"No!" Ben shouted, terrorized, but no sound came.

The shapeshifter did not see him. Instead, Ben realized he saw the creature that lived within its branches. Bordock left, and now it was the other's turn to look up.

General Zoltar spoke sharply at the creature in the tree. *"Come!"* he ordered, fire reflecting in his eyes.

Ben screamed.

* * *

Lord Crawford tapped him on the cheek. "Benarcher, Benarcher," he repeated.

Ben lay sprawled on the ground.

"Drink," the Toreq lawyer said, lifting Ben so he could gulp from a cup. The fresh liquid invigorated him.

The stool had fallen on its side. The attorney's papers lay strewn on the ground. Ben barely noticed. He was stricken. "Zoltar!" he gasped. "It was Zoltar!"

"Tsk, tsk," Lord Crawford said. "You've had a bit of a shock. I've seen it before, in prisoners awaiting a trial that could lead to a death sentence. It is quite common." He stood, picked up Ben's rickety stool and left the cup on the wooden table. Then he slipped with ease through the force field in the middle of the room—confirming Ben's idea that the virtual bars had been designed to keep only him trapped inside.

"Now, now," the lawyer said, glancing at the

mess on the floor. "This is quite unfortunate. It will take me days to put our defence together again." He sighed. "I will send someone to pick this up. In the meantime, I suggest you get some rest. You will need to pull yourself together, Benarcher, or your attitude will lose you this trial."

CHAPTER 10 *The Judge*

Ben paced his cell, biting his knuckles.

Zoltar!

The name branded in his mind. It had been General Zoltar who had sent an assassin to kill Mesmo and his crew eighteen months ago. It had been Zoltar who had been behind the start of his whole adventure. If not for Zoltar, Bordock would never have come to Earth, and he would never have shot down Mesmo's spaceship. Or Kaia's. Kaia wouldn't have died, and she wouldn't have given Ben her skill.

Mesmo had suspected Bordock had not acted on his own. He'd suspected that a powerful Toreq had been behind the attack on his crew. And now that powerful Toreq was right here, in the alien warship, attacking Earth...

But that doesn't make sense!

Zoltar had told Bordock he didn't want Earth to be attacked. It was the whole reason he had sent Bordock in the first place. So why was he doing so now? Ben couldn't fit the pieces together. Was General Zoltar on Earth's side or not? He strongly leaned towards the latter.

So, now what? What was he supposed to do with this information? Who could he confide in? And what difference would it make?

He thought of Lord Crawford, but the attorney seemed oblivious to what was going on in the bigger picture. What about Tuli? But who was she? And what did she want?

That left Torka, who claimed to be Mesmo's friend. Ben stopped pacing and thought about him some more. Although Torka had accused him of being a thief and a liar, Ben felt he could trust the plastered-haired alien. After all, if he truly were Mesmo's friend, it would be logical for him to see Ben as an enemy: one who had 'stolen' Kaia's skill and who was 'hiding' Mesmo's location.

Torka, then.

But how was he going to get the alien's attention? It wasn't like he could make a phone call and say, "Operator, patch me through to Torka."

Ben curled up on the bed and crossed his arms over his chest, squeezing tight. Because, above all these questions, another major one loomed: who, or *what* had sent him this vision?

* * *

Two impossibly long Toreq days passed. Lord Crawford had put his stack of papers together again. He was revising them with Ben one at a time, and Ben began to wonder if this was some form of excruciating torture imagined by General Zoltar. He also wondered why his attorney was using paper in the first place, to which Lord Crawford answered that this was all part of the process to make him feel more comfortable. "We have the greatest respect for the ways of other life forms and are striving to make the proceedings as similar to the A'hmun ones as possible, so you do not feel cheated."

How charming...

Ben tried to find out if he could have visitors, to which Lord Crawford answered visitors were strictly forbidden before the court hearing.

So that meant both Tuli and Torka had broken the rules. Was that something to his advantage? Ben wondered about this as he stared out the window after Lord Crawford had finally left. He had found the tiny, round window upon waking from a restless sleep. It was one thing for which he could thank his attorney.

But looking through the window had not brought the solace he had hoped for. Before him drifted the other Toreq warships, dark and forbidding, as they lurked beside the Moon. Only once did they glide up far enough from behind the rocky satellite for Earth to appear. Ben's heart bulged at seeing his home planet, bright and blue and beautiful, yet so far out of reach. Strange cloud formations covered North America, the most impressive being a big, flat circle with a hole in the middle.

A hurricane! Ben stared, stomach twisting. The thing was massive. It covered half of the Northern Atlantic Ocean. *What's going on down there?* Good thing his mom would be home on the other side of the American continent and miles away from this monster storm!

A shuffling sound made him turn, and he found Lord Crawford entering his cell with two Toreq soldiers.

"It is time," the attorney said.

Ben's legs shook as he tried to get up.

I'm not ready!

He wanted to shout the words, beg for a delay, claim his innocence to whoever would hear. But there lay the problem. He couldn't claim his innocence. The Toreq were right: he had submitted a living creature to his skill. He had bent the Arabian horse to his will with a force that even he could not comprehend.

I'm guilty!

The thought flashed in his mind while Lord Crawford disintegrated the force field containing the metal bars.

"Lord Crawford!" he said in a wave of panic. "May I have a Toreq translation device?"

His attorney frowned, "But you don't nee..."

"Please!" Ben insisted. Maybe the translation device would remove some pressure off his skill. Maybe it would help him keep the skill in tow. "I... er... I'm kind of nervous, and I want to make sure I understand the entire proceedings."

Lord Crawford stared at him, then shrugged.

After providing him with the small black dot, which Lord Crawford placed behind his ear, the soldiers led Ben out of his cell and down the corridors. He didn't have far to go. Turning to the right, Ben found himself walking down a row of trees with leaves and roots that intertwined in such a way that they formed a vast alley, ending in a white wall. To his surprise, the two soldiers passed right through the solid-looking surface, and Ben realized the wall was actually made up of some sort of diffused light.

Lord Crawford urged him to follow, and Ben found himself in a massive, egg-shaped room. He was going to step forward when Lord Crawford held him back. Ben frowned at him and saw one of the soldiers swipe at a hovering screen.

The dome's surface filled with small, colourful blocks that fitted into each other like the pixels of a huge image, until suddenly it was as if he'd been dropped into a different location. Ben gasped as he found himself at the edge of a narrow balcony, staring several feet down into an auditorium. He jumped back to avoid falling over the railing.

"What do you think of our courtroom?" Lord Crawford asked, thrusting his chest out. "It was recreated based on my extensive research into A'hmun history."

Ben stared at the deep burgundy carpets and gold decorations. Rows of chairs with dark red covering led to the front of the room and were split down the middle by an aisle. Right at the front, there was a stage. He squished his eyebrows together. If this was a courtroom, why was there a stage with curtains dropping from the ceiling?

His eyes widened, and he understood. The fancy auditorium with a balcony bordering half of the dome, the stage, the curtains...

This is a theatre!

Ben blinked, not sure whether he should laugh or cry. Did the Toreq really think a theatre was a courtroom? Well, it fit the occasion. Was this all not a show, anyway?

Ben didn't feel the urge to mention this absurd mistake because the Toreq who filled the audience had their eyes turned on him. About fifty pairs of eyes, maybe more.

Lord Crawford indicated he should head to his left, to the end of the balcony that overlooked the stage. Ben sighed inwardly, relieved that he did not have to sit up front with the whole audience watching.

Ben could understand the attorney's misinterpretation of the theatre. He began to understand that the left side of the balcony was his, while, on the opposite balcony, a middle-aged Toreq woman with long white hair took a seat.

The plaintiff!

This woman must be the one who had taken action against him and brought him to court!

It wasn't long before the curtains raised, and

ten wrinkled-faced Toreq took a seat in chairs set up in a single row on the stage. The ten elderly men and women each wore a burgundy cape attached by a gold pin at the neck. A bigger, empty chair split them into two groups of five. Ben wrung his hands in his lap and glanced at his attorney, who sat beside him with an air of self-confidence. He hoped the man truly knew what he was doing.

In spite of the filled auditorium, silence prevailed, the air feeling tense and muffled.

Ben held his breath.

One of the elderly women stood and spoke with a clear voice that carried over the audience. *"This court is now in session. All rise."*

Lord Crawford whispered proudly in Ben's ear, "I told her to say that!"

Everyone stood.

Ben tried to get up, but his legs wouldn't hold him. Lord Crawford dug a couple of fingers into his shoulder, urging him to stand.

Ben did, though he had to hold on to the railing to sustain him. His cheeks flushed as the woman looked at him, then returned to her seat.

"Now comes the judge," Lord Crawford whispered.

He had barely spoken when a tall man with a flowing silver cape made his entrance. The judge reached the big chair in the middle and addressed the audience in a loud, deep voice. *"Ladies and gentlemen of the jury, this day begins the Toreq State vs. Benarcher case."* He glanced to the balconies to his right and left. *"Lord Crawford, Captain Daria, you may begin."*

Ben tumbled into his chair.

It was General Zoltar.

CHAPTER 11 *Ping-Pong*

Zoltar, of all people!

With the General as the judge, all hope was lost. Not that Ben had had much hope to begin with. But wasn't the General supposed to be busy attacking Earth?

As if hearing his silent question, Lord Crawford whispered in his ear, "Can you believe it? General Zoltar personally offered to be the judge in this case. You couldn't have asked for a higher-ranking Toreq. A great honour indeed!"

Indeed...

Goosebumps rose on Ben's arms.

While the two attorneys spoke back-and-forth, battling with words to advance their case, Ben's eyes were glued on the General. A cold sweat broke out on his brows as he thought of the fire in Zoltar's eyes when he had glanced up at the creature in the tree, and a creepy idea began to form in his mind, one that sent shivers up his spine. What if it had been this creature that Ben had heard moaning in pain? What if it had been trying to communicate with him—asking for help? Ben stared at General Zoltar. Was this man capable of harming such a precious living being?

He shuddered again.

Why did he feel a connection to the General? Why did he have fleeting moments of recognition, of familiarity, with the man? Was it because of the memories that the creature had sent him?

A mumble broke through the crowd, interrupting his thoughts.

The other attorney—the one called Captain Daria—stood at the other end of the balcony, addressing the attendees. At the same time, before the judge and jury, a three-dimensional globe of Earth expanded until it filled a quarter of the room.

"The anomaly was detected fifteen star-rises ago," Captain Daria spoke in Toreq. *"Our sensors captured a ripple in the fabric of space-time and pinpointed it to this location."*

The Earth rolled slowly on its axis until a red beam emanated from the ground into space. The powerful beam came from a spot in the Middle East...

Ben hunkered into his chair.

"We all know what this reading means," Captain Daria said. *"This is the typical signal of a skill gone awry. A team was sent to locate the suspect of this unpardonable mismanagement of the skill. Please consider evidence 972-3."*

The Earth disappeared, and the outline of Ben's form took its place. Billions of moving particles vibrated within him, releasing a red substance. The red substance was matched to the red beam until they superimposed in perfect harmony.

Captain Daria faced the stage. *"This evidence shows that the accused is indeed the holder of the translation skill, which he abused fifteen star-rises ago."*

Shocked exclamations rose from the audience.

Ben sank deeper into the chair.

General Zoltar lifted his head in his direction. *"Do you have anything to add, Lord Crawford?"*

Ben's attorney sprang to his feet. *"I do, General Zoltar. It seems my opponent conveniently forgets a critical piece of evidence. The accused is an underaged child. He cannot be held responsible for his actions. Toreq law states that children under the age of ten are the responsibility of their mentor and cannot be charged as an adult. And this child here, in Toreq years, is only eight-and-a-half."*

Ben straightened. He stared at his attorney, a flicker of hope rising in his chest. Could it be Lord Crawford knew what he was doing after all?

Captain Daria sat and deliberated with her consorts, then nodded.

Ben held his breath.

"Esteemed jury," she said, standing and facing the stage again. *"Lord Crawford's argument does not stand, for the simple reason that this child is not a Toreq. He is A'hmun. He is thirteen-Earth-years-old and responsible for his actions. He submitted a wild creature to the translation skill, making it suffer, perhaps even killing it. This goes against our fundamental laws. We demand that he be sentenced with the death penalty."*

The blood drained from Ben's face. He slumped back, feeling crushed.

His attorney sat, too, breathing heavily through his nose.

"So, that's it, then," Ben said in a low voice while the opposing attorney continued to speak.

Lord Crawford balled his fists. "You just wait,

Benarcher. I still have a few tricks up my sleeve."

"What's the point?" Ben argued. "Is everyone going to play ping-pong with my life? Going back and forth between A'hmun and Toreq laws, depending on which one suits you best? In their eyes, I'm an A'hmun adult, yet they want to apply a Toreq punishment. Where's the fairness in that?"

The court proceedings continued, but Ben no longer paid attention. He stared at Zoltar, anger welling up inside, and wished the General would look up so he could make it clear that he knew what was going on.

But General Zoltar remained impassible, listening to both attorneys as they duelled.

Then something behind the General caught Ben's eye. He squinted, wondering if the old theatre came with a ghost. Sure enough, there she was...

Tuli!

The pale girl peeked from the sides but must have sensed his gaze because she lifted her eyes.

Ben frowned at her, trying to send a silent question to find out why she was spying.

She lifted a finger to her lips as she had done before, the blue end of her braid shining, then turned her attention to the auditorium again.

CHAPTER 12 *The Eye of the Storm*

"We're back online, Miss," a soldier said, startling Laura out of her thoughts. She had been staring at the cream pattern in her latte, thinking of the ferocious hurricane raging above ground.

Days had passed, and the unnatural storm had continued to feed hungrily off merging hot-and-cold currents in the Atlantic. Never in history had a hurricane lasted this long above one area, and Laura had heard whispers of the insurmountable loss to human life and property.

The ground of the Bunker cafeteria rumbled beneath them. Laura and the soldier glanced around, their eyes wide. This had happened several times already, and Laura did not like the sound of it at all. Tremors travelled from the floor through the soles of her shoes, then quietened down, leaving her with a dry mouth and stiff spine.

The soldier straightened and cleared his throat, trying to hide his fear. "We don't have long," he said. "We'll be in the eye of the storm for an estimated ninety-seven minutes before winds pick up again."

Laura's stomach squeezed. She had never experienced a hurricane before.

During a subdued lunch earlier on, Jeremy had explained the phenomenon to her. He had taken a white paper plate and stuck the tip of his pen through its middle, making a small hole. "If this plate is the hurricane, then this hole in the middle is the *eye of the storm*," he had said. He had drawn a long arrow from the edge of the plate towards the middle. "We just spent the past days going through the first half of the hurricane, and in a few hours, we'll reach the eye." He had pointed to the hole in the middle. "Winds are constantly rotating around the eye of the storm, and the closer we get to the eye, the stronger the winds. Yet, when we arrive right in the very middle, we will reach a calm zone." He had lifted the plate and peeked through the hole. "Winds will die down, and we may even see some sunlight. We'll be under the impression that the worst is over. But it won't be."

He had then continued his original arrow, this time going from the middle of the plate to the other edge. "We will still need to survive the other half of the hurricane.

"Usually, the force of a hurricane lessens as the storm pushes against the land," Jeremy had said. "But this is no normal hurricane..."

Laura pushed away her latte and shuddered as she remembered Jeremy's words.

The eye of the storm.

They would be in the eye for the next ninety-seven minutes. Ninety-seven minutes of calm before they entered the other half of the hurricane. A brief respite—just enough time to try and connect to the internet, gather as much news as possible, call loved ones, reinforce barriers.

Laura left the cafeteria and headed to the operations room, where everyone was talking over each other on multiple phones. She caught Jeremy snapping away with his camera. At this point, no-one seemed to care whether the reporter was supposed to be there or not.

"Laura." Hao grabbed her arm. He was holding up his mobile phone. "This message just came in from the Dugout."

She took it from him and stared at the screen. PATIENT CONSCIOUS. PLEASE ADVISE.

Laura's eyes widened. "Mesmo's awake?" she gasped.

Hao nodded.

She grabbed her phone but found it unresponsive. Clearly, Hao's captured a better signal.

"This is all I've got," Hao said, crushing her hopes. "My calls won't get through."

Laura looked at him, and she knew they were both thinking the same thing. "We need to get above ground," she said, already moving.

They were heading up the stairs when they found Jeremy puffing behind them.

"What do you think you're doing, Mr. Busybody?" Hao snapped.

"Doing my job just like you, Mr. Bigshot," Jeremy retorted as he continued to trail them.

They rushed outside the UN building and came to a dead stop.

"Oh, no!" Laura exclaimed before she could help herself.

Jeremy made a strange hiccupping sound.

Hao grasped his hair with his hands.

New York lay in shambles. Skeleton skyscrapers surrounded them. Few windows remained. The sea lapped at the edge of Garden Court, threatening to overflow it. Poles that had held the flags of the world's nations lay twisted on the ground. A ray of sunlight cast a web of shadows over the city while, out in the ocean, a dark wall of clouds and rain advanced relentlessly towards them.

"The other half of the storm," Hao breathed. "Do you really think the Toreq are provoking this hurricane?"

"Yes," Laura said without hesitating.

Hao nodded. "Then we'd better do something about it," he said before wandering off with his phone stuck to his ear.

At the same moment, Laura's phone buzzed in her trouser pocket. She picked it up in a hurry. "Hello?"

"Laura?" Mesmo's voice sounded so close she had to sit on a boulder in shock.

"Mesmo! You're awake!" she exclaimed, shutting her eyes to try and control her emotions.

"Of course, I am. You won't get rid of me that easily."

Laura bit her lip hard. "Mesmo, they took Ben," she managed.

"I know."

Laura closed her eyes and swallowed. "Look, I'm in New York with Inspector Hao. The Toreq were here three weeks ago. We think they'll be back in another week. I'll be waiting for them. I'll convince them to take me to Ben."

"No, Laura! I won't allow it. Einar has teamed up with a faction of my people. They are extremely dangerous and will stop at nothing to see the A'hmun exterminated. They tried to kill me and destroyed my spaceship. I won't let you fall into their hands, as well. I need to speak to the leader of the Toreq army. I suspect he is not aware of this rebellious group. I may be able to reason with him."

"But how, Mesmo? You don't have a spaceship!"

"In fact, I do," he said. "Inspector Hao gave me the idea. His team has done a pretty decent job pasting together salvaged parts from the two crashed spaceships. I think I can work with that."

Laura remembered the craft caught within a web of scaffolds at the bottom of the Dugout. She gasped. "But that thing's a wreck!"

Someone shouted in the distance. A soldier was waving her over. She glanced out at sea, and her heart almost stopped.

The dark wall of clouds and rain loomed before her, approaching much faster than expected. The sun disappeared like a light passing at the end of a tunnel. The wind lifted, and she had to press her hand to her ear to hear Mesmo on the other end. His voice crackled. "It will hold," he said. "I know about the hurricane. Hang tight! I need a day. Tw... at the most. Then I'll come f... you."

Laura swallowed as she watched the approaching deluge.

"No," she said.

"Laur...? I can't hea... y..."

"There's no time!" she shouted into the receiver, wind whipping at her hair.

"Wha...?"

"Don't pick me up. Tell your people to stop the hurricane! Get Ben!" she yelled, running toward the UN building, her heart pounding. "Get Ben!" she repeated several times, needing to make him understand. She rushed into the lobby, wind chasing her through the shattered glass doors.

"A... right..."

Thick raindrops splattered into the lobby while waves lapped at the seawall.

"Laura," Mesmo said. "I lo... y..."

The line went dead.

CHAPTER 13 *Defence*

"No! Please... Please... no..." the voice begged in Ben's mind. He squirmed, wishing to be released from this nightmare. But he was stuck in the same shaft as before, resting on Echis' mind, listening to the moans of despair coming from the nearby room.

Echis!

Ben called the snake, but it didn't budge.

Echis? What's the matter?

The snake didn't respond.

The voice whimpered through the shaft like a lost soul, sending shivers down Ben's spine. He desperately wanted to help the suffering creature, but this being a nightmare, he also wanted to flee as far away as possible from whoever was causing such harm. He squirmed and twisted in his bed, tearing himself from his sleep. Even then, the moaning followed him into the cell, echoing in its walls.

Heavy sobs left Ben's chest. Sobs that belonged to the suffering creature but were also his own. He grasped his head and cried for all the people on Earth who were getting hammered by droughts and storms and winds. And he cried for himself because even though he had known from the beginning there was no way out, it still hurt to know the end was near. Today the attorneys would plead their case; the jury would deliver their sentence.

Lord Crawford had said that the sentence would be swift. The Toreq had things to do, and many were glued to the proceedings instead of fulfilling their tasks. The case was becoming too much of a distraction and needed to be rushed.

This afternoon, then. This afternoon he'd be ejected into space like a bothersome speck of dust.

The day went by in a blur. Ben's head buzzed as he was taken from the cell to the egg-shaped dome. He had barely slept, and echoes of the moaning voice nagged at the back of his mind, messing with his thoughts.

He sat in a daze as Captain Daria pleaded her

case against him with strong, believable arguments. Ben watched the audience hang on to her every word with zeal.

Something buzzed in front of Captain Daria's face. It was a small drone-like object that Ben had seen hovering throughout the case. At first, he'd thought it was some kind of security device, but now he realized it was a lot more than that.

He turned to his attorney, who was wringing his hands together in his lap. Ben had noticed Lord Crawford's nervous twitches increasing over the past days, and a pit in his stomach deepened as his worst fear was confirmed: the attorney was losing the case.

"Lord Crawford," Ben whispered.

"Hm?"

"Are we being broadcast live?"

Lord Crawford spoke in a hushed tone. "Of course! The whole fleet is watching us right now. There has not been a Toreq versus A'hmun case since *The Great War of the Kins*. You can imagine how thrilled the fleet is to watch and see how this will turn out. Fascinating! Fascinating, indeed..." He drifted off into a mumble that Ben couldn't make out.

Ben leaned back, feeling dead inside. He watched the audience as if he were just another mini-drone filming passively for the pleasure of others.

On the other side of the room, a man sat beside Captain Daria, listening to her defence. It was Einar. Ben barely twitched. *Who cares that Einar is there?* He was just another pawn out to get him. And near the entrance of the dome, several soldiers marched to form a line. The end of the proceedings was near. Were they expecting Ben to make a run for it? Come to think of it: maybe he *would* panic and run.

He'd unconsciously placed his hopes in Lord Crawford, but now they were at the end of the proceedings. He stared at the auditorium as if from a distance, realizing he had nothing left to lose. That thought sparked the beginning of an idea within him. He straightened. *It's too late for me, but what if... what if it wasn't too late for Earth....?*

Captain Daria finished speaking and glanced his way with a satisfied air.

Ben swallowed. "Lord Crawford?"

"Shush!" the attorney urged. "It's my turn to speak."

"But... Lord Crawford..."

From the stage, General Zoltar spoke in Toreq. *"Thank you for presenting us with your defence, Captain Daria."* He turned towards Lord

Crawford. *"We are ready to hear yours, Lord Crawford."*

Three little drones flew into place before Ben and his attorney.

Lord Crawford cleared his throat and was about to stand when Ben held him back. "Wait! Lord Crawford, please listen!"

"Not now, Benarcher!" the attorney growled, then paused. He turned to Ben and said more gently, "Do not fear; I have studied hundreds of Toreq defences. I know what I'm doing." Ben looked into the attorney's eyes and saw doubt reflected there.

"Lord Crawford," General Zoltar's voice boomed from the stage. *"Is there a problem?"*

"Uh... no, no. No problem at all, General." He stood.

Ben jumped to his feet beside him. *"Wait!"* His hands buzzed from the skill as he spoke with Toreq words. His heart beat so fast it hurt, but he knew what he was supposed to do. He'd been tired of not being in control. Now he could change that. *"I want to speak in my own defence!"* he burst out.

Lord Crawford tensed like an ice-pick. The jury glanced at each other. Voices rose among the audience.

"Silence!" General Zoltar snapped before

facing Ben and Lord Crawford again.

Lord Crawford stuttered, *"Uh, G-General. There is a m-mistake. I wish to confer with my client..."*

"There is no mistake," Ben said loudly, pushing away his attorney, who was trying to hold him back. *"On Earth, an accused has the right to plead in his own defence."*

"What are you doing?" Lord Crawford squeaked beside him. "Do you want to get yourself killed?"

* * *

Torka stopped working on his spaceship in the main hangar of the warship. He straightened from his crouching position and looked into his cockpit at a hovering screen that was showing the proceedings.

"Hey, Qu'ira! Are you hearing this?" he shouted.

A short-haired Toreq woman slid from under the belly of her spaceship and joined him. *"What's up?"*

Torka shook his head in disbelief. *"The A'hmun child has lost it. He wants to defend himself!"*

Qu'ira frowned and stared at the screen.

Torka shook his head again. *"What a stupid move. I'm actually starting to feel sorry for him."*

Qu'ira's face hardened. *"You're misjudging him, Torka. He already knows he's lost. I don't think he cares who says what at this point."*

Torka glanced at her in surprise. He did not doubt Qu'ira's insight. She was skilled in telepathy, and even without reading a person's thoughts, she had a knack for judging them by sight.

"You know," he said. *"I have to admit I've been wondering about that Einar. The fact that the A'hmun child mentioned him has been bothering me ever since I spoke to him in his cell. I should have gone back."*

Qu'ira gave him a wry smile. *"It's a bit late for that, Torka. The child will be gone by..."*

Alarms blared.

Toreq soldiers scrambled into the hangar. Three spaceships rose into the air and shot out into space.

Qu'ira grabbed Torka's arm as they searched for the source of danger.

"Kaani, Panaï! What's going on?" Torka yelled, spotting two of his friends running after the soldiers.

"Unidentified incoming craft!" Kaani yelled

back at him.

Torka and Qu'ira ran after the two brothers.

The soldiers took position, Torka and his friends doing likewise.

It didn't take long for the three spaceships to return, flanking a fourth craft that barely seemed to hold together. It hiccupped in the air, and a piece of it detached, crashing to the floor below it.

"Whoa!" Torka yelled. *"Stand back!"*

The mysterious craft attempted a landing but lost its hovering capacity, sending it spinning to the ground.

Panaï thrust his glowing hand before him, sending a gust of air below the craft to soften its fall, but still, the craft smashed to the ground, taking out Torka's spaceship with an imploding crunch.

Torka swore and rushed to the scene after the soldiers, while others were quick to blow out flames and smoke. All waited, alert and silent, their glowing hands raised and ready to strike the craft's occupants if needed.

A tense minute passed, then the craft's door groaned open, and a tall Toreq with white, wavy hair stepped out. He wore strange, human garments, but Torka would have recognized him anywhere. *"Mesmo!"* he exclaimed.

The soldiers backed down and stared at each

other. Then a whisper spread among them. *"It's the Observer!"* they said. *"The Observer has returned!"*

The news spread like wildfire.

Torka sprang forward. He stopped before Mesmo, placed his three middle fingers to his forehead and bowed. *"It's so good to see you, Mesmo! We feared the worst!"*

Mesmo placed his hand on his friend's shoulder, and they greeted each other head to head. *"It's good to see you, too, Torka,"* he said.

"Mesmo!" Qu'ira said, breathless, coming up beside Torka. She, too, saluted Mesmo head to head. *"You're alive!"* she said. *"We looked for you everywhere but couldn't find you."*

Torka noticed his bandaged hands. *"Mesmo, what happened?"*

"I'm fine," Mesmo said, wincing as he dropped his hands to his side. *"I'll tell you later. I need to know first: do I still have authority around here?"*

Torka raised an eyebrow and glanced at the excited soldiers around them. *"What kind of a question is that? Of course, you do, Mesmo. You are the Arch Council's appointed Observer..."* he trailed off, checking Mesmo up-and-down. *"Though... you may want to rethink your outfit. You'll have a hard time giving orders in that."*

Mesmo dismissed his comment with a wave of a hand. *"I need to talk to your General. I believe he is holding a human child on board the fleet. I wish for this child to be brought to me at once!"*

Torka and Qu'ira exchanged a glance.

Torka puffed his cheeks. *"I'm sorry, Mesmo, but you're a bit late for that."*

CHAPTER 14 *The Last Word*

Ben didn't quite know what he'd gotten himself into. Here he was: an insignificant earthling speaking to an auditorium filled with high-ranking aliens who wanted to get rid of him and the rest of his species. His throat tightened, and he almost gave up, but his eyes rested on General Zoltar, and that ignited a wave of anger within him that spoke louder than his fear.

This man had sent an assassin to kill Kaia; he had tried to kill Mesmo—perhaps, even succeeded. He was torturing a poor alien creature somewhere deep in the warship's belly, and he'd toyed with Ben for days, making him suffer through this absurd trial.

Well, so be it, but I'll have the last word.

The two attorneys and the judge gathered at the front and argued for a while until it was agreed: the law did indeed allow Ben to plead his case.

Ben saw Einar smirk from the other side of the balcony—enjoying watching him dig his own grave, no doubt.

Everyone took their place again, and General Zoltar turned to face him. *"You have the floor. You may speak."*

Ben couldn't tell if General Zoltar was happy or angry about this fact. As if on cue, Tuli appeared on the sidelines. She had a habit of showing up when something odd was about to happen. For some reason, though, the sight of her brought Ben a sense of calm that allowed him to speak.

"I wish to thank Lord Crawford for his excellent service," he began. *"He is the most professional and knowledgeable attorney I have ever met, and I would have him defend me again in a heartbeat."*

Lord Crawford made a little nervous jump beside him. *"Oh, um... Ha, ha, ha."*

"However," Ben continued. *"I know that what I'm about to say will go against his wise advice."* He held his breath as the cameras closed in on his face. *"I plead guilty."*

Lord Crawford froze by his side, letting out

an almost inaudible, pained groan. Exclamations arose from the audience. The jury gasped. General Zoltar called for silence.

When enough calm returned, Ben kept his eyes on General Zoltar and continued. *"I used the translation skill to submit a creature to my will. I made it suffer."* He paused and swallowed. *"I can still hear it pleading for me to release it. It was the worst day of my life, and I wish I could take it back."*

Murmurs echoed through the auditorium.

Ben hadn't meant to cry, but tears streamed down his face anyway. He stared at Zoltar, thinking of the suffering creature in the belly of the ship. *"None should make a creature suffer like that. The Toreq laws are righteous, and anyone who is caught doing such a vile act should be punished—no matter their rank or origin."*

Ben stared at Zoltar as he said this, but the General's face was unreadable.

"I know you decided my guilt long before this trial even started. I know this is all a setup to keep you entertained. Fine, then! Do what you wish with me. But I will say this: while you sit here debating and wasting time, millions of creatures down on Earth are crying for help, suffering by your hand. Soon Earth will be as barren and lifeless as our ancient planet of Taranis."

Ben stared at the auditorium. *"That's right. I know about Taranis. I know humans originated there. I know you wiped out all life on that planet during The Great War of the Kins. And now you are doing the same to Earth.*

"So when all is done, and you have gotten rid of us, WHO THEN WILL JUDGE YOU?" He thrust the words into the audience and let them hang long enough to make an impact.

"Mesmo once told me the Toreq were a just and peaceful civilization, but just and peaceful at what cost to others? Who are you to decide who lives and who dies? Who are you to condemn a brother civilization before you even know what it will accomplish? It seems to me you are so focused on your old enemies that you have forgotten how to make new friends. You hunker behind the Moon and attack defenceless people with skills that we could never match. I beg you to reconsider your actions! Go down and meet us. We're not that bad once you get to know us, you know?"

His shoulders dropped, and he unwound his fists. *"If I were granted one last wish, then that would be it: I would wish for you to go down and meet us, face to face. Just talk to us."* He dropped his head and said, *"That is all."*

* * *

Torka paused the screen on the A'hmun child's face. He checked on his long-lost friend out of the corner of his eye.

Mesmo had become as pale as a ghost. Without taking his eyes off the screen, Mesmo said, *"I need to get in there."*

Torka glanced at Qu'ira, Panaï and Kaani, who stood around the Observer. *"You know that's not possible, Mesmo,"* Torka said gently. *"No one gets into the dome while proceedings are ongoing. There's no way to get messages in or out. The people in there don't even know you've returned."*

Mesmo rubbed his face with his hand. *"Qu'ira, Panaï, Kaani,"* he said, deep lines appearing on his forehead. The three friends straightened. *"I don't care how you do it, but find me a way into that dome. And, Torka..."* he turned, *"...give me all you've got on this trial."*

CHAPTER 15 *The Toreq Son*

"Guilty," a juror said.

"Guilty," another one said.

"Innocent."

"Innocent."

"Guilty."

Ben leaned the back of his head against the chair and closed his eyes.

"That was the stupidest thing I have ever heard in my life," Lord Crawford muttered for the hundredth time. "You were supposed to defend *yourself*, not your *people*! What a waste, what a waste..."

"Innocent."

"Guilty."

"Innocent."

There was a pause.

Ben opened his eyes.

"Guilty."

Goosebumps rose on Ben's arms.

The last juror stood, hesitated for a lifetime, then said, *"Innocent."*

Gasps from the audience.

"What just happened?" Ben said, sitting up.

"Well, I'll be!" Lord Crawford exclaimed. "I think your speech moved them! It's a tie!"

"A tie? What does that mean? What happens now?"

"All stand," a juror said.

"Stand up!" Lord Crawford urged. Ben hurried to his feet.

The juror said, *"Five jurors have voted in favour of the accused, five have voted against him. The last vote is yours, General Zoltar."*

"WHAT?" Ben almost fainted.

"An eleventh vote must be cast," Lord Crawford said excitedly. "The General's vote weighs above all. It's unheard of! Fascinating, fascinating!"

Ben didn't have time to think how fascinating that was. The juror spoke. *"General Zoltar, in the Toreq State vs. Benarcher case, do you vote the accused guilty or innocent of unlawful possession of a Toreq skill? Do you vote the accused guilty or innocent of misuse of the translation skill to the first degree?"*

Ben's stomach turned rock hard. He found himself searching for Tuli, but she was nowhere to be seen. That made him panic even more. Was this the time when he was supposed to make a run for it?

General Zoltar closed his eyes for a moment, and when he opened them, he looked straight at Ben, fire burning from within.

Ben braced himself.

"STOOOP!"

The cry came from the back of the theatre. All eyes whirled around, searching for its source. Wide doors to the side of the dome had slid open, momentarily letting in bright light from beyond. Soldiers scrambled to block the way, clearly taken by surprise: they had expected problems to surge from within the theatre, not without. Five shadows were visible in the entrance, the tallest one leading the others down the central aisle.

Ben grasped the railing in shock, his heart leaping into his throat.

"The Observer!" Whispers rose from the audience. *"It's the Observer!"*

Mesmo walked to the front without

acknowledging Ben.

General Zoltar rose slowly from his seat. *"You're alive!"* he exclaimed.

Mesmo gasped. *"General!"* he said. He stopped before Zoltar, and both bowed deeply.

Captain Daria jumped to her feet, her face ashen. *"What is this? General Zoltar, arrest this individual at once! An insurgence in the dome is highly unlawful! We are at the end of the proceedings. Declare the accused guilty already!"*

"Enough, Daria!" Mesmo snapped, his voice cold as ice. *"This charade ends here."*

General Zoltar sat again. *"Captain Daria is right, Mesmo. Before we speak further, I must close off this trial."*

"That won't be necessary," Mesmo said. *"I have come to tell you that this trial is annulled."*

Loud murmurs rose from the crowd.

Ben watched Torka rush to Mesmo's side, a hovering screen surging from the palm of his hand. Mesmo swiped at it and said, *"I ask you to consider the following document as evidence."*

"What?" Captain Daria roared. *"We cannot accept new ev..."*

Too late. Hovering screens sprang up before all attendees, including Lord Crawford. Everyone leaned forward for a closer look.

"Ooh...!" Lord Crawford uttered in shock.

"What?" Ben cried, stricken. He craned his neck but couldn't tell what the document said.

Exclamations rose from the jurors. Captain Daria shook in rage. Shouts broke out.

"How dare you!"

"This annuls the trial!"

"It's a fake!"

"What?" Ben shouted in fear. *"What does it say?"*

"Silence!" General Zoltar's shout got lost in the racket.

Scuffling broke out.

"Get the accused out of here!" someone shouted.

Hands grabbed Ben by the arms, dragging him away. *"Lord Crawford!"* he yelled, struggling. *"What does it say?"*

Lord Crawford's eyes darted left-and-right, his voice not carrying over the commotion.

Ben fought hard but was no match for the soldiers who pulled him away. He caught a glimpse of Torka and three others closing in around Mesmo to protect him. "Mesmo!" he shouted before being dragged out of the dome.

* * *

Ben paced his cell, frantic. He'd had time to bite his nails to stubs half-a-dozen times.

Mesmo's alive! What's going on? Is he okay? What's in the document?

A million excruciating thoughts roared through his head. He'd go mad if he had to wait for another second...

The door to his cell slid open. Lord Crawford stepped inside. The attorney was unrecognizable. His spectacles lay crooked on top of his head; his rolls of white hair stuck out, dishevelled; his face was so red Ben thought it would explode. Never had he seen his attorney more excited. He thrust his arms apart. "It's done!" he cried. "You're free!"

Ben gawked at him.

Lord Crawford stood there, then dropped his arms awkwardly to his side. "Oh! Ha, ha, ha. I forgot." He held up a single piece of paper before Ben. "See for yourself." He grinned from ear to ear.

Ben stared at the Toreq symbols printed on the page. He stared at Lord Crawford, shaking his head.

His attorney looked like he was about to burst. "Don't you see? He adopted you!" he cried.

Ben stared blankly from the paper to the attorney.

Lord Crawford nodded vigorously. "The Observer adopted you! Benarcher, you have become the Observer's lawful Toreq son!"

CHAPTER 16 *Catching Up*

"A brilliant move! Absolutely brilliant!"

Lord Crawford paced the outside of the cell with such vigour it made Ben's head sway. The Observer had officially adopted Ben as his son, he said. The news had had a tsunami effect throughout the fleet. He'd never seen anything like it.

"With that one act, the Observer has single-handedly rendered both accusations pointless. As a Toreq, you are entitled to a skill. And as a Toreq, you are considered underaged, hence, not responsible for your actions. The capital death penalty is no longer applicable. The opposing party's arguments have been shoved right back into their faces!" Lord Crawford finally stopped pacing and said, beaming, "Benarcher, you are free!"

Ben hadn't moved an inch.

Mesmo adopted me!

The words flew around in his head on repeat.

Mesmo's alive. And he adopted me!

The news wouldn't sink in. It was too good to be true.

Something pinged on Lord Crawford's device. "See? What did I tell you? The release papers have arrived. You may go."

Ben stared at him from behind the bars.

Lord Crawford made a little jump. "Oh! Forgive me. Ha, ha, ha. Where is my head? It's all the excitement." He swiped at the computer near the door, and the cell disintegrated before Ben's eyes, leaving him in one of those whitewashed rooms with nothing in it.

Torka appeared and leaned against the doorway.

Lord Crawford stepped forward and took Ben by the shoulders. "Benarcher, we are going to be in the history books, you and I—in that great Toreq library I was telling you about. That is payment enough for me. It was a pleasure doing business with you, even if you are just an A'hmun." He gestured towards Torka and added, "This gentleman will take you to your new quarters. You are heading up in the world, Benarcher. Congratulations!" He shook Ben's hand limply. "Now, if you will excuse me, I have been called by some important officials to celebrate..." He whirled and left, leaving Ben alone with Torka.

Ben tensed, but Torka smiled. *"Aren't you glad to get that buffoon out of the way?"* He shook his head. *"I owe you an apology,"* he said. *"I am sorry for calling you a liar and a thief—among other things. I was worried about Mesmo and lashed out at you."*

Ben nodded, too shook up to speak.

"Come on. He's waiting for you," Torka said.

"Mesmo?"

"Of course! Who else?" Torka grinned as he left the cell.

Ben hurried after him, wanting to burst into tears, but he held it together as they entered a type of elevator that overlooked the main hall and which took them to the top floor of the warship.

"How do you know Mesmo?" he asked, trying feverishly to sound casual, but his legs shook, and his heart almost beat out of his chest.

Mesmo adopted me!

Torka raised his glowing hand at him. *"Water skill,"* he said. *"We trained together. I've always been jealous of him; he'd win at everything."* He grinned and lowered his hand as the elevator arrived. But when the door opened, he added, *"Though that may have changed."*

"What do you mean?"

Torka's face fell. *"I shouldn't have said anything. I'm sure Mesmo will tell you himself."*

They left the elevator, and Ben sprinted after the alien. Torka waved his hand, and double doors slid open, revealing a comfortable apartment within. Torka gestured for him to enter and, before leaving, winked. *"Get some well-earned rest now, son of Mesmo."*

Ben watched him go, then entered the apartment.

Mesmo stood at the other end of it, surrounded by half-a-dozen Toreq. One of them was attaching a silver cape with a pin over Mesmo's shoulders and the customary Toreq outfit.

Ben caught his breath. He remembered having found Mesmo dressed this way, long ago, after the alien had crashed near his grandfather's house.

The short-haired woman who had healed Ben's blistered lip in Dubai was holding her glowing hand over Mesmo's palms, her eyes glazed in concentration. Even from where he stood, Ben could see the damaged skin on Mesmo's hands.

Mesmo turned and saw him. *"Thank you, Liana,"* he said.

The short-haired woman spotted Ben and smiled.

"Leave us," Mesmo ordered.

The group of Toreq saluted with three middle fingers placed on the forehead and hurried out. The short-haired woman winked at Ben. *"You did well,"* she said, stepping out of the apartment. Then the door slid shut behind her.

Ben hadn't taken his eyes off Mesmo. They hadn't seen each other since... since —Ben's mind whirled —*since the day of our hike a million years ago!* Ben had forgotten how tall the alien looked, more so with his Toreq outfit and white, wavy hair.

Mesmo's eyes twinkled. His mouth curled into a smile.

Ben grinned.

Mesmo took a couple of large strides across the room. Ben did likewise, and they fell into each other's arms. Ben squeezed hard, needing reassurance that this was real. He still couldn't believe it.

Mesmo's alive!

"It's okay. You're safe now," Mesmo said.

Unable to speak, Ben let go of his emotions. Mesmo wrapped his arms tighter, wincing in the process, but continued to hold on without uttering a word. Ben wasn't sure how long they stood there, but Mesmo only let go when he stopped shaking.

The alien pulled back and scanned him with his eyes, forehead creasing. "Are you all right?"

Ben sniffed and nodded through a watery smile.

"Good," he said. "Come." He led Ben to some seats by a window overlooking the Moon and a sliver of the Earth.

"Mesmo, your hands…" Ben uttered.

"It's fine," Mesmo said. "Nothing Liana can't cure. It's you I'm worried about. I'm sorry you had to go through this, Benjamin. I came as soon as I could. And…" His eyebrows knitted together.

"What?" Ben urged him on.

Mesmo shook his head. "I never meant to impose anything on you, Benjamin. I'm sorry about the adoption. I never meant to do something like this without your consent. But I was going to do it anyway, and I was running out of time, and I… I…"

Ben's heart burst out of his chest. "Don't you dare apologize! There's nothing I've ever wanted more in my whole life!"

"Are… are you sure?"

Ben pulled back and laughed. "Are you

kidding? I get to be on a real spaceship with real aliens and... and will you just look at this view? I mean, seriously! Who's got a view like this? I can't wait to post a selfie; *all* my friends will be so jealous..."

Mesmo raised an eyebrow. "Not long ago, I might have felt offended," he teased. His face became sombre again. "I missed your humour, *son.*"

"And I missed yours... *Daaad.*"

They stared at each other and grinned.

"What about mom?" Ben asked. "Is she here, too?"

"She's fine. But no, she's not here. She wanted me to get you as soon as I could. And good thing I did, too..."

Ben shuddered.

"And in any case," Mesmo continued, "it's better this way. You know the Toreq would see it with a bad eye if I brought another life companion on board—especially an A'hmun one."

"Yeah, what's with that, anyway?" Ben grumbled. "It's not your fault your first wife died. Why wouldn't you be allowed to love someone else? It still doesn't make sense to me."

Mesmo smiled. "Believe it or not, there are good reasons for it. My home planet is a safe and healthy place. Mortality rates are low, and it is common for life companions to live together for many, many years. It is almost unheard of and a great tragedy for one to lose their life-companion at an early age.

"When you know you can only have one life-companion with whom you'll spend the rest of your days, you choose very carefully. You give yourself completely into the relationship—heart and soul. The respect you show for the other is the same respect you would give yourself. You become one. There can be no other."

Ben groaned. "Okay, okay. I've heard enough. No more lovey-dovey stuff."

"Fine." Mesmo smiled. "Then it's your turn. I want to know everything," he said. "Start from the beginning, and don't leave anything out."

"No," Ben argued. "You go first. I want to know about this..." He pointed at Mesmo's hands.

So Mesmo told Ben how he'd gone after Einar, thinking the Wise One had kidnapped Ben, only to have fallen into a trap himself.

Ben's eyes widened. "But where are Captain Daria and Einar now?"

Mesmo swiped at a small table, and a hovering robot arrived with trays of the most interesting food. Mesmo munched on something that looked like a walnut and pointed out the window at the other warships. "Don't worry about those two. As soon as they realized I had returned and they had lost the trial, they fled to Captain Daria's ship. They won't dare act now that their treachery is known."

Ben stared at the warships, wondering whether he felt good about that.

"I have good news," Mesmo continued. "The Toreq were moved by your speech. They can't believe you used up your time to defend humans instead of defending yourself. The captains of the five warships have agreed to stop the attack until I've debriefed them. I've convinced them to wait until *The Great Gathering*. They will want to hear what the animals have to say. If the creatures of Earth confirm that they stand by humans, then the Toreq will have to back down."

Ben whooped. "That's excellent news!"

Mesmo nodded. "We have allies here, Benjamin. Daria and Einar have a following, but their extreme line of thought has set them apart. For instance, did you know the dome is impenetrable once a trial is ongoing?"

Ben shook his head.

"Well," Mesmo continued, munching on another walnut. "I feared I would not be able to enter and stop the proceedings, yet as soon as I arrived, the doors to the dome opened."

Ben frowned.

Mesmo cast away the nutshell and pointed at Ben. "Somebody opened the dome from the inside. Whoever it was, knew I was coming!"

Ben gasped.

Mesmo shook his head, thinking. "This person doesn't want to be unmasked, and that's fine. At least we know there are people on our side."

Ben wondered briefly if Lord Crawford had had something to do with it, but the attorney did not seem the kind of man to execute hidden agendas.

Mesmo wanted to hear about his adventures, so Ben recounted his experiences out in the desert, which had ended with him submitting the Arabian horse to his skill. He raised his hands before him. "My hands, they glowed red. I've never seen anything like it, Mesmo. The skill has never acted like that. I mean, when I talk to Echis, it's not like that at all..."

"Echis?" Mesmo interrupted.

"Oh, right. I have to tell you about Echis. It's a venomous snake I picked up in the desert. He's on this ship somewhere." Mesmo raised an eyebrow, so Ben added quickly, "Oh, but don't worry, he won't bite anyone. Just don't stare at him; it makes him edgy... Anyway, when I use the skill to talk to Echis, my hands glow blue, you know, the normal way, and I can have a normal conversation with him. But with Sadalbari..." His voice faltered. "With Sadalbari, it was different. The skill was so powerful I couldn't hold it back. It lashed out at the horse, and it wanted to... it..." He swallowed. "It *wanted* to control the horse..." He dropped his head and shut his eyes. "I feel so bad, Mesmo. It was like the skill was controlling me instead of the other way round, and I..." He opened his eyes and looked at Mesmo. "I wouldn't use the skill ever again if I could help it..."

Mesmo stared at him gravely. "Benjamin," he began. "I'm stumped. I never thought the skill would reach such a level of power in you. I can count on my fingers the number of times this has happened in Toreq history. It's that rare. That's why I never mentioned it to you. I didn't see the point." He rubbed his chin. "But, listen, there's something else... I know you want to go home, but you're going to have to be patient."

Ben frowned. "Why?"

"We are playing a delicate game right now. We are on Toreq territory and have the upper hand, but only as long as we play by Toreq rules.

Becoming a Toreq saved you from execution, but that doesn't mean there are no consequences to your actions.

"On my planet, once a child discovers his skill, he is appointed a mentor to guide him. The jury has concluded that you need a mentor, as any normal Toreq child would. What I'm saying is that, until *The Great Gathering*, it has been decided that you will fall under a mentor's supervision."

Ben's eyes widened. "Are you telling me you're sending me to alien school?"

Mesmo grinned. "Something like that. The point is, you don't have to worry anymore. You have so many questions about your skill, and now you'll have this incredible opportunity to learn from the very best. Even I couldn't have dreamed of giving you the lessons your mentor will teach you. I'm excited for you to meet him. In fact, here he is right now..."

The doors to the apartment opened, and General Zoltar stepped in.

CHAPTER 17 *Inheritance*

Mesmo stood and rushed to greet the General head to head, hands on each other's shoulders.

"You're going to get me all emotional again, Mesmo. It's not proper for an old General like me," Zoltar said, smiling.

"I think that's acceptable, just this once, considering," Mesmo said, returning the smile. "But come, I want you to meet my son."

They approached Ben, who felt like he had just been dumped into a pool of ice. He sat glued to his seat, stricken.

"Benjamin," Mesmo said. "I want you to meet my father, General Zoltar." He looked at the General and added, "Father, this is Benjamin Archer. You know all about him already."

Ben gawked. *His WHAT?*

Somehow, Ben managed to stand. As soon as he did so, General Zoltar put his hands on Ben's shoulders and rested his forehead on Ben's own as if he, too, were a long-lost son.

Ben felt like a scorpion had just hugged him.

"At last!" Zoltar said, backing away, eyes twinkling. "I feared this moment would never come. I insisted on being the judge in your case to make sure nothing happened to you, but when you claimed your guilt, I... well, you threw me off guard. You have no idea how relieved I am to see you safe and under our protection. I welcome you to my family with open arms."

Ben's eyes travelled from Zoltar to Mesmo.

Did I just go crazy?

"Your f-f...?" he stuttered. He couldn't match the two together. Brave, loyal Mesmo and... and *Zoltar?* This was another nightmare. It had to be! He'd wake up, back in his cell.

Mesmo beamed. "Yes, my father. Crazy, isn't it? But our luck has turned, Benjamin. When I didn't come home, the Arch Council decided to send an army to attack the A'hmun, and my father insisted on being appointed General of the fleet. That means the five warships are under his command. He is the one who ordered a stop to the attack on Earth as soon as I arrived."

Ben's brain hadn't caught up yet. "Your f-f...?" Hot and cold flashes washed over him in waves.

"Oh dear, oh dear," Zoltar said. "Mesmo, have you been feeding this child? He looks like he's seen a ghost. Come and sit down." He led Ben back to the seats by the window.

Mesmo and Zoltar. Zoltar and Mesmo. Light and darkness. Day and night. Both peered at him, frowning. The high cheekbones, the long nose, the shape of their honey-brown eyes...

Of course! Why didn't I see it before?

"Too many emotions for one day, eh?" Mesmo said gently.

Zoltar straightened. "Give the child some rest, Mesmo. We can talk about the mentoring tomorrow."

"Mentoring?" Ben's voice squeaked.

Mesmo grinned. "Of course! Toreq skills are hereditary. From where do you think Kaia got hers?"

"Y... you...?" Ben pointed at Zoltar.

Zoltar nodded and smiled. "I, too, have the translation skill, yes." His gaze dropped. "I dearly miss my granddaughter..." He looked at Ben again. "...but could think of no one better than you to have inherited her skill."

Ben stared at them, dumbfounded.

"Come on," Mesmo said gently, leading Ben into one of the apartment's bedrooms. "I was so happy to see you; I kind of forgot it's way past your bedtime."

Ben was too traumatized to point out he wasn't six anymore.

The bedroom left him speechless. He stepped through the door and found himself in his bedroom back home in Chilliwack: two wide windows that let in a warm breeze of a summer night, light blue walls, his grandfather's telescope on a shelf...

After a silence, Mesmo said, "Too much?"

Ben swallowed and nodded. He couldn't handle the idea of home right now, not when he was so impossibly far from it. "Can you just, um, make it more... Toreq-like?"

"Of course." Mesmo activated a hovering screen near the door and gave the computer some instructions.

The bedroom washed away in a wave of pixels and was replaced by a curved window that covered most of the left side, giving Ben a daunting view into space. In the middle, a king-sized bed awaited and, to the right, a small room appeared that Ben guessed was some kind of bathroom.

"I have to leave a human touch, Benjamin. Toreq furniture would confuse you, and I want you to have a good night's rest."

Ben didn't object, focusing on the bed. He kicked off his sneakers and sank into the gorgeous mattress. He glanced out the bedroom door into the living room, where he spotted Zoltar still sitting in the same spot.

Mesmo pulled a bedsheet over him. "Are you okay?" he asked. "You're shivering!"

No, I'm not okay. There's a murderer in your living-room. There's a traitor who's out to get us. And he's your FATHER!

Ben held his breath. He couldn't say those words, could he? Mesmo had received the General in his private apartment with open arms. Mesmo was still glowing with pride and happiness from having found both Ben and his father again. He'd think Ben had lost a screw.

And maybe I have...

That was a real possibility. But too many things clashed in his brain right now for him to figure it out.

"Mesmo?" Ben said.

"Hm?"

"I'm scared."

Mesmo stopped arranging the covers. He

came around and sat at the edge of the bed. "It's okay to be scared. You've experienced more things than anyone I know—human *or* Toreq. So I'm going to ask you to do something for me."

Ben turned his gaze away from the living-room and looked at Mesmo. "What's that?"

Mesmo smiled and looked him straight in the eye. "Be a child for a while. Let me be the adult. I know it might sound absurd considering everything, but let's pretend you can be carefree for a while. Remove those burdens from your shoulders and give them to me. You are too young to be thinking about war, peace and political debates. Those are my responsibilities. Your responsibility now is to learn to master your skill. That's all I ask of you. Isn't that what your mom would tell you? To study well at school? Well, I'm asking you to do the same."

Ben bit his lip. "You mean, study with Zoltar?"

Mesmo gave a little laugh. "Yes, that's all you have to do for now. I know he can seem intimidating at first, but he does that on purpose. Remember, he has a military fleet to run. That's no small task! But you'll figure him out soon enough. You'll see he's really just a big-hearted softy when he thinks no-one's looking." Mesmo grinned.

Ben swallowed. *When no-one's looking...*

"Anyway, you're supposed to be sleeping. I have several things to take care of, but you can always call me through the computer there. It will also let you know your schedule for tomorrow. Don't worry; you don't have anything until the afternoon. So go ahead and explore the ship. No-one will stop you. You can go anywhere and talk to anyone, ask any questions. You are quite simply the General's grandson now and will be treated as such."

* * *

"Is he alright?" Zoltar asked in a low voice.

Mesmo glanced towards Ben's bedroom, then placed a hand on his father's shoulder as he sat beside him. *"He's a little shook up, but he's strong. He'll be fine."*

"Your timing could not have been better, son. I am relieved by the outcome."

"So am I," Mesmo said. *"Never in a million years did I imagine I would see you again, Father. This is a good day, indeed."*

They stared at each other, smiling and enjoying the moment.

Zoltar looked down. *"I don't deny I feared the worst for you, Mesmo. When you sent Bordock's body through the wormhole but did not return yourself, I was convinced the A'hmun had subverted you. It would never have occurred to me that you had stayed of your own free will. I can't explain the dread and outrage I felt towards the A'hmun for taking you away from me. I needed to come to Earth and lay my wrath upon them. I attacked them with full force as soon as I arrived; such was my appetite for vengeance. The Arch Council should probably not have sent such a hot-headed General at the head of the fleet."*

Mesmo smiled. *"I admit I never thought the Arch Council would send a fleet to attack Earth without me having sent them the seven keys first. It is unusual for the Arch Council to have made such a drastic decision at the last minute. But you think too lowly of yourself, Father. You know very well you are the best leader the Toreq could have asked for. You did what you thought was right with the information you had at the time. Your heart is in the right place. Proof is that you did your best to remain calm during Ben's trial; you looked for justice, where people like Daria only saw blind hate. And you also put an end to your attack on Earth as soon as you heard my story."*

Zoltar stared at his hands. *"I do my best, Mesmo, but I will always think back on the day the*

Arch Council appointed Kaia to go to Earth. She was so young! And then you insisted on being appointed the Observer so that you could accompany and protect your daughter. They should have picked me, not her. Then you and she would have been safe, back on Torequ'ai. I will regret that day for the rest of my life."

Mesmo placed his hand on his father's arm. *"I don't blame you, Father,"* he said softly. *"You know there was no other way."*

Tears spilled out of Zoltar's eyes. *"No,"* he said. *"There was no other way."*

CHAPTER 18 *A Major Theft*

The ground rumbled around the Emergency Operations Bunker of the United Nations. Laura glanced worriedly at Hao, catching him look around briefly before diving back into an in-depth conversation with a superintendent. If he was as nervous as she about the recurring shaking in the walls and thin cracks appearing in the concrete, he did not show it.

She sat back, shifting her thoughts to Mesmo and Ben. Had Mesmo found Ben? Were they safe? She took a gulp from her asthma inhaler. A dark pit grew in her stomach as time went by. The longer the hurricane remained stationed above New York, the more it meant the Toreq had not abandoned their onslaught—meaning Mesmo had failed to speak to his people.

Everyone in the Bunker was on edge. Their shirts were stained at the armpits, and sleepless souls paced the concrete cafeteria, gulping down coffee.

Secretary-General Adhira Prabakhar was the only one who seemed centred. She came in from her private quarters within the Bunker, holding a laptop, looking fresh and posed, her high heels clicking and her grey-white hair tied in a neat bun at the back of her head. "I know you struggled to get a hold of your loved ones while we were in the eye of the storm. I know you witnessed some distressing sights above ground or from what news you could gather on your devices." She looked at each person in turn.

Throats were tight, and eyes glistened. Someone blew their nose.

Adhira's voice softened. "When this hurricane blows over, people out there will need us. Together, we are stronger than this monster. Together, we will rebuild, one home at a time." She paused. "But to do this, I must tell you things as they are—no matter how hard they are to hear—so you are better prepared." She shuffled some papers. "I have spoken to the President of the United States. It is estimated that thirty-nine percent of New York City is destroyed. By the time the hurricane blows over, this percentage could reach over fifty."

Someone whimpered.

Adhira raised her voice. "I also want you to prepare for a possible evacuation."

Laura's heart constricted.

Adhira's voice didn't falter. "While we were in the eye of the storm, I asked a team to check out our building above us." She paused. "A crack has appeared across the building. This crack is causing instability in the foundations surrounding us, which in turn is causing the rumbling sounds you have been hearing." She raised her hand to calm the commotion and almost had to yell. "The foundations are strong! The Bunker is strong! They will hold until this blows over, but I must tell you that if the emergency alarms go off, we will all need to head out..."

"Out? And go where?" someone shouted.

"That's madness!"

Laura jumped to her feet. "She said 'if'! We're not there yet! We'll be fine!" She wasn't sure anyone heard her over the panicked voices.

It took a full hour of back-and-forth arguing before everyone left the operations room. Only Adhira, Laura, Hao and Jeremy remained.

Adhira was focused on her laptop, so they

prepared to leave to give her some privacy.

"Wait," she said, holding up her hand without taking her eyes off the screen. For the first time, Adhira looked crestfallen. She lifted her head and said, "There's something I need you to see."

Laura and Hao exchanged a look.

"What is it?" Hao asked.

Adhira sent a video from her laptop to the large screen. "My people managed to access a live feed, which I just watched. Rather than tell you what happened, I think it is best you see it for yourselves." She pressed the play button, and they all turned their attention to the screen.

The video was shot with night vision, and the images were hard to discern, but after a while, Laura realized they were looking at several hangar-like buildings. Sudden flashes, like powerful lightningbolts, made the camera go blind several times.

"What are we looking at?" Hao asked.

"This is a military facility in New Mexico..." Adhira explained. "A *nuclear* facility."

Laura's head snapped from the screen to the woman.

Adhira continued. "It is under attack as we speak. You might be able to help me determine by whom and how they are doing it."

"Doing what, Secretary-General?" Hao asked, alarmed.

Adhira leaned forward, "Stealing a nuclear warhead."

Stunned silence. Laura gawked. Even Jeremy stopped taking pictures.

Adhira looked at them one at a time. "What do you think?"

The images froze, then continued, then turned to static. Communications worsened.

Laura glanced at Hao. "You think this has something to do with the Toreq?"

They watched fires raging through the collapsing hangars and soldiers running in all directions. Then the image changed to the inside of a silo with an ominous-looking cylinder that Laura knew must hold the nuclear warhead.

They watched, aghast, as the bomb rose in the silo. There was a blinding flash, static, then the image balanced. The bomb was gone.

"Whoa!" Hao breathed.

Laura scanned the outskirts of the video. "There!" she said. "Can you zoom in?" She pointed at the bottom right corner of the screen, at metal stairs following the inner wall of the silo.

Adhira zoomed into the corner, and the rough outline of two people appeared. One was a woman with long white hair flowing to her hips; the other was a tall, well-built man with a beard and braids above the ears.

"I'd recognize him anywhere," Laura gasped, then said, "That's Einar!"

CHAPTER 19 *The Prisoner*

Ben didn't want to be mentored by Zoltar.

Mesmo had left early. He was going to have to deal with a million things after his miraculous return, which meant Ben wouldn't get a chance to cautiously approach the subject that gnawed at his mind. He lingered around the apartment, not knowing how to deal with the clashing images in his mind: Zoltar, ordering Bordock to kill Mesmo; and Zoltar, Mesmo's loving father. How could a single person be such opposing things at once?

Ben thought about this while trying to figure out how to use the bathroom because the 'shower' didn't use any water. Instead, a circle of energy scanned him up-and-down and, although he felt refreshed and clean at the end, he already knew he was going to miss hot showers from home.

No sooner was he done, when a Toreq garment slid out of a hidden wardrobe and landed in his arms. The material felt soft and sturdy. Ben hesitated, then figured he'd best blend in. The pants and raised collar t-shirt fused at the seams around his hips. There was a type of cardigan as well, but Ben decided to wear his hoodie sweater instead, so he could cover his brown hair if need be. While Mesmo stood out like a sore thumb back on Earth because of his white hair, here it was Ben's brown hair that stood out among the Toreq. The other things he refused to go without were his black sneakers. No way was he going to wear silver space-boots.

He'd slept in late, and by now, judging from the computer that was pinging at him to get ready for his mentoring class, it was afternoon.

His stomach twisted again.

He couldn't get himself to face Zoltar. The General must be wringing his hands together, scheming his next notorious plot. Ben wondered how bad Mesmo's return had messed with Zoltar's plans and how long he was going to pretend to be the nice guy.

A whirring sound pulled him out of his thoughts. A small, floating tray crossed the room and stopped before him. On it, Ben found a round, silver object made from the same material as his clothes, as well as a note.

"Wear this on your wrist. Dad," the note said.

Ben picked up the object, and it split open on one side, latching on to his wrist. It looked a bit like a tennis wristband, but its use became apparent when a small, hovering screen deployed out of it. The device made a low, pinging sound like the computer and indicated it wanted to guide him to his rendezvous point with Zoltar across the main hall.

I don't want to go there.

Ben exited the apartment, half expecting to be ambushed or held back, but nothing happened. Toreq men and women went about their business, mostly ignoring him, though some made a little bow and three-fingered gesture as they passed him by. This was nothing compared to the first time he had been brought on board. Feeling slightly relieved, Ben gathered courage and began exploring the warship, heading as far away from Zoltar as possible.

The place was confusing. The central hall looked nothing like a ship designed to wage war. Trees hugged the walls, with vines dropping from the tallest branches to the ground, while strange and colourful birds soared near the roof. An artificial orange sun shone and warmed his cheeks. The air smelled of rich, humid earth, and edible fruits and greens grew at arms reach, hanging down the balconies that overlooked the hall.

Mesmo had told him long ago that the Toreq did not do well in confined spaces, and he wondered if this was the reason for the unexpected layout. Perhaps this was the place where the Toreq came to gather energy by pretending they were back on their home planet, out in the open. He had seen Mesmo do this many times back home.

He found a sturdy tree and climbed up one of its thick branches, finding a quiet spot to take in this alien landscape and munch on the fruit of the tree that he recognized from his cell.

"You're still here," a voice said in Toreq speech.

Ben whirled and found Tuli staring at him from a balcony at his level.

The girl hopped over the side and stepped lightly on to a branch without losing her balance.

Ben had a hard time ignoring her translucent blue eyes. *"Does that bother you?"* he asked, in reference to her question.

She skipped onto his branch and hopped over next to him. *"Yes, it does. We told you to leave."*

She didn't say it in a nasty way—well, at least, not that he could tell, but he still felt offended.

"Sorry to disappoint you, Your Highnesses, but I'm staying."

Not that I have a choice...

She remained silent, and he wondered if he'd hurt her feelings. But then she said, *"Then it will have been in vain."*

"What will?"

She sat down beside him, legs swinging. *"We let in your friend—the one you call Mesmo—so he could save you from the trial and so you could flee. Yet, you remain."*

Ben paused, his teeth already crunching into the fruit. Then it hit him. *"You mean, you're the one who let Mesmo into the courtroom?"*

She nodded.

"How did you do that?"

She stroked her long, white braid, the end of it shining a bright blue like her eyes. *"We have our ways."*

Ben snorted. Her answers were beginning to annoy him. He wasn't going to get anything out of her. *But she saved me... "Thank you,"* he said, not sure what she was trying to achieve.

She glared at him. *"Didn't you hear what we*

said? We told you to leave before the translation skill gets you killed! If we were you, we'd be halfway across the galaxy by now."

Ben stopped munching on the fruit. It became a hard lump in his throat. *"I don't even know what you're talking about."*

Her eyes glued on his. *"Yes, you do!"*

Ben froze. The branch suddenly felt unstable, as if it were swaying. He felt woozy. The moaning echoed in the walls of the ship, the pleading creature begging to be released. The fruit slipped out of his hand. He slowly wiped his mouth with the back of his sleeve, never taking his eyes off Tuli's.

She sprang to her feet. *"Come with us!"* she ordered.

"Wh... where?" He scrambled to his feet, then remembered he wasn't as nimble. His foot slipped, and he almost toppled out of the tree, but then he grabbed onto the branch in the nick of time.

She glanced at him, skipping away. *"See you on the ground,"* she said, then descended swiftly down the trunk.

Ben wasn't very successful at trying to appear surefooted as he climbed down after her. *"Where are we going?"* he asked again when he landed on his feet.

She had the decency to wait for him. *"You don't believe us. So we're going to show you."*

A chill ran down Ben's back, but he suspected she wouldn't say more if he pressed for details, so he sprinted after her, away from the daylight, into colder, duller corridors.

It wasn't long before the true nature of the warship revealed itself. Tuli took him down a level, where they ended up in a cavernous hangar filled with sleek spaceships of all shapes and sizes. Toreq men worked on a ship's carcass, building up the hull with the sole use of their skill. Their hands glowed as they manipulated the material from which the craft was made, directing the curves with their palms and sealing together loose ends by the touch of their fingers.

"This way," Tuli said, grabbing Ben's arm and tearing him away from the fascinating sight.

She led him down two more levels: one replete with hovering screens, another with tight corridors filled with endless pipes and hissing vents. A heaviness hung in the air, and it became harder to see in the dim light.

A sense of foreboding tickled the back of Ben's mind, and he wondered whether he was walking into a trap. What did he know of Tuli, anyway?

Absolutely nothing.

Ben began to sweat, fully aware that he was hopelessly lost. But then he remembered the wristband. He glanced at its miniature screen and saw with relief that it indicated where he was.

Near the heart of the ship...

It became harder to advance. The way forward was narrow and full of obstacles. They ended up crouching, and Ben realized that Tuli was not taking 'official' routes, but rather, following service areas—like a rat would follow back alleys or sewage lines.

...or like Echis would a shaft.

He breathed harder.

I don't like this. I don't like this at all.

"Tuli..." Ben began.

"Shush!" she snapped, then added in a barely audible voice. *"We're here."*

Ben swallowed.

She crawled on all fours and advanced with caution, watching where she placed her hands and making sure her foot didn't drag and snag something.

Ben followed with even greater care, dread building up with each movement until he found himself on a circular platform with small holes and a bigger one in its center. An orange glow similar to a slow-burning fire reflected through the holes. He crawled after Tuli, trying to determine what was down there: a large room with something in its middle. Something *alive*.

Ben tried to stifle a gasp of fear.

Tuli shot him a look that said, 'Be quiet!'

This was his nightmare! This was the place he'd glimpsed when using his skill to see through Echis' eyes. Only, the snake had approached the room from a shaft below, while Ben now crouched above it. This was the place inhabited by the moaning creature—which meant its captor could be here, too.

Ben froze.

Tuli had reached the edge of the bigger hole. She placed a finger to her lips, then pointed down.

Going against his every instinct, Ben crawled forward on his stomach and peered over the edge. His eyes widened.

The glow did not come from a fire. It came from a creature—a bird—resting on a perch. 'Bird' was not the right term. Ben tried to come up with a definition for it, so his mind would accept what he was seeing. The beast was more like a winged dragon, a blazing creature made of fire. It did not move but sat with its beak hunched in on itself, yet its mere presence was sublime and unnerving. Ben felt eerily drawn to it.

He sensed more than saw Tuli crawl away from the hole, but his eyes were glued on the bird. Even in its sleeping state, there was something magnificent and terrifying about it, and Ben could barely grasp what it must be like in waking.

Then Ben thought of Echis, wondering if the snake was stuck somewhere in a shaft not far from this powerful creature. The snake had an innate fear of birds, but if Ben reached out for it with his mind, would he inadvertently catch the attention of the fire-beast, instead?

The bird stirred.

Ben's hands began to glow.

Fingers wrapped around his ankle. Ben flinched and turned to find Tuli tugging at his leg, urging him away. It was time to go.

Ben followed her without a word, the hairs on the back of his neck rising at the thought the creature could wake and come after them through the narrow tunnels. But even more frightening was the thought that someone possessed a power strong enough to keep such a beast prisoner at the heart of the warship.

CHAPTER 20 *Lifegiver*

"What was that?" Ben had been holding on to the question until he deemed it safe to speak—which meant he'd had to wait until they had reached the hangar with the spaceships.

"It is a Lifegiver," Tuli said. *"It is the material manifestation of a being born at the heart of a galaxy within the folds of a black hole. Its life is fueled by the substances and energies consumed by its gargantuan appetite, yet it is also a spreader of the seeds of life, leaving trails of star clusters in its wake, where life can form and prosper. It is the Giver and the Taker, which is why you feel attracted, yet also repelled by it."*

Ben tried to hide his stupefaction. *"And you know this, how?"* he tried to sound as casual as possible, but inside he was rattled.

A shadow crossed before Tuli's eyes. It was gone in a blink. She did not answer his question. Instead, she stroked her braid and said, *"If you stay, both the captor and the prisoner will set their eyes on you."* Her blue eyes pierced through him. *"Do you want to be around when that happens?"*

Ben's pulse raced. *The captor and the prisoner... She meant Zoltar and the Lifegiver...*

"But why? How do you know?" he asked.

The wristband pinged at him.

Tuli pointed at his arm. *"You should answer that,"* she said.

Ben glanced at the small screen and saw Mesmo's face. He was being hailed. A message said: "Where are you? Meet me at the apartment."

Ben shook his head, annoyed. *"Come on, Tuli! Just answer the question, will y..."* he began, then broke off when he lifted his head and found her gone.

"Tuli!" he groaned. *"Hey! Come back!"*

How convenient. Make him aware of a potentially life-threatening situation, then vanish, leaving him with more questions than before. *"Tuli!"* he called, searching around the stationed spaceships.

"Hey, son of Mesmo!" someone called.

Ben whirled and found Torka walking up to him. *"What are you doing here? Aren't you supposed to be with General Zoltar?"*

Fear made Ben jumpy and impatient. *"Why do you want to know? Are you my babysitter or something?"*

Torka lifted his hands. *"Whoa! Take it easy, Benarcher. I was just curious."*

Ben dropped his shoulders. Great, now he regretted lashing out. *"I'm sorry. You can just call me Ben. And yes, I'm supposed to be with General Zoltar."*

"Well, he's off doing more important things now. It's not like he could wait around for you. Come on, Mesmo was asking if I'd seen you." He led Ben to an elevator.

"I can find my own way back..."

"Of course you can. And I'll come with you," Torka said, showing him into the elevator.

"But you're not my babysitter, right?" Ben poked.

Torka smiled. *"No. But I am Mesmo's eyes and ears. He needs people he can trust. I won't have another Captain Daria or Einar make an attempt on his life—or yours for that matter. I'm taking precautions, is all."*

That came as a shock. Ben stared at the alien,

reminding himself he and Mesmo needed people they could trust.

"And do you trust General Zoltar?" he asked carefully.

Torka looked at him as if he had just barked. *"What kind of a question is that? General Zoltar is by far the most experienced and noble Toreq out there. The Arch Council couldn't have appointed a better General for this mission."* He patted Ben's shoulder. *"You'll see. With him and Mesmo at the helm, good things will come."*

Crap...

So he, too, thought Zoltar was a superstar. Did that mean Tuli was the only one besides him who seemed to know what was really going on? That didn't help at all. The girl kept appearing and disappearing on a whim.

They reached the apartment, and Torka followed Ben inside. Several people were standing around, waiting for their turn to speak to Mesmo, who was deep in conversation with a caped Toreq. The woman called Liana was there, focusing on healing his hands.

"Here's your lost apprentice, Mesmo," Torka said, interrupting the conversation.

"Thank you, Torka," Mesmo replied, taking his leave of the caped man.

Torka winked at Ben. *"See you later,"* he said as he turned to leave.

Ben didn't know why he would be seeing Torka later, but he nodded, more preoccupied with what Mesmo was going to say.

Mesmo excused himself and led Ben out of earshot from the others.

Ben braced himself for a sermon. He'd have to tell Mesmo he hadn't gone to Zoltar's mentoring, and then Mesmo would want to know why...

Instead, Mesmo's forehead creased, and he said, "Are you okay?"

Ben wrung his hands together behind his back. "Uh-huh."

Mesmo leaned against a table and crossed his arms. "Look, I don't know what's going on in that little head of yours, and I wish I could spend more time with you. But things being what they are, I have to trust you'll talk to me if you need to."

Ben looked at his feet.

Mesmo continued. "I understand you've been through a lot and might need some time. So whatever your excuse for not seeing my father today, is acceptable, but I think there's something you don't quite understand, son."

Ben looked up at him. "What's that?"

Mesmo glanced at the people in the room,

then approached him to speak in a low voice. "The fleet has accepted that you are a Toreq now, but that doesn't mean everybody is happy with it. Arranging a mentorship with my father was the deal made between different factions, some who would have rather seen you ejected into space."

Ben gulped.

Mesmo continued. "We don't want to ruffle feathers the wrong way, Benjamin. You need to go to your lessons. In fact, I don't understand why you don't want to go. It's only for a week. And you can finally exchange experiences with someone who fully understands what you've been through and can guide you."

Someone tried to catch Mesmo's attention, but Mesmo held up his hand to make them wait.

"Will you try at least?" he asked Ben.

Ben squeezed his hands behind his back so hard they hurt. *How can I refuse that?* "Sure, Dad," he said, testing the word again to see how it felt.

"Good." Mesmo smiled. "So what did you do all day, anyway?"

Ben shrugged. "Nothing special. Just visiting the ship with Tuli."

"Tuli?"

"Yeah, it's a girl I met. She knows her way around."

Mesmo frowned. "A girl?"

Ben nodded.

Mesmo shook his head. "I don't think so, Benjamin. There are no children on board. This is a warship, remember? We would never accept children."

Ben stared at him. "Well, I was with her for the better part of the afternoon."

"Hm, okay. If you say so. Bring her around next time. I'd like to meet her."

The person, still waiting, coughed extra hard in his hand.

Mesmo sighed. "Look, I have to go. But hang around, will you? I'd like you to meet some of my friends tonight..." he bent and whispered in Ben's ear, "...as soon as I get rid of this eavesdropper."

Ben grinned.

* * *

They headed to the spaceship hangar that evening. A small group of Toreq men and women were waiting for them, sitting in a circle with a virtual fire floating in their midst.

Ben stared. He knew all of them—sort of. They were the ones who had picked him up in Dubai. Torka grinned his way. Then there were the twins, each with a single braid down their back—Panaï, *air skill* and Kaani, *moulding skill*—and finally, the short-haired woman, Qu'ira, *telepathy skill.*

The four of them greeted him in the customary way. Ben did the same, feeling awkward as he sat amongst them. At least they no longer looked at him like he was an 'anomaly,' the way they had before, though Qu'ira stared at him intensely.

Ben broke into a sweat. Was she reading his thoughts?

She noticed his discomfort. *"I apologize for staring, but I have not yet gotten used to seeing such dark hair and eyes. It is most unusual."*

"Get used to it, Qu'ira," Mesmo said. *"Humans have the widest variety of characteristics. It is most refreshing. It is we who are quite dull."*

Torka jumped in. *"And I can't get used to you referring to the A'hmun as humans, Mesmo."*

"The A'hmun ceased to exist after they were banished to Earth, Torka. We are dealing with a new species that is barely getting to know itself. That is why we cannot treat them the way we would have our old enemies," Mesmo explained.

Qu'ira crossed her arms. *"Can we change the subject? We've been talking politics all week. I need a break."*

"Yes," Kaani agreed, passing around a bowl of juicy nuts. *"Where's Liana? I thought she was coming?"*

"She had an emergency on the Qu'Tué. She should be here shortly," Qu'ira said.

Ben zoned out of the conversation. He didn't quite catch everything they were saying but enjoyed the friendly atmosphere. They chatted back-and-forth, sharing old memories about growing up together and completing something called an 'exit race' in their last training year. Ben glanced at his new dad. The alien looked relaxed and comfortable, which was a nice change after so much tension in the past days.

He watched the faces of the Toreq that sat around the fire and knew they could be trusted. These were Mesmo's longtime friends. No wonder they had been so tense when they had picked him up in Dubai. They had been overly anxious about their friend.

Ben started wondering whether this was a good time to speak. Only he didn't know how to approach the subject. Blurting *General Zoltar is a traitor* amid their lighthearted conversation probably wouldn't end well. He still didn't understand how everyone could be so oblivious to

Zoltar's true nature. It constantly made him second-guess himself.

After struggling to find the right words, he gave up and stood, saying he needed to stretch his legs. There was a small round window on the other side of the hangar, from which he could see a sliver of the Earth.

Mesmo came up beside him and placed a hand on his shoulder, startling him. "That must have been impossibly boring."

"Oh, no!" Ben said. "Not at all. You have some great friends."

"The best," Mesmo agreed. "I didn't think I would ever see them again. We had a lot of catching up to do."

They stared at the blue planet.

"Do you think Mom's okay down there?" Ben whispered.

"Of course she is," Mesmo said. "You know her. She's probably talking up a storm with world leaders right now, convincing them to come to *The Great Gathering*."

Ben sighed. "I hope you're right."

Mesmo squeezed his shoulder. "I know I am. Hang in there, son. You'll see her in a week."

"So will you," Ben said, but Mesmo didn't answer.

"Hey, guys!" Torka shouted behind them. *"Liana's here. Can we get going?"*

Ben frowned. "Are we going somewhere?"

"We sure are." Mesmo grinned. "You're going to like this!"

CHAPTER 21 *The Exit Race*

"Well, come on," Kaani said. *"This may be the only chance we get!"*

Mesmo's friends had put on spacesuits and held helmets under their arms.

"Be gentle, now. This is my son's first exit race," Mesmo said.

Ben's head snapped up. *Exit race?*

"Not a chance," Torka said, slipping the helmet over his head. *"I'm on my own. He's riding with you, so his chances are as good as ours."* He grinned and gave the customary Toreq salute, then headed for a sharp-pointed spaceship that looked a bit like the paper planes Ben made when he was little—only this one looked like it could have been made from liquid silver.

The others put on their helmets and picked similar spaceships: Liana with Panaï and Qu'ira with Kaani.

"Are you ready?" Mesmo asked Ben, eyes twinkling.

"Are we going in one of those?" Ben gaped, pointing at the knife-edged spaceships.

"Only if you want to."

Ben's eyes popped out of his head. "Are you kidding? What are we waiting for?"

"We need spacesuits for this kind of craft," Mesmo explained. "It's called a speeder. It's not like our other spacecraft that have inbuilt gravity and air. This is going to be a totally different experience!"

Ben grinned, accepting a spacesuit and helmet, then took a seat in the narrow craft: Mesmo in front while he was at the back.

"What happens now?" Ben asked.

Mesmo said from the front, "You hang on tight!"

Ben held on tight, but even that didn't prepare him for the jolt as the craft went from zero to crushing speeds in seconds. The speeder slipped out of the warship in a blur.

"Argh!" Ben yelled.

"Are you still with me?"

Ben's heart travelled to the end of his feet. "Uh-huh!"

Mesmo laughed.

Torka's voice entered the cockpit. *"The point of the exit race is to travel from the front of the warship to the back. The first one to arrive, wins."*

Ben glanced at the mammoth warship with control towers and wings sticking out of it everywhere. *"Er... but isn't it surrounded by obstacles?"*

"That's the whole point!"

Torka's craft flew up beside them, and they joined the other two right at the front of the warship.

Ben swallowed as they faced the dark nose of the warcraft that looked like a massive submarine. A metallic voice crackled into the cockpit.

"Whoops! They're onto us!" Panaï said.

"Who is?" Ben gasped.

"The crew," Mesmo said. *"They know we're stealing the speeders."*

"Borrowing, Mesmo," Torka corrected. *"We're just borrowing them."*

"Dad?" Ben said, aghast.

"There's no time to waste," Mesmo said. *"On my mark: three... two... one...."*

The spaceship's thrusters rumbled into

action, flinging the speeder forward, and for a moment, Ben felt flattened like a pancake. The four ships sped off across the warship's hull, zigzagging to avoid protruding parts. Ben wished he could shut his eyes, but they were stuck open by the pressure.

"Are you still with me?" Mesmo yelled excitedly over his shoulder.

Ben gurgled something.

Torka laughed. *"He's still there! Way to go, son of Mesmo."*

Ben thought he was going to pass out, but the pressure lessened somewhat, and he was able to catch his breath. A control tower zoomed by to his right, so close he might have been able to touch it if he'd stretched out his arm. He gritted his teeth and hung on to his seat for dear life.

"Out of practice, Observer?" Qu'ira shouted, zooming by on their left. They were starting to lag.

"Faster, Dad!" Ben yelled.

"Are you sure?"

"Yes! What are you waiting for?"

Ben braced himself as Mesmo steered the speeder in curves, masterfully avoiding the warship's control towers and small protruding wings.

"The pressure becomes less as the spaceship

adapts to the speed," Mesmo explained. "Can you feel it?"

"Uh-huh." Ben could. His thoughts cleared, and he was able to focus more on his surroundings. The end of the warship was near. "We're winning!" he shouted.

At the last moment, Torka's ship sped by from behind one of the warship's tails, propelling him to the front with a lead of a microsecond.

Torka whooped.

The others groaned.

"Nice try, Mesmo," Torka said. *"But I'm afraid you've become old and rusty."*

Mesmo laughed. *"It's nothing like that, Torka. I let you win."*

The others chipped in, but Mesmo turned his head as far back as possible to look at Ben. *"Are you okay?"*

Adrenaline rushed through Ben's body. His breathing came out in gasps. *"Can we do that again? Please?"*

The others cheered.

Mesmo grinned. *"One more round before they stop us. What do you think?"* he asked the others.

"Taking position," Panaï said. The others followed.

"What's that?" Ben asked, noticing needles of blue light emanating from the warship.

"Stunners!" Torka said.

"Things are about to get a lot more interesting," Qu'ira said excitedly.

"Stunners," Mesmo explained in English, "means that the crew is going to try and paralyze our ships as we fly past."

"We are in so much trouble," Liana said, though there wasn't a trace of regret in her voice.

"Let's do this," Torka added, counting from three to one.

A burst of power, then a crushing weight as the ship sped off. Trying to remain conscious, Ben took in small gulps of air. The four speeders zoomed back across the warship, zigzagging even more now that they were the target of the stunners.

"Do you want to win?" Mesmo asked Ben.

"Yes!" he yelled.

"Then watch this!"

To Ben's surprise, Mesmo veered to the left, lagging behind the others as he rolled all the way to the underbelly of the warship.

Ben gasped, then understood why Mesmo had done this: the belly of the warship was much smoother. Mesmo only had to concentrate on the stunners.

"Guys, they got me!" Qu'ira said. *"See you in detentio..."* Her voice broke off.

Mesmo didn't react, focusing on avoiding one stunner after another. Ben held his breath.

Then they were at the other end, soaring up in front of the nose of the warship where they almost smashed into the two other incoming speeders. An invisible force field around the speeders sent them spinning away from each other.

Ben shut his eyes and grabbed his head, forgetting he was wearing a helmet.

The three remaining speeders stabilized and turned around to face the warship again. Spaceships were exiting the hangar and heading towards them.

"Fun's over, friends," Liana said.

"Welcome to the fleet, Ben," Torka said.

"Yes," Panaï spoke. *"Welcome to the fleet. You're one of us now."*

Ben glowed.

The spaceships surrounded them, and metallic voices ordered them to follow obediently. Communications with the others shut down.

"So? What do you think?" Mesmo asked.

"Can we do that again tomorrow?" Ben burst out.

Mesmo laughed. "I highly doubt it. This is a

once-in-a-lifetime thing. We've all done an exit race at one point or another in our youth. It's a kind of unofficial rite of passage. It drives the captains crazy. But I didn't want you to miss out."

"Wow! Thanks!" Ben breathed. "Are we in big trouble now?" The larger ships escorted them back to the hangar.

"Nothing I can't handle," Mesmo reassured him. "Hang on." He dipped the speeder straight into the hangar towards the floor, sending Ben's stomach to his throat. As if following a signal, the other two speeders did the same, slipping away from their guards. They all landed a few inches from the ground at the same time, while the bigger, clumsier ships lagged above them.

"Get out," Mesmo ordered.

Ben half tumbled out of the speeder, his legs feeling like jelly as he landed on the floor.

Mesmo jumped next to him. "Go," he said, picking him up and urging him to head for a door.

"But..." Ben protested.

A handful of soldiers spilled out of the first ship, rushing towards them.

Liana, Panaï and Torka placed themselves in front of Ben.

"Go on!" Mesmo repeated as he joined his friends.

Torka stood shoulder to shoulder next to him and crossed his arms. "I won—again," he told Mesmo.

"No, you didn't," Mesmo retorted. He turned his head and winked at Ben with a half-smile.

Understanding that they were allowing him to escape, Ben grinned and slipped through the door.

CHAPTER 22 *The Garden*

Ben couldn't sleep that night. The race played over and over in his mind, levels of excitement impossible to contain. He wanted to talk over every detail with Mesmo. Also, he wanted to make sure Mesmo and his friends hadn't gotten into too much trouble.

But Mesmo didn't arrive, and Ben fell into a restless sleep filled with speeding spaceships, cheering onlookers, and, in the background, the sound of a moaning creature that distorted his dreams.

His wristband beeped at him, waking him with plenty of time to get ready for Zoltar's mentoring.

Mesmo had left him a message: "In detention

for the rest of the week. LOL! Nothing bad. C U tonight."

Ben lifted an eyebrow as he stared at the piece of paper. Was that really how the Toreq were punished for misbehaving? It was funny and a bit worrisome at the same time. Mesmo had known what he was getting himself into when he took Ben for a ride in the speeders, and he'd known he'd get punished. Yet he had done it anyway.

Ben smiled. Poor Mesmo. He could picture his new father scrubbing away at the floor or something tedious like that. They'd have to remember not to tell his mom about this! He sighed. Mesmo had done something for him. Now he needed to do something for Mesmo. He needed to face Zoltar.

I promised...

It was time he got over his fear of the General. This was Mesmo's father, and Mesmo had great respect for him. The last thing Ben wanted was for Mesmo to lose his father or become disappointed in him. If General Zoltar truly was embroiled in shady plots, maybe Ben could reason with him. He needed to get Zoltar to talk to him so he could bring him back on the right track.

Getting dressed was a lot quicker that morning—faster than he would have liked. He managed to produce some decent food, but he wasn't really hungry. Seeing as there was nothing left for him to do, Ben followed the instructions on his wristband to get to his meeting point: double doors somewhere at the end of the great hall, tucked away in a small corridor.

Not knowing whether he was supposed to knock or wait, Ben passed his hand before the door the way he'd seen Torka do. His wristband beeped, turned green, and the door disintegrated.

Ben held his breath.

"Draft!" someone yelled. "Close the door!"

Ben hurried inside and waved his arms like crazy, hoping to activate a closing mechanism. It worked. He turned and faced a marvellous, confusing garden. His ears buzzed and the skill vibrated under the skin of his hands. A cacophony of sounds entered his mind, and he had to do a quick mental trick to shut out the noise.

He blinked and realized why the garden seemed so confusing. It was teeming with living creatures that mingled with the vegetation. From bug-like insects to critters no bigger than squirrels, they buzzed, scampered, or flew over plants and trees of all colours and sizes. Ben took in large breaths of air, his nose trying to determine the wonderful and unknown smells coming from the flowers.

"Is that you, child?"

Ben stiffened. It was Zoltar who had spoken in English, but he couldn't locate the General in the beautiful chaos.

"Over here," Zoltar called, and Ben spotted a patch of his silver cape. "Hurry! I need your help."

He hurried to Zoltar's side and gasped.

For a split second, he thought Zoltar was torturing some poor creature, holding it down with both hands, but he said, "Quick! I need you to calm her down so I can set her leg."

Ben blinked, suddenly understanding the situation. The furry creature had a broken leg. "Wh... what should I do?" he stuttered. He had not expected to be setting broken bones in the first five minutes of his lesson.

"Talk to her. Calm her down. Just get her to focus on anything besides the pain in her leg."

Ben had no idea how to go about this, but he raised his glowing hands, placed them an inch from the creature's head and gazed into the most stricken eyes he had ever seen in his life. He wavered.

"Hey, now. Focus!" Zoltar warned. "Don't get sucked in. You can't save a creature if you're going to feel its every emotion. It's relying on us to save it, so show some self-confidence. Showing reassurance is half the battle won."

"Oh… er… Right. Sorry." Ben tried to look confident. He shifted to his knees and placed his hands above the creature's head again, staring into the pained eyes. He didn't give the animal time to transfer its physical distress to him. Instead, he sent it images of ocean waves breaking on a beach. One wave. Another wave. And again.

The creature stopped squeaking and stared at him, stunned. It had never seen waves before, and it rested its mind on Ben's, trying to figure out what these repetitive images and their soothing sound meant.

Ben held on to the image, focusing all he had on the details, then allowed the waves to become gentler, more spread out.

The creature relaxed, its heartbeat slowed, and Ben made sure to keep it utterly entranced so it would not return to a state of panic.

"There," Zoltar said, startling him. The General pulled back and added. "It's done. You can let go now, child."

Ben stared at the General, blinking several times. "Already?" he said.

Zoltar smiled—something that blew Ben's mind because it did not match the image of the surly General that he had created in his head.

"When you are absorbed by a task you love, time ceases to exist," Zoltar said. "You did well, child. Extraordinarily well. Mesmo was right about you."

"Right about what?" Ben asked.

Zoltar's eyes twinkled. "You are a natural. Kaia chose well!"

Ben blushed.

Zoltar bent down to check on the creature's bandaged leg. It stretched a paw and placed it on Ben's nose, then hurried to lick its fur contentedly.

Zoltar hummed as he stood and called forth a hovering device that allowed him to clean his hands.

Ben watched, his mind in turmoil. Where was the terrifying General who had ordered Mesmo's murder? Where were Zoltar's fiery eyes as he prepared to condemn Ben to a death sentence?

He saw nothing of that here.

"Did you enjoy the exit race?" Zoltar asked, drying his hands.

"Yes, it was amazing..." Ben blurted out before catching himself. He looked up at Zoltar.

Shoot!

The General turned and gave him a sideways smile. "Good," he said. "Congratulations are in order, then. Welcome to the fleet."

* * *

There was plenty to do in the garden. The creatures within were cared for by a group of Toreq whose sole task it was to follow Zoltar's orders. Ben figured they could be called gardeners. These Toreq raised the creatures until they were ready for release into the halls of the five warships. These animals were the pollinators of the plants and flowers and were a vital part of the fleet's survival. Without the critters, bugs and birds, the vegetation in the hall could not regenerate or provide nutrition.

Zoltar spent hours explaining how creatures and plants were interconnected. For example, one plant with red tube-like flowers fed one bug species, on which another type of critter revelled. These critters, in turn, burrowed in the ground, making the earth soft enough for the plant to grow in.

Zoltar's knowledge of multicoloured butterflies, long-beaked birds, bright blue-leaved shrubs and everything else that Ben laid his eyes on, was endless. He marvelled at the General's ability to determine each and every living thing's place in the whole biosphere.

"Take away this six-winged fly or this camouflaged mushroom, and the whole ecosystem falls apart," Zoltar explained. "Diversity is what makes an ecosystem strong. My task here is to make sure one species does not override the other and to negotiate with the culprit when such a thing occurs. In the end, that is the ultimate goal of the bearer of the translation skill: to maintain a balance among all living things. It's one thing to heal a broken bone, but it takes a whole array of knowledge and many years of practice to understand how to maintain a balance between so many living creatures."

Ben raised an eyebrow. "That sounds like a big responsibility!" He glanced at the hundreds of species around him. "And that would mean that an ecosystem could only be healthy if the skill bearer is wise and respectful."

Zoltar smiled broadly. "Absolutely! Well said, child. Only a skill bearer who is healthy in body and mind could influence the balance of an ecosystem in a positive way."

Ben muttered, "Sounds a bit like playing God to me."

"Hmm?"

Ben cleared his throat. "What I meant to say

is, how can one determine if a skill bearer is healthy in body and mind?"

Zoltar nodded gravely. "A fundamental question, indeed. Fortunately, there is an easy way to determine that."

Ben's eyes widened. "How?"

Zoltar's eyes twinkled. "Just look around you."

Ben did. Flowers cascaded from the rocks; birds frolicked above them, ant-like creatures carried big chunks of dry honey on their backs...

Zoltar bent down and spoke into Ben's ear. "I don't mean to brag, but if an ecosystem is doing well, then the skill bearer might just be doing a good job, too." He winked at Ben, then walked off, humming.

Ben stared after him.

As the days passed, Zoltar put him to work with all kinds of strange creatures, teaching him how to listen to them, help them, and showing him the bigger picture of how everything was interconnected. Realizing he was only receiving a fraction of Zoltar's knowledge, Ben found himself wishing the mentorship could continue for several months or even years.

While scrubbing a large bowl clean that had contained water for the birds, Ben said, "I was thinking of home and how much your teachings could help humans. I wish you could go down and see for yourself."

Zoltar was focused on a tiny, multicoloured bird, which rested on the palm of his hand. "Oh, I've seen plenty," he said vaguely, becoming engrossed in a conversation with the bird and leaving Ben wondering about what he'd meant.

Tomorrow was going to be his last day of mentoring, and he hadn't yet approached the major questions to which he needed answers. "Can you do what I did with the skill?" he asked.

Zoltar continued to speak with the tiny bird, and Ben wasn't sure he'd heard him. "You mean, submit a creature to my will?" Zoltar said finally, gently stroking the bird's back.

"Yes." Ben watched him closely, forgetting to scrub.

"Of course," Zoltar said. "But that is not a path one wants to wander down."

"Why?"

"Because once that power over other living things is unleashed, there is no turning back. The skill turns into greed—irresistible, gargantuan greed that is never satisfied." He stared at the bird.

Ben shuddered. Zoltar had just told him that he was also capable of submitting other creatures to his will and that, once he'd had a taste of that power, there was no turning back. "So, are you saying there's no hope for me? That if I submitted one creature, I might do it again?"

"Most likely," Zoltar said.

Ben gawked.

Zoltar blinked and glanced at him. "Oh, child. I'm sorry. I didn't mean to frighten you. No, of course, it won't happen to you again. Hard training and practice using the skill builds walls that fend off evil thoughts. By the time you reach adulthood, you will be armoured against that kind of danger."

Ben wasn't reassured at all. How was he going to reach that level of mastery? Not to mention Zoltar himself. Was the man armoured enough to avoid submitting creatures to his skill? Like, a certain Lifegiver, for instance?

The thought that he was supposed to find out Mesmo's father's true intentions gave him courage. "Are you and Mesmo close?" Ben asked, pretending to focus on his scrubbing while his stomach twisted because he was afraid of the answer.

"What a strange question..." Zoltar said. The bird fluttered its wings, looking as though it wanted to take off. Zoltar closed his hand over it, imprisoning it. He turned to face Ben; his eyes had lost their glimmer. Ben suddenly felt like the

General was about to cast him a guilty judgement again. "Why would you ask something like that?"

Ben swallowed. "It's just that, when I first met you, you didn't seem very worried about finding him." He could tell the bird was frantically trying to get out. He started to sweat, but he ploughed on. "I had a disappointing relationship with my human father. I was afraid... well, I was afraid you and Mesmo might be having the same experience."

Zoltar let the bird go. He stared at Ben. "You are a strange child," he said. "You insinuate things that would deeply offend any other Toreq parent. I raised Mesmo well, gave him all the tools he would need in life. It is a Toreq parent's greatest pride to let their child go so he can follow his path into adulthood. Mesmo is capable of taking care of himself; therefore, I was not worried." He stretched his back and checked his wristband. "Ah," he sighed. "Duty calls. Duty always calls." He surveyed the lush garden. "If it were up to me, I would do this all day."

Ben frowned. "You don't like being a General?"

"One time, perhaps, when I was younger and full of energy, it would have made me proud to become a General. But right now, I would far prefer tending to the gardens of the Arch Council."

Ben didn't know what to say to that. Zoltar never ceased to amaze him. He couldn't match the two General's together: the gardener standing before him now and the one scheming with Bordock. "So why did you accept this position?"

The alien's neck twitched, and Ben felt an inexplicable chill. "I had no choice," Zoltar said. He cast dull eyes on Ben. "Soon, perhaps, you will understand."

Ben shuddered. He wasn't sure he wanted to understand. He'd touched a nerve, he could feel it, but Zoltar would say no more, so they headed off in separate directions, with Ben acutely aware that Zoltar had not confirmed he felt close to Mesmo.

CHAPTER 23 *The Quratis*

Ben wandered off, half hoping he would run into Tuli. He hadn't seen her all week. When he didn't find her, he headed back to the apartment and waited for Mesmo.

He tried to connect with Echis again. He'd been worried sick for the snake, who hadn't sought him out or sent him any kind of signal. Ben felt really bad for the venomous viper. Perhaps it was lost somewhere, terrified, way down in the lower level of the warship. How was he going to find it and get it out? He laid back, dozing off a little.

He found Echis in the same place as before, in the shaft near the room where the Lifegiver was being held. Ben shivered, knowing the snake was so close to such a beast.

Echis?

The snake didn't reply. What was wrong with it?

Echis? Can you hear me? I need you to come back to me.

"Aarrgh!"

A cry made Ben jump out of his skin. It had come from so close; Ben thought it had been Echis who had yelled in pain. But no, the moaning came from the other side of the shaft, right at Echis' level.

"No... please! No..." the voice moaned.

"Benjamin?"

Ben squirmed.

"Son, wake up!"

Ben woke with a start. Mesmo stood over him. "You just had a bad dream," he said.

Ben sat up, trying to calm down his beating heart.

"You know you don't have to keep working after your lessons, right?" Mesmo said, pointing at his glowing hands.

"It wasn't a dream!" Ben said out loud.

"What?" Mesmo asked distractedly, because Torka came in just then.

"Are you ready?" Torka asked. *"They are waiting for us."*

"Just a minute." Mesmo turned to Ben.

"There's a reunion between the warships' captains. *The Great Gathering* is in two days, and we want to go over the details. Do you want to join me? As the Observer's son, you are authorized to be there, but maybe you've had a long day?"

Ben struggled to shake off the whimpering voice. "I... I actually need to talk to you..."

"Mesmo," Torka urged. "We're late."

Mesmo asked Ben, "Can it wait until after the meeting? This is really important. I want all the captains to be on the same page when we go back to Earth."

Ben rubbed his hands on his trouser, then nodded. "I'll come with you," he said. He'd had such a hard time getting a hold of Mesmo in the past week. He'd pull Mesmo aside as soon as the meeting was over. Maybe he would even take Mesmo down to the lower levels and show him the Lifegiver.

"Good," Mesmo smiled.

The three of them headed out.

"Besides," Mesmo added. "You're going to witness something very special at the meeting."

"What's that?"

"You'll see," Mesmo said as he and Torka exchanged a mysterious smile.

Ben wasn't sure he was up for surprises right

now, especially when they headed to a place Ben knew well: it was the white egg-shaped dome where he had been on trial.

"Oh," he groaned. "Not the theatre again!"

Mesmo laughed. "No, not the theatre. The captains are attending the meeting virtually from their warships. The dome simply takes on any format for which it is needed. You won't even recognize it."

They passed through the whitewashed force field, and Ben gasped.

Mesmo led him to the left, where they found a spot to sit on the ground among a circle of imposing Toreq men and women. In their midst, a child-sized crystal shimmered. Above them towered the branches of a mighty tree with a potato-shaped moon chasing away a blood-orange sun.

"I've been here before..." Ben said, staring up at the branches.

Mesmo didn't hear him because he was greeting his neighbour. Then he leaned back toward Ben and said, "Welcome to Torequ'ai, my home planet. This is a hologram of course, but it copies the meeting place of the Arch Council to the minutest detail. We feel comfortable meeting in familiar surroundings."

Ben gaped at the otherworldly setting, half expecting Bordock to be sneaking behind the tree trunk.

Mesmo continued. "Do you see the ones wearing capes with a golden pin? They are the captains. See, on your left? That's Captain Anaris of the warship Maq, and there, Captain Yigis of the warship Codo, Captain Olin of the Qu'Tué..."

Ben gasped. "And is that...?"

Mesmo's voice lowered. "Yes, that is Captain Daria of the warship Zul. Don't worry; she and Einar are only present as a hologram. They can't hurt us."

"But how can they be allowed to attend this meeting after what they did to you?"

"Daria is still a captain appointed by the Arch Council, and she is well-respected. If my father arrests her, he could end up facing a mutiny. He thought it safer to keep her in the role of captain, though at a distance from the rest of the fleet. She is still under his orders and must obey him, so we can rest assured she won't go astray..."

Ben stared at him as if he'd just made the worst joke of his life.

"...and my father is the captain of this warship, which is called the Ob, after a famous General from the time of the *Great War of the*

Kins," Mesmo finished.

Ben was no longer listening: Zoltar had made his appearance. He drew in a sharp breath of air. "Wooow!"

"See?" Mesmo said. "I told you you'd want to come along!"

Zoltar took his place among the circle at the far end. On Zoltar's shoulder rested the fire-beast, the magnificent bird Ben had seen in the belly of the warship. It seemed to have shrunk in size as it was just a little bigger than the man's head, its plumage shining like a thousand suns in golds and reds and yellows. Its blue eyes pierced the room, its sharp beak resembling that of a bald eagle. Long tail-feathers wrapped around Zoltar's neck and ended in iridescent blue and green.

The bird took flight, its wings almost too bright to look at. It rested on one of the branches of the tree, close to Zoltar.

Men and women murmured in awe at the sight.

"We call it a Quratis," Mesmo whispered. "It means..."

"...Lifegiver," Ben finished.

"Ah. I see my father has already told you. I only found out myself that it was in the warship a couple of days ago. The Quratis came to my father shortly before I left for my mission to Earth. It was just an apparition at first. My father did not recognize it, but he says it became stronger after I left. I don't know if you realize the importance of this creature, Ben. The last time the Toreq saw such a being was during *The Great War of the Kins*."

Ben gasped.

Mesmo nodded. "Crazy, isn't it? They say these mystical creatures appear in a civilization's time of need. Their wisdom—which is sometimes as ancient as the age of a galaxy—helps civilizations get through rough patches. It is thought the Quratis helped end the *Great War*. Unfortunately, my father says it has been unwell and has not been able to guide him as needed, so it's a good sign to see it here!"

A good sign?

Ben stared from Mesmo to the bird. He didn't see this as a good sign at all. Not if Zoltar was controlling the creature.

CHAPTER 24 *Playing by the Rules*

Ben couldn't concentrate on the meeting.

General Zoltar made a tedious opening speech that gave the Quratis plenty of time to focus on Ben. He didn't notice it right away. He thought the bird was scanning the attendees, but no, it was looking at him. Only at him.

A cold sweat broke out over his brow. There was something fundamentally unnerving about the creature. Ben found he could not look at it directly in the eyes because there was an immensity lying within them that his human brain couldn't handle. Even more, he felt that if he looked too long, he would be swallowed into that gaze, never to return.

He focused on Zoltar instead, but that only made things harder because even out of the corner of his eye, he could sense the creature watching him. There was something odd about it, too. Maybe it was the ruffled feathers, the faltering hops it made on the branch or its stooped posture.

It's in pain...

Goosebumps rose on his arms.

Was the Quratis asking him for help? Why didn't it speak to him, then?

The idea was terrifying because he instinctively knew that the bird's mind would swallow him whole if he tried to connect with it. There was nothing about it that Ben comprehended, only that it was ancient and wise and powerful. It was like a stray lion that had been mistreated by its master, but if Ben reached out his hand to help, it would lash out at him before he even had time to say a gentle word.

"Tomorrow, thirty star-rises will have passed," Zoltar was saying. *"It is the day we have agreed to meet with the A'hmun leaders, should any of them still live. I have asked Captain Olin to send a team to Earth to pick up these leaders."* Zoltar's hands began to glow. He half-closed his eyes and seemed to enter into a trance. Above him, the bird swung from side-to-side on its branch.

Ben sweated profusely. Even while averting its gaze, he could feel the Quratis' blue eyes piercing him. Unable to control himself, he found his attention shifting from Zoltar to the bird again. Their eyes locked, and...

Zoltar woke from his trance. *"After consultation with the Quratis, it is decided that we will hold the meeting with the A'hmun leaders on the Qu'Tué tomorrow. Are you in agreement, Captain Olin?"*

...Ben saw...

"Of course, General," Captain Olin said.

...an explosion of a terrifying magnitude. The Qu'Tué ripped apart in a catastrophic blast. Pieces flying through space, followed by an aftershock that expanded as brilliant light, swallowing the whole warship...

"NO!" Ben shouted, his cry echoing around the dome.

Attendees swung their heads around and stared at him, confused.

Ben looked from one to the other, eyes wide with terror. *Don't they see? Don't they know?*

"Benjamin?" Mesmo said beside him, startled.

"The Quratis! That's not what it said!" Ben said in alarm, the skill vibrating in his hands. *"Zoltar's lying!"* He hadn't meant to speak out so loudly. Gasps of outrage rippled around the room.

"Benjamin!" Mesmo's shocked voice jolted

him. His father sprang to his feet, pulling Ben up with him, then glanced around at the attendees. *"Forgive my son,"* he said. *"There is a misunderstanding. Benjamin still has much to learn."*

Words lashed out at them.

Overcome with terrifying images of the exploding warship, Ben insisted, *"But, he's ly..."*

"Benjamin!" Mesmo snapped again, pulling him by the arm so fast Ben had to sprint after him to keep up.

"Wait!" Ben yelled, but they were already exiting the dome. As the force field closed behind them, Ben caught the forlorn expression of the Quratis—a sad, hopeless look that lingered with him long after the dome closed.

"WHAT was that?" Mesmo spoke sharply, switching to English, his face pale as a ghost's.

Ben had never seen him this angry before. "He's lying!" he repeated desperately. "Your father's lying!"

"Benjamin!" Utter shock carried through Mesmo's voice. "How could you say such a thing?"

Ben pushed on, "I've been trying to tell you..."

Mesmo shook his head, not listening. "Do you realize what you just did? Half that room wants you dead! My father and I are the only ones standing in their way. Do you have any idea what it took for him to convince them to let you live? By accusing my father, you just tore apart that safety net! I can't believe you did that, after everything my father's done for you, and knowing he is the most honest, brave man you'll ever meet."

Despair washed over Ben. "Just... wait! Please... Let me explain!" How was he going to say this? How was he going to convince Mesmo of Zoltar's treachery? His chin shook, and he had trouble finding his voice. "I've been trying to find a way to tell you this. Please, please listen to me!" His throat constricted. He held his breath, then plunged on. "Zoltar is the one who sent Bordock to kill you!"

Mesmo tensed. He straightened, the blood draining from his face.

Ben waited, terrified.

Mesmo took a step away from him.

That simple gesture filled Ben with anguish. He ploughed on, panic-stricken. "Listen to me! Do you remember when you told me a powerful Toreq must have sent Bordock through the wormhole to kill you and your crew? You were wondering who it was..." He tried desperately to form the words. "I *know* who it was. It was Zoltar!"

Mesmo didn't move an inch.

Ben could tell he was preaching to a brick

wall, but it was too late, so he continued. "There's going to be an attack on the Qu'Tué. An explosion! I saw it with my own eyes. The Quratis showed me…" He lifted his hands, "…with the skill."

The corner of Mesmo's eyes tightened. He stared at Ben as if he were speaking some weird language. Then he shook his head slowly. "You are mistaken, Benjamin. The Quratis couldn't have spoken to you. It speaks to one master only, and it has chosen Zoltar." Mesmo's voice was so strained Ben realized how much he was containing himself.

"I'm telling you the truth!" Ben said, his voice diminishing. "I know you don't want to hear it. I know he's your father, and you trust him. But I don't. Not at all! I swear: Zoltar sent Bordock after you. I don't know why, but he did. Please believe me!"

Mesmo bent down on one knee to be level with Ben. He placed his hand on Ben's arm and spoke with a restrained voice. "I don't know what you think you saw, Benjamin, but my father is not a liar, and I am disappointed in you for not using some common sense. We will talk about this later. Right now, I must return to the meeting and try to patch up the damage with the attendees—if they have not removed their confidence in you already."

"But…"

"For now, I want you to go to your room."

"But…"

"Go—to—your—room."

Ben took a step back, shocked by Mesmo's rejection. His dad wouldn't even contemplate a treasonous Zoltar. Not in a million years. There was so much more Ben wanted to say, so many ways he wanted to convince Mesmo, but he didn't know how. His shoulders sagged. "I just wish…" he stammered. "I just wish we could go back to being the way we were: just you and me and mom. The three of us, back on Earth…"

Mesmo's eyes dimmed, and he suddenly looked as if he were carrying the weight of the world. "I'm not going back to live on Earth, Benjamin," he said, his voice dull.

Ben's jaw dropped. "What?"

"I warned you before: we are on Toreq territory," Mesmo said. "We have to play by their rules. Toreq laws forbid me to take on another wife. If I go back to live on Earth with you, I will be branded a human. And if I am branded a human, then you will be, too. And then we are back to square one."

Ben's heart sank to the bottom of his feet. "Back to the trial…?" he whispered.

Mesmo nodded. "That was the price of adopting you," he said. "I'm sorry, Benjamin. I had hoped to tell you this in a gentler way."

They stared at each other.

"Now go to your room," Mesmo repeated. He stood, glanced sadly at Ben, then headed back into the dome.

Ben whirled and fled down the hall.

CHAPTER 25 *Deadly Schemes*

Laura heard a clicking sound. She lifted her head from her crossed arms where she had dozed off and found Jeremy aiming his camera at her.

"Will you stop that already?" she complained without really meaning it.

Crunching sounds echoed around the Bunker, making them stare at each other. Jeremy lowered his camera and sat beside her at a table in the middle of the cafeteria. "Sorry," he said. "I tend to take more pictures when I'm nervous."

Laura smiled, sliding the camera her way.

"Do you think we'll get out of here soon?" Jeremy asked, checking the concrete roof and walls.

Laura took a couple of pictures of him. "I asked Adhira again just now, but even though the hurricane died down four days ago, she says it's not safe enough yet. There's still too much rain and flooding." She lowered the camera and sighed. "In any case, flooding or not, I'm heading out tomorrow."

"You are?"

Laura nodded. "The Toreq said they'd come back in thirty star-rises. That would be tomorrow."

Jeremy let out a heavy, "Ah!" before falling silent.

To calm her thoughts, Laura turned her attention to the camera. She scrolled over the reporter's hundreds of photographs: a focus on Adhira's composed face, Laura in deep discussion with Hao, blood-chilling pictures of New York skyscrapers that looked like dead carcasses, close-ups of the screen showing Einar and the Toreq woman in the nuclear facility...

"These are really good," Laura commented, mesmerized by Jeremy's ability to capture intense moments.

"Thank you," he said, wringing his hands together as if he longed to get his camera back.

Laura paused on a particular picture. Jeremy had caught her with her gaze lost in the distance, and even though she was surrounded by dozens of people in the operations room, she seemed alone.

She stared at the pockets under her eyes, the deepening lines on her forehead, her pale cheeks.

"You worry for Ben," Jeremy said softly.

She didn't have time to reply. Hao joined them in the cafeteria. "Hey, Mr. Busybody," he said to Jeremy, grabbing a chair opposite them and sitting heavily. "The Secretary-General is granting you an exclusive interview. She's waiting for you in the operations room."

"Look at you!" Laura teased Jeremy. "Mr. Bigshot reporter…"

Jeremy puffed out his chest.

A terrible rumble shook the ground beneath Laura's feet. Sirens screamed.

"Argh!" Laura gasped, thrusting her hands to her ears. Lights flickered off, leaving them in total darkness.

"Evacuate!" a voice yelled above the blaring alarm.

"Laura!" Hao cried, grabbing on to her arm from across the cafeteria table.

"I'm here!" Laura called. "Jeremy?" She reached out to the reporter next to her, but a gushing sound made her heart skip a beat.

"There's a breach!" someone screamed.

"Water's coming in!" Hao yelled in alarm. "Go, go, go!"

They rushed through the dark, tripping over chairs, frantically searching for the way out. The sound of fast-flowing water approached from the main corridor.

"Get out! Get out!" Hao urged.

They made it to the stairs, where ice-cold liquid splashed around their feet.

"The ocean's risen over the seawall," someone shouted. "We're being flooded!"

"Evacuate!"

Laura tripped and fell into the water, her breath cut short by the cold.

Hao was by her side, then Jeremy on the other. They pulled her up.

A deep rumble came from far down the corridor behind them.

"The bunker's collapsing!"

Another voice cried, "No! The whole *building's* collapsing!"

They all froze.

Seawater gushed relentlessly down the steps, swirling around their feet and legs.

"We'll be drowned like rats in a sewer if we stay!" Hao yelled. "We have no choice. Head out, now!"

They pushed on up the stairs, the flow of people almost carrying Laura.

Emergency lights flickered on.

"Wait! Jeremy!" she shrieked.

The reporter turned, eyes wild at her sudden cry. "What?"

"Your camera!"

Jeremy's eyes nearly popped out of his head. He searched for the camera he always had strapped around his shoulder. It wasn't there. His mouth dropped open.

"The cafeteria!" Laura cried. "I left it in the cafeteria!"

"Too late now!" Hao yelled from higher up.

Laura could see the panic rising in Jeremy's eyes. He was considering going back.

Hao grabbed his jacket. "Don't even think about it, Jeremy!" he growled, dragging the reporter up the stairs.

The reporter turned and shouted at Laura, "Leave it!"

Laura took a step forward, then stopped. People bumped into her as they fled, but she stayed rooted to the spot, her voice lost in her throat. The pictures! The ones incriminating Einar and the Toreq woman! The ones showing them stealing the nuclear warhead... they were on Jeremy's camera. They had no other evidence.

"James!" she breathed, willing the Inspector

to turn around, but he was already way up. "James!" she cried.

He turned and saw her.

"The camera!" she yelled, wishing she could explain over the noise.

His eyes widened.

Laura didn't wait. She whirled and headed back down through the panicked crowd and rising water.

"LAURA!" Hao bellowed after her, through the rumbling noise.

* * *

"I'm not going back to Earth." Mesmo's words bounced in Ben's head as he ran down the great hall. Ben didn't know what hurt more: that Mesmo didn't believe him or that the three of them couldn't be together again.

All because of me.

If the Toreq cast Mesmo away, it would mean they considered him to be a human. And if that happened, then Ben would also be considered a human again.

And once that happens—Ben sobbed—*once that happens, Captain Daria and Einar can revert the trial and get rid of us.*

Ben reached the apartment, then realized he didn't want to be there. He didn't want to run into Mesmo and see the disappointment on his face. He spun around, took an elevator down to the hall and ran to the tree that hugged the wall, half hoping Tuli would be there. She wasn't. He clambered up the trunk and took refuge on a big branch where it was safe to cry without being seen.

How long had Mesmo known? When had he realized he couldn't go back to Earth?

From the beginning.

As soon as Mesmo arranged for the adoption, the alien had known he wouldn't be able to go back to Laura.

She'll be heartbroken—because of me!

Ben cried for his mother, and he cried for the look of disappointment Mesmo had set on him earlier. A look that had broken something sacred between them. A bond of trust. Ben flung his hands through his hair. Where had things gone wrong? How could Mesmo be so sure Zoltar was truthful, while Ben was not? Was Ben misinterpreting Zoltar? Had he missed something?

That thought took him to the Quratis. The bird needed his help. He was going to have to free it on his own. Would that convince Mesmo?

Ben checked the map on his wristband, trying

to figure out how to get to the belly of the ship again. He had just pinpointed the location when the wristband buzzed. Mesmo was calling him.

Ben watched his father's face blink on the screen, waiting for him to answer. He pulled off the wristband, scrunched it up in his hands, and flung it down the tree. Anger and pain welled up inside. Why didn't Mesmo believe him? Couldn't he at least have listened?

Biting his trembling lip, Ben thought over-and-over about what had happened at the meeting until, exhausted by emotions, he fell into a restless sleep.

* * *

"The A'hmun child suspects something," Zoltar said, his eyes aflame.

Ben found himself cringing on the floor. He watched as Zoltar lifted his hand and stroked the Quratis' head. The bird rested on the man's arm.

Curiously, Zoltar did not notice Ben.

Ben tried to flee, but he remained there, stuck to the floor, peeking out from behind some pipes into the room at the belly of the warship. His heart lurched as he realized he had connected with Echis...

Einar entered Ben's field of vision, then retracted when the Quratis shuffled its wings. The Norseman eyed the bird nervously. *"Do you think the creature told him?"*

Zoltar fed the winged creature a critter from the garden. *"The Quratis?"* His face broke into a half-grin. *"No. The Quratis and I have an agreement, don't we, dear?"* He stroked the bird's chest.

"Are you referring to his outburst at the meeting, General?" Captain Daria asked, appearing from behind some boxes.

Ben cringed. So Zoltar had allowed the two foes to sneak on board the warship...

Zoltar paused. *"Yes, it's as if he knew,"* he replied.

"Begging your pardon, but what if he told the Observer? We can't take such a risk, General," Captain Daria ventured.

Zoltar dropped the bird on its perch and paced the room with his hands behind his back.

Ben watched from the shadows, resting on Echis' mind.

Echis? Why aren't you answering?

The snake worried him. Why wasn't it moving or speaking back?

"We need to act quickly," Zoltar said. *"I've*

had enough of the Observer and his son. They have single-handedly turned half the fleet in their favour, forcing me to pause the war against the A'hmun. It's time we gave the Toreq an unquestionable reason to attack our enemy. The nuclear bomb will do that. When you launch it at the Qu'Tué tomorrow, make sure you can provide proof that places suspicion on the A'hmun. That will get the fleet on our side again."

"*What about the Observer?*" Einar asked.

"*Don't worry about him. I have calmed his worries about the child's accusations and am sending him to the Qu'Tué. He won't trouble us again.*"

Ben reeled.

Echis!

Maybe the snake twitched, or perhaps it was bad luck, but just then, Captain Daria turned her gaze towards the pipes. "*What's that?*" she exclaimed, rushing towards the snake. She bent down, slightly to Echis' right, further along the wall, and picked something up from the floor. She held it up to the light.

Zoltar and Einar peered closer at the long object.

"*Strange,*" Zoltar said. "*I wonder what it is.*"

"*I know what that is,*" Einar gasped, taking the

object from Daria's hands. *"It's a snake's skin,"* he said.

"Can you be more specific, Einar?" Daria rumbled.

"A snake is an animal that slithers on the ground, back on Earth. Once in a while, it sheds its skin and grows a new one."

"You mean, there's an Earth creature lying around here somewhere?" Daria questioned.

They peered at the item, then turned and searched the ground.

"This snakeskin didn't get here on its own," Einar said. *"Its owner must be slithering around in the shadows."*

Zoltar's eyes burned bright. *"Find it!"* he said. *"We may have found ourselves a spy."*

Ben yelled.

He woke up and almost fell out of the tree. He sat up, puffing like a locomotive. With his heart almost beating out of his chest, it took him a full ten minutes to calm down.

Daria, Einar, Zoltar; they were in the belly of the warship, preparing for a major coup. And Mesmo would be caught in the middle of it.

Ben sprang to his feet, half-climbing, half-tumbling out of the tree in his haste. He crossed the hall and rushed to the dome. The place was empty;

the meeting had ended. He thought to call Mesmo on his wristband, then remembered he had thrown it away. Fear grasping his chest, he sprinted back down the hall, quickly checking for his wristband along the way but not finding it, then took an elevator to the apartment. He barged inside, searching up-and-down. Mesmo wasn't there. He was about to head out when a piece of paper on the table caught his attention. He read the note.

"Was looking for you. Have to go to the Qu'Tué for negotiations. We must talk when I get back. Dad"

Not "Love, Dad," but at least, "Dad."

Ben rushed to the window, pressing his face against it. He could see the Qu'Tué from here: Captain Olin's warship hid part of the Moon and the Earth. A pinpoint of light from a small spaceship headed towards it.

"No!" Ben breathed.

Behind him, the door to the apartment opened—Zoltar's tall form reflected in the windowpane. Ben froze.

The General stepped inside, the door shutting behind him. A moment of crushing silence passed. "So," he said finally, "it's just you and me now."

Goosebumps rose on Ben's arms. He watched

Mesmo's ship speed further and further away from him. He took a step back, away from the window. Breathing hard, he tried to sound defiant. "I know about Bordock," he said, clenching his fists. He turned slowly to face the General. "And I know about the bomb."

Zoltar didn't move. Then he laced the fingers of his hands before him in a calm manner. He spoke in a low hush. "Of course, you do."

Captain Daria stepped out from behind him, hands glowing. Her skill sent Ben flying through the air and crashing into the wall.

CHAPTER 26 *The Qu'Tué*

Mesmo was glad to be flying a spaceship again. The model was the same as the one he had lost, but bigger because Kaani, Panaï, Liana and Qu'ira were accompanying him this time. They whizzed through space in the shadow of the Moon, the warship Qu'Tué growing bigger before them.

His friends remained at their controls, not saying a word. Mesmo knew they didn't dare to speak—not after what had happened at the meeting. They didn't know what Ben had told him outside the dome but were perceptive enough to know not to ask.

Questions spun around in Mesmo's head. He wished he'd had time to talk with Ben before leaving, but his father needed someone to supervise the meeting with the human leaders on the Qu'Tué. He'd been glad to accept. Not that there had been any choice after Ben's little stunt. The meeting had ended better than Mesmo had expected, with his father toning down the attendee's angry reactions at Ben's accusation. Once again, Mesmo realized how lucky he was to have his father on his side. Had the fleet been led by anyone else, Ben and he would never have made it this far.

"I'll take care of Ben," Zoltar had told him. *"We'll see you tomorrow at The Great Gathering."*

Mesmo had left, intent on fulfilling his tasks, because the survival of the human race depended on what would happen in these two days. Yet, the further he raced across space, the more troubled he became. He input a command to call Torka.

"Miss me already?" Torka said from the warship they had just left behind.

Mesmo wasn't in the mood for jesting. *"Did you find him?"* he asked.

"It's not like I have anything else to do, Mesmo," Torka said. *"You'd think your son would be more interested in helping me prepare for our trip to The Great Gathering tomorrow..."*

"Torka!"

"Er... sorry. No, I haven't found your son—or

your father, for that matter. They weren't in your apartment."

"Keep looking," Mesmo said, then cut off communications.

"I'm sure he just needs some time to himself..." Liana began but stopped when Mesmo's knuckles turned white from balling his fists too hard.

He couldn't shake the feeling that something was off. Memories kept replaying in his mind, the trials that he and Ben had been through, their mutual understanding of things, their common goal. But to accuse his own father of sending out an assassin to kill him... Well, Ben had gone too far. It was impossible; unthinkable. Never in a million years would Zoltar do something like that.

But Ben... Well, Ben was Ben, and he wouldn't blurt out something shocking like that for no reason.

Mesmo knew, deep down, that Ben was convinced of something. Whatever Ben thought he had heard or seen, he had misinterpreted it, no doubt, but still, something had sparked this absurd theory.

And then Mesmo had let slip that he would not be able to return to Earth. He hadn't meant to say it bluntly like that. Knowing Ben, Mesmo realized he'd just broken his son's heart. He'd be sulking somewhere, feeling miserable.

As they approached the Qu'Tué, Mesmo felt worse and worse. He knew he shouldn't have turned away from Ben like that. After all, Ben was in a strange environment, surrounded by a way of life he did not fully understand. It would have been normal for him to reach the wrong conclusions based on inexperienced observations. He should have taken more time to figure out where Ben had gone astray. Then they would have figured it out together.

Only time had run out, and now he was off to the Qu'Tué. He almost turned the spaceship around. He was convinced, now, that Ben had heard or seen something abnormal, something he deemed dangerous and imminent. Some kind of threat.

His mind whirled: Daria and Einar. What if they had something to do with this? It was the only thing that made sense. Maybe the two accomplices had somehow managed to plant this absurd idea in Ben's mind. It seemed far-fetched, but the more he thought about it, the more it became crystal clear to Mesmo that he needed to heed Ben's warning.

They were approaching the ramp into the Qu'Tué's hangar.

Mesmo slowed down.

"We have clearance to land," Qu'ira said.

Mesmo slowed down even more.

"Mesmo?" she insisted. *"We have clearance."*

Mesmo entered the huge opening to the hangar. He flew on, not stopping.

"Er... Hello? You missed the landing spot!"

Mesmo ignored Qu'ira and flew straight through the hangar, exiting back into space on the other side.

"Mesmo? What are you doing?" Panaï asked.

Mesmo didn't answer. He flew along the flank of the warship up to the command level.

"We're being hailed," Liana shouted. *"Mesmo, I hope you have a good reason for this."*

Mesmo slowed down the spaceship at the height of the command level. *"Hail Captain Olin for me. Now!"* he ordered, staring at the command level of the Qu'Tué.

Liana glanced at him with raised eyebrows but obliged.

After a pause, Captain Olin appeared on a screen before Mesmo.

"Observer," Olin said, greeting Mesmo.

Mesmo gestured to him as well. *"Are we on a secure channel, Captain Olin?"*

"We are."

"Good," Mesmo said. *"Captain Olin, do you trust me?"*

Olin seemed taken aback by the question. *"Of course, Mesmo. I have the deepest respect for you and your father."* He hesitated. *"Are... are you questioning my loyalty?"*

"Not at all, Captain," Mesmo said. *"But you are going to question mine."* He held his breath for a fraction of a second, then said, *"I want you to abandon ship."*

Liana gasped beside him. Kaani and Panai approached, whispering tensely to one another.

Captain Olin blinked. *"Eh... excuse me?"*

Mesmo straightened. *"You heard me, Captain Olin. I want you to abandon ship. The Qu'Tué will fall victim to a fatal attack—I don't know when or how, but my intel is sound."*

Captain Olin looked left-and-right as if someone was about to pounce on him. *"Mesmo, this is a serious accusation. You know very well I can't abandon the Qu'Tué. I need to confer with your father about this."*

"My father doesn't know," Mesmo said.

Captain Olin gawked at him.

Mesmo continued. *"I need you to evacuate in stealth mode and wait for instructions on the Moon. Have the Qu'Tué scanned from top to bottom, search every corner. The strike could come from anywhere and take on any form. All I know is your crew will die if you do not act quickly."*

"I..." Olin began. *"I don't know, Mesmo. I..."*

"Captain Olin," Mesmo interrupted. *"As the Observer, appointed by the Arch Council, I am giving you a direct order: abandon ship!"*

Barely audible, Liana whispered under her breath, *"What are you doing, Mesmo?"*

Captain Olin saluted. *"At your orders, Observer. I will evacuate my crew in stealth mode and tell them to take refuge on the Moon. However,"* he added. *"The command crew—myself included—will stay."*

Mesmo stared at the man. *"Olin..."*

"I am staying, Mesmo," Olin insisted. *"Forgive me for going against your direct order. You can have me arrested, but as captain, I cannot leave the Qu'Tué."*

Mesmo put his head down, then said, *"I understand, Olin. I implore you to be vigilant until I figure this out. In the meantime, I will join your crew on the Moon and meet the A'hmun leaders there."*

"About that," Olin said. *"There will be no meeting."*

"Why?"

"I sent my commander with a small crew down to Earth to pick up the A'hmun leaders, but he has reported that none have made it to the appointed location. He is still on Earth, awaiting my orders. I was hoping to confer with you about our next step."

"What?" Mesmo exclaimed. *"How is that possible?"*

Olin continued. *"I guess Captain Daria's crew was particularly efficient when attacking the planet before you called for a truce. My commander down on the ground says the area is destroyed."*

Mesmo's blood went cold. *"Which area is that, Captain Olin? Show me!"*

A 3D image of Earth appeared on his screen, rolled over and zoomed in on the Atlantic Coast of North America, which was now filled with scattered clouds.

Mesmo's mouth went dry. *"New York,"* he breathed.

"I'm sorry?" Olin said. *"Please repeat…"*

Mesmo wasn't listening anymore. An empty pit opened up under his feet.

Laura's down there.

"Mesmo?" Olin was calling him. *"What are your orders?"*

Mesmo set his jaw. *"Evacuate your crew, Captain,"* he said. *"And do it quietly."*

He cut the communication, staring fixedly at the virtual Earth hovering before him. Then he input some coordinates, initiated the thrusters, and sped away from the Qu'Tué.

"Uh... Mesmo?" Panaï ventured. *"Where are we going?"*

CHAPTER 27 *The Culprit*

Ben came to, with his arms dangling down over his head. He tried to focus, but everything swayed, to-and-fro, to-and-fro. Voices mumbled through his ringing ears. He knew these voices...

Too weak to move, he watched the back of a man's shoes walk below him, and for a second, he lost all sense of direction, then realized somebody was carrying him over their shoulder.

The shoes stopped, and a hollow sensation in Ben's stomach told him they were heading down in an elevator.

Down to the belly of the ship...

Ben wanted to move or yell, but his head throbbed too much, and his eyes wouldn't focus.

It didn't take long after that to reach the room

where the Quratis was being held.

Ben's stomach twisted at the bird's overpowering presence even though he couldn't see it from this uncomfortable position. He was lifted into the air and dropped on the floor like a sack of potatoes.

"Now what?" Einar said. The man's shoes moved away from Ben's field of vision.

"Leave us," Zoltar said. *"You have your orders."*

"What about the Observer?" Daria asked from the doorway.

"He is already on the Qu'Tué," Zoltar said. *"This is the time to strike. Go now. I will meet you at The Great Gathering."*

"Is that still necessary?" Einar questioned. *"Our little scheme on the Qu'Tué should be enough..."*

"I am leaving nothing to chance," Zoltar said. *"Now go. Time is precious."*

Ben's ears picked up Daria and Einar's receding footsteps. The door shut.

There was a long silence, except for a low humming machine. The floor was cold and hard. The stillness terrified Ben. He knew Zoltar and the Quratis were both in the room. What were they doing? Ben risked moving his head and found the strangest sight unfolding before him.

Zoltar stood with his back to Ben, facing the Quratis. Zoltar's hands glowed a deep red, and both man and mystical creature stared at each other as if in a deep, muted conversation. Zoltar's rigid stance made Ben's skin crawl. There was something unnervingly creepy about the whole thing. Zoltar seemed transfixed in time until, without warning, a tail feather from the Quratis unfurled from Zoltar's neck like a lasso.

The tension in Zoltar's body loosened, and he crumpled to the ground.

Ben jerked in fright.

One instant, Zoltar had stood tall and imposing before the bird; the next, he lay in a heap on the floor, moaning. *"No, please... No. Not the child... please."*

It felt like spiders were crawling all over Ben's skin.

Zoltar whimpered, buckled down on himself like a rag doll. Towering over him, the Quratis shone brighter and brighter. No longer did it limp or stoop. No longer did it look forlorn and submissive.

And Ben understood too late that he had been tricked: *the captor and the prisoner...* He had gotten it all wrong. It was not General Zoltar who was submitting the Quratis to his will. It was the other way around! It had not been the Quratis who he had heard moan and cry in his dreams; it had been Zoltar! All along, it had been Mesmo's father who had been suffering under the beast's domination, begging for help...

Anguish washed over Ben. He rolled onto his back, struggling to his knees. *"Zoltar!"* he cried.

Mesmo's father wrapped his arms around his head and moaned, *"Not the child... please!"*

Ben crawled to Zoltar's aid, but the Quratis had grown in size, its feathers gleaming in blinding flames of gold and red and orange. It extended its wings to reveal its true might, its presence so overwhelming it became hard to breathe. And the fear that Ben had once sensed from the suffering prisoner now became his, tenfold.

Like the tentacle of a poisonous jellyfish, one of the bird's tail feathers unfurled, coiling around Ben's neck like a whip, releasing red filaments that entered through his skin and wrapped around his brain. That single touch, from that single tentacle, scalded him. Images flashed before his eyes: stars, a thousand times brighter than the Sun; swirling galaxies; a bug crawling on the earth of a distant planet; life, born and gone in the blink of an eye...

Ben fell to his knees, squirming, his brain

exploding with images. *"No!"* he screamed. *"Please... no!"*

The Quratis spoke with a voice resonating in a thousand wave-lengths, echoing, repeating, bouncing off the walls and the farthest planet. *Young and fragile,* it spoke in his mind as it considered the minute, shivering life form before it. *And yet, bearer of the skill. Welcome, Ben Archer.*

* * *

Mesmo knew he had been going too fast. The controls indicated the spaceship's outer hull was reaching dangerous temperatures as it hurtled into the Earth's atmosphere. He couldn't help it. The single thought that he could lose Laura wiped away all his previous resolve. It was easier, knowing Ben and Laura were safe when he remained among the Toreq. But the idea that he could lose either of them permanently rendered his careful plans meaningless.

Goal number one: save Laura. It no longer mattered what the Toreq would think or that he could be cast away. Once Laura was safe, he'd have to improvise.

Clenching his teeth, Mesmo descended to the

ocean level, advancing towards the City of New York. Skyscrapers reached for the sky like fingers scratching the clouds. Patches of sunlight made it to the ground while dark grey waves travelled relentlessly to shore.

Liana, Kaani, Panaï and Qu'ira approached the window, gazing at the scene in awe.

Mesmo located the spaceship sent by Captain Olin to pick up human leaders and found it stationed at the edge of a river, next to a low building that was split in two. Half of the building had crumbled, while behind it, a taller building with shattered remnants of windows shadowed the first one. Waves spilled over the seawall and reached the entrance of the first building.

A small band of survivors huddled under a makeshift shelter on the roof of the remaining half of the building, trying to escape the rain that came and went at the whim of the constantly changing weather.

Mesmo hovered the spaceship at the height of the roof, so he could hop across and join the humans and the Toreq who had gathered there.

The Toreq commander greeted him. *"Observer,"* he said. *"I'm glad Captain Olin sent you. Perhaps you can make more sense of what it is we should do now that there are no A'hmun leaders here."*

Mesmo nodded.

Qu'ira joined him and whispered, *"Mesmo, are you going to tell us what we're doing here?"*

"I need to set things right," he said half to himself, too focused on finding Laura among the group. The human survivors parted and let him in, glancing at him with fearful eyes.

An older woman stepped before him. "I am Adhira Prabhakar," she said. "Head of the United Nations. Who are you?"

Mesmo turned and said, *"Liana, provide the Secretary-General with a translation device."*

Liana nodded and placed a button-sized black object behind Adhira's ear, then handed some to Kaani to distribute.

Mesmo greeted Adhira in English. "I am Mesmo, also known as the Observer. My father is General Zoltar of the Toreq fleet."

The woman nodded. "If you come for our leaders, you will not find them here," she said icily. "They are scrambling to save their subjects from your people's onslaughts. They could not make it to New York. And as you can see, we are barely surviving, ourselves."

"Mesmo," someone called, pulling his attention away from the woman.

Mesmo glanced through the faces and at the edge of the circle saw a haggard Inspector Hao looking up at him. Their eyes met. Mesmo rushed over to him and knelt. "Where is she?" he breathed. "She was with you, wasn't she?"

Hao's face dulled. "I take it you convinced your people to stop the hurricane, Mesmo. But it was too late. She didn't make it. She's still under there." He pointed at the crumpled side of the building.

Mesmo stared in horror from the man to the mounds of broken concrete. He left the group and approached the edge of the split roof, rain slipping over the thin layer of blue light emanating from his body, his cape billowing in the wind. He glanced down at the destruction below.

* * *

Ben tried to use every trick he knew to keep the Quratis out of his mind. Though Ben had only once used the skill to submit a creature to his will, the Quratis was an expert at it. It had had millions of years of practice, and there was nothing Ben could do.

The bird scanned his mind with its tentacles, taking its time, planning, scheming, and all Ben wanted was to get those whiplike fingers out of his head before they destroyed him.

I now have two translation skills at my mercy, the Quratis said. *It has happened before, on Torequ'ai. Zoltar and his granddaughter Kaia: both holders of the translation skill. I chose to connect with Zoltar: he was powerful and well esteemed by his people. They would listen to him. He could start a war, if necessary. But the girl... The girl began to suspect me. Yes, she was smart, that one. I had to get rid of her. I made Zoltar send her to Earth, then sent Bordock after her. How amusing that I managed to get rid of the girl, but not her skill. For here it still lives, within you...*

Ben shuddered. He didn't want the skill; he hated the skill; he wanted it out of him forever, just so the pain would stop.

What an unexpected situation, the Quratis said in its hundreds of reverberating voices, relishing its options. *Zoltar is old and a nuisance, always whining. It bores me. You, on the other hand, are young and malleable. We could accomplish many great things together. I will teach you.* It paused, then added, *After all, this was to be your last day of mentorship, was it not?*

Ben squirmed. He didn't want to learn. Not from this monster.

Let me show you all the great things I have achieved. When you know my power, you will understand, and you will join me in my quest.

Images, accompanied by smell and taste and sound, crashed into Ben's mind.

No! Please... no!

CHAPTER 28 *The Rubble of War*

Mesmo turned to face the group of humans and Toreq, who waited for his reaction by the shelter. Anger that he had never thought possible welled inside. He balled his fists, casting raindrops away from him. *"Kaani, Qu'ira, Panaï..."* His three friends straightened. *"Follow me."*

The four of them rushed down through the wrecked building. When they exited the stairwell, their feet sank into several inches of freezing seawater. Mesmo opened up a dry pathway for them with his water skill.

"Qu'ira," he said. *"I need you to use your telepathy skill to scan below the rubble. Look for any signs of life."*

Qu'ira nodded and set to work.

"Kaani, can you use your moulding skill to remove some of the bigger boulders? I need to find a way under there," Mesmo continued. *"Panaï, if your air skill can help in any way, use it!"*

The brothers saluted briefly and were off.

Mesmo set his jaw. He called forth his skill again, the palms of his hands stinging from the remaining burn marks on his hands. He pushed through the rain and invading seawater, calling the liquid away from the rubble, extracting it from whatever structure lay below ground.

They worked like that for the better part of an hour.

Some survivors came down from the roof and helped where they could, all of them silent and muted. Mesmo knew they were helping, not out of hope for finding Laura, but out of respect for his grief.

He struggled with his water skill. It kept snuffing out after long stretches of use, allowing the sea to conquer the land again.

"Mesmo," Liana came up to him and placed her hand on his arm. *"I don't know who you think you will find here, but whoever it is, it's too late for them."*

Mesmo ignored her comment and spread his hands before her. *"Liana, I need your skill,"* he said.

"Heal them."

Liana covered his hands with her own, sending soothing waves into them, but shook her head. *"This is not a solution, Mesmo. All I can do is lessen the pain temporarily. You will need to continue in-depth healing to avoid permanent damage."*

Mesmo pulled his hands away. *"Later,"* he said, pushing at the seawater again. Half the group had abandoned their search, but he wouldn't give up.

"Here!" Qu'ira yelled suddenly. She held out her hand for them to be silent while scanning the mountain of rubble below her with the other.

Mesmo waited in apprehension.

Qu'ira looked at him. *"There's someone, here."*

They rushed up the pile of concrete blocks to join her.

Qu'ira shook her head. *"I sense a woman. She's barely alive. She's deep down... right here."* She stared at Mesmo. *"This is an A'hmun woman, Mesmo. Why are we looking for an A'hmun woman?"*

Mesmo turned and yelled at Kaani. *"Can you lift the rocks and make a path through this?"*

Kaani nodded.

"Move away!" Mesmo yelled, but Qu'ira remained on the spot, still scanning the ground with her hand.

"She has you in her mind, Mesmo," she said, making him catch his breath. She looked at him. *"This is the mother of your son, is it not?"*

"It is," he admitted.

Qu'ira hopped down the rubble after him, casting a strange look his way.

They pulled back and watched as Kaani's hands glowed with an almost unbearable glare, smothering concrete to dust, while Panaï lifted other blocks into the air with powerful gusts of wind. A gaping hole formed before them, leading down into the Bunker. Water spilled down, then pulled back as Mesmo struggled to retrieve it. He approached the opening they had made with their skills and headed into the darkness.

* * *

Time ceased to exist in the world of the Quratis. All was one, and one was all. The Quratis cast its web over the galaxy, bonding star clusters, meteor belts, nebulae, colliding gas giants... And in its center, in the folds of time and space itself, lurking behind the deepest, impenetrable darkness, lay its den. Like a camouflaged, carnivorous monster sucking in anything that came within its path, the Quratis grew and took shape until it was strong enough to leave its home.

The Quratis spied on its subjects, studied them, watched their civilizations bloom and decay. And all the while, Ben sensed a great emptiness within it: a void that it opted to fill with war. It revelled in it! It found the bearers of the translation skill and whispered in their ear, planting an image, a thought; twisting reality.

Then suddenly Ben was on Torequ'ai, perched in the great tree of the Arch Council, watching the ghostly forms of men and women sitting in a circle below him. Some were tall with white hair and honey-coloured eyes; others had black hair or golden beards, light or dark skin, green or brown eyes. The Toreq and the A'hmun gathered one last time to try and stop the total annihilation of their planets. Smoke billowed from the plains, and the sky was dark with ominous clouds. Torequ'ai was burning.

Ben gasped.

This was an ancient memory. One from eons ago. One that meant everything...

Watch... The Quratis breathed the word into his mind—as if Ben had the choice not to. For there was nothing he could do except watch the end of *The Great War of the Kins* unfold before him.

The Quratis spread its wings and let itself drop onto the shoulder of an old man, wrapping its tail feathers loosely around the Toreq's neck.

Ben flinched inwardly at what he now knew to be a wicked gesture.

The Quratis spoke. *Meet Counsel Okra. He was a great and wise Toreq skilled in translation—the ancestor of the skill you now bear... He was my 'trusted ally' in The Great War of the Kins.* The beast laughed cruelly at the word 'ally.' *See, there, on the other side? That is Captain Ob—the one who unknowingly put the end in motion. Even to this day, the Toreq both loathe and revere him. They believe he allowed the Toreq to win the War, with an unforgivable deed...*

Ben looked through the eyes of the Quratis at the other side of the assembled Toreq and A'hmun. An important-looking Toreq with a trimmed white beard—an unusual trait for Toreq men—was looking straight at him. Ben cringed, for Captain Ob had an intelligent gaze, one that made Ben think he could see right through him. A flicker passed through the man's body, and Ben realized Captain Ob was attending the meeting virtually.

Old Counsel Okra spoke to those assembled

with words that the Quratis placed in his mouth. *"We have all agreed to disagree. That is one thing we can count on. With the crushing losses on either side, it is highly unlikely that we will ever make peace with one another as individuals. However, I ask that you think of future generations and work together with them in mind. We, here, may never make peace, but let us lay out the foundations so our children and grandchildren may find a way to do what we could not."*

The Quratis spoke to Ben over the unfolding memory. *Do these words not sound innocent and peace-loving? The Toreq and the A'hmun respect Counsel Okra; he gives them hope—I give them hope. Those are my words that they are hearing. They truly believe Counsel Okra will bring a peaceful end to the War.*

The Quratis cackled. *The Toreq and the A'hmun have been tearing each other apart for years. Their planets and their civilizations lie in shambles, yet still, they gather one last time in the hopes of reaching peace. Does it not give you great elation to watch these insignificant life-forms gather against all odds, betting on a minuscule glimmer of hope, only to have that hope snuffed out in a second—by me?*

The Quratis breathed hard, intoxicated by its

clever design. *Captain Ob is skilled in strategy. His military fleet is positioned around Taranis—the planet of your ancestors. He has the whole A'hmun civilian fleet at his mercy. The problem is that I know Captain Ob; he will not fire on civilians. He has ignored Counsel Okra's orders—my orders—to attack them. He merely surrounds them to force the negotiations to continue here on Torequ'ai. So, I have had to find a way to force his hand... Back then, I could not corrupt Captain Ob, but I was able to corrupt his Lieutenant, a dutiful, obedient soldier...*

Ben watched a younger Toreq appear behind Captain Ob.

Captain Ob does not yet understand that Lieutenant Saprakas will betray him. Captain Ob did not listen to me, but Saprakas did. He knows what his orders are...

Lieutenant Saprakas glanced at the Quratis, gave a tiny smile and bow, then vanished from the meeting.

The Quratis whispered in Ben's mind. *Watch the screens...*

Ben watched the hovering screens around the meeting. He could see a yellowish planet and Toreq warships surrounding smaller spaceships. He reeled inside, horrified by what he knew he was about to see.

A blinding flash of light emanating from one of the Toreq warships; travelled silently over a stretch of space and crashed into one of the A'hmun ships. It was pulverized in an instant.

Both Toreq and A'hmun, gathered under the Arch Council Tree, wailed in shock at the sight. Captain Ob's mouth dropped in horror. An A'hmun sitting opposite him staggered to a standing position, lifted his index finger at Ob, took in a huge breath and shrieked, "TRAITOR!" Then all hell broke loose under the great tree of the Arch Council, where the Toreq and A'hmun, who had been trying to negotiate peace, turned against each other.

The Quratis took flight, watching the end of the *Great War* unfold below it, relishing in the destruction. The land burned, warships battled in the sky, and Torequ'ai was all but flattened to the ground.

Captain Ob died in the final battle, of course. To this day, the Toreq hail him as a savior; they believe he destroyed the A'hmun. Others detest him; they say he murdered innocent, defenceless people. It is quite comical that he has gone down in history as a war hero when, in fact, it was his Lieutenant who committed the deed...

Ben felt broken inside. *You caused it all! You caused The Great War of the Kins! But why? And why are you showing me this?*

I am showing you the possibilities, the Quratis spoke in his head. *The Great War of the Kins was my greatest creation, the greatest downfall of two civilizations. Now, millennia later, I was both pleased and surprised to discover how well the Toreq and the A'hmun have risen from the ashes of war.*

Zoltar is no longer of use to me. But you and I have a new opportunity. You momentarily stopped the attack of the Toreq on your planet. But no matter, you have only made it more enjoyable for me. You will now assist me, as did Counsel Okra...

Ben squirmed. *Assist you with what?*

Shh... the Quratis soothed him. *All in good time.*

I don't understand. Why use Zoltar? Why use Bordock? That memory of their meeting. You sent that to me, didn't you? Why did Zoltar defend humans then, only to attack them later?

The Quratis shrugged. *Bordock, Zoltar, Daria... What does it matter whose side they are on? The game is to stoke the fires of war, which must be done on both sides.*

Ben shuddered. *But why stoke fires of war? Are you not a Lifegiver?*

To his horror, the Quratis burst into a horrible laugh that shook his brain. *Lifegiver or Lifetaker? Are they not one and the same? Does death not give rise to life? Does the vulture not feed off the carcass, the mushroom off the rotting branch, the seed off the cooling lava? Do not judge, Ben Archer, for you know nothing of me.*

But Ben did. He could feel it with his skill: the empty heart of the Quratis beat in the void, a void that the Quratis sought to fill with emotions of pain, loss, hate, courage and loyalty. These strong emotions emanated from species like A'hmun and Toreq—emotions denied to the Quratis due to its nature.

The Quratis swooped across the black firmament, observing the fight for life on minute planets, the struggle to be born and thrive, the bonds of hate and love between creatures, tiny and large. It saw all this, and Ben noted that it was always from a distance; the Quratis never really belonged. Ben sensed its jealousy, for it could not take part in the joys and sorrows experienced by its subjects. *You are lonely!* he finally breathed. *There is no one like you out there.*

At Ben's words, dark anger simmered within

the bird. Ben should have paid closer attention to it but was too stunned by what the Quratis had revealed.

Ben watched the scene inside his head, helpless, unable to close his eyes, as Taranis and Torequ'ai burned, and he knew the Quratis wanted him to revel in its genius, in its craftsmanship, in its ability to manipulate others. But all Ben could think of was the empty feeling the bird hid behind its warmongering greed.

You have never known love, he said.

The Quratis roared. It thrust Ben out of its mind and flung him to the ground, hard.

CHAPTER 29 *Back from the Dark*

Mesmo descended into the remnants of the Bunker, the only light coming from his glowing hands. Then another light illuminated beside him in one swift stream.

Hao waved a flashlight into the darkness, then glanced at him when Mesmo stopped. "What?" Hao said. "You weren't planning on doing this on your own, were you?"

A second flashlight came on next to Hao.

Mesmo stared at a young man with curly hair. "I know you," he said. "You're…"

"Jeremy Michaels, Provincial Times reporter," the man nodded. He glanced at Hao and squished his face. "What? Is there only room for bigshots down here?"

Hao rolled his eyes and shrugged. "Bringing Jeremy along was Laura's idea," he told Mesmo, nudging his head the reporter's way. "Too long to explain."

Qu'ira and Kaani followed behind the trio.

They searched the darkness, sloshing through a layer of ice-cold water. When Jeremy lit up the walls, they could tell how high the water had risen. Almost to the top.

Qu'ira shook her head. *"I'm not sensing her anymore."*

Mesmo yelled, "Laura!" His voice echoed down the corridors.

Something rumbled to their left, and a slab of wall crashed to the ground, barely missing them.

"Jeez!" Hao growled, adjusting the translation device behind his ear. "This place isn't going to hold for long."

"The entire structure is unstable," Kaani agreed.

Mesmo grabbed the flashlight from Jeremy's hands and rushed forward. The others sprinted after him. He searched everywhere: the cafeteria, the control room, the sleeping quarters, calling Laura's name. Still, they found no trace of her.

"Mesmo," Qu'ira said after a while. *"You have to stop this madness. The A'hmun woman is gone."*

"No!" Mesmo cried, setting his sight on Qu'ira with a fire that burned hot inside him. *"You sensed her! She's alive, and she needs help."* His begging eyes revealed more than they should have, he was sure, but he ploughed on. *"Please, Qu'ira. Find her!"*

Qu'ira considered him for a moment before nodding. She took a deep breath, raised a glowing blue hand, and closed her eyes. After a brief silence, she opened her eyes again, and her hand moved to the right. *"There,"* she said, hurrying past them to the elevator. *"In there."*

"Kaani!" Mesmo yelled, urging his friend to use his skill.

Without answering, Kaani dipped his glowing fingers into the metal of the door, which melted under his touch. The material dripped down like thick paint until only a puddle of metal remained on the floor.

Hao illuminated the inside of the elevator, but there was nothing.

The four of them stared, incredulous.

Qu'ira glanced, wide-eyed, at Mesmo. *"I'm sorry. I thought... I thought..."* She broke off.

Hao lowered the flashlight.

They backed away, leaving Mesmo standing with his fists clenched, staring at the empty elevator. He couldn't make himself leave. Qu'ira had heard Laura; he was sure of it. Laura was smart. She would have known the water would rise and that elevators were unsafe in an emergency. She would have looked for higher ground...

"Wait!" he yelled.

Hao swung the flashlight around, back into the empty elevator.

Mesmo stepped inside and used Jeremy's flashlight to illuminate the roof. Then he saw it: a piece of clothing sticking through an emergency trap door in the ceiling. *"She tried to escape the flooding!"* he yelled. *"Get me up there!"* Mesmo stepped in Kaani's linked fingers so his friend could heave him up. He pushed the trap door and popped his head through to look inside the dark shaft. Laura's lifeless body lay to the side.

"Laura," he gasped, feverishly reaching for her and pulling her towards the opening. The others reached out to catch her as she slid down.

Mesmo jumped back down into the elevator, then picked Laura up, his blood going cold as he caught sight of her ashen face and blue lips. Jeremy's camera lay strung around her shoulder over her damp clothes. He pulled the camera off her and handed it to the reporter.

Laura's fingers closed on the front of his cape, and he cocked his head to listen as her lips parted.

"What took you so long?" she breathed.

"Hang on, Laura," he said through gritted teeth, sprinting out of the elevator and up the stairs, sloshing through the water that was returning down into the Bunker.

Anxious to reach the spaceship, he rushed up the stairwell of the UN building with Laura's head pressing against his chest. Her body had gone limp again.

He hopped into the spaceship, yelling, "Liana!" as he placed Laura on a horizontal energy field in a room at the back.

Liana rushed to his side and shoved him aside. *"This is where I come in,"* she said sternly, indicating Mesmo needed to back away so she could apply her healing skill.

Mesmo did so reluctantly. *"Will she live?"* he asked.

Liana glanced at him without answering, concentrating on passing her glowing hand over Laura's body, then entering in a trance-like concentration.

"Mesmo," Hao said beside him, startling him. "I know the timing sucks, but I need to talk to you in private."

Mesmo set his jaw, concentrating on Laura.

"Mesmo," Hao insisted. "This is urgent."

Mesmo set his jaw but left the room and followed Hao out of the spaceship. Hao gestured towards the middle-aged woman Mesmo had seen earlier—the one called Adhira. She joined them, followed closely by Jeremy.

Hao turned to the middle-aged woman. "Ma'am, do you have it?" he asked.

She nodded and took the camera from Jeremy's hands. "I cannot show you the full video," she said. "But our intrepid reporter was smart enough to take pictures of it."

Jeremy beamed.

Adhira continued. "Before we evacuated the Bunker, I was informed of a very troubling incident: a nuclear warhead was stolen from a high-security facility in New Mexico. We have pictures of the thieves on this camera. This camera is the reason Laura returned to the Bunker. She went back to retrieve it because she said you would know the culprits." She turned the camera around to show Mesmo pictures of the underground nuclear silo with two shadows in the corner. She enlarged the image.

"Captain Daria!" Mesmo exclaimed.

"And that one," Hao said, pointing at the other individual, "is Einar."

"This incident is of a major concern, Mister

Mesmo," Adhira said. "We have no idea where the nuclear bomb is or who or what it could be used against."

Mesmo's eyes widened as he stared from Hao to Adhira, a lightning-bolt of dread coursing through his body. "I do!" he said, aghast. He turned and sprinted back into the spaceship, dashed to the front, and called up Captain Olin.

The captain appeared on his screen. *"Observer,"* Olin saluted.

"Captain Olin!" Mesmo yelled. *"Evacuate NOW!"*

Captain Olin wasn't listening. Somebody was shouting something behind him. His face turned ashen, he glanced at Mesmo, eyes bulging, and then the screen went blank.

* * *

How dare you! The Quratis pulled away from Ben, angry sparks flying from its magnificent plumage. Its tail-feathers crackled.

Ben watched it cautiously, unable to move from the floor after the creature had sucked the energy out of him. So... it did not know love. It had grown up, hiding in the folds of its own black hole, unique in its kind—alone, while its anger festered.

The Quratis ruffled its feathers bitterly, then gathered itself and turned its attention to the whimpering Zoltar, wrapping its tail feather around the man.

It took a fraction of a second: Zoltar stopped moaning, lifted himself off the ground, and stood straight as an arrow.

Like a puppet brought to life... Ben shuddered.

The Quratis communicated with Zoltar. Ben sensed it rather than heard it, the bird having cast him away from its thoughts.

Zoltar turned and stared at Ben, an inner fire burning in his eyes, then, in a few strides, he crossed the room. Ben tried to scramble away, but Zoltar had him on his feet in an instant, dragging him to a window and pressing his face against the glass.

"Watch and learn," Zoltar said in a dull voice.

The blast ripped through the warship Qu'Tué in a light so bright Ben thought he'd be blinded even though he'd shut his eyes. It took a couple of breaths, then the blast reached them and sent them sprawling to the ground.

* * *

Thoughts crashed into Ben's throbbing head as he came to, lying on the floor.

The explosion! Mesmo!

Pressing his hands against his mouth to stifle a sob, he found the Quratis hunched in on itself as if sleeping. Its brilliance had dimmed somewhat, and it looked less threatening than in waking.

How could it be sleeping? How long have I been out?

There was no trace of the terrible blast. He rolled onto his back, pain searing through every muscle, and found Zoltar standing right beside him, still as a stone, eyes glazed. Ben froze, then realized Zoltar was still in the Quratis' grasp, obliged to stand there like a robot that had been switched off.

Mesmo!

A huge void opened up in Ben's chest. Zoltar had seen the explosion, too. Zoltar had just lost his son.

With his heart constricted with grief, Ben reached out and took Zoltar's hand. Perhaps Zoltar could feel his connection. A subtle buzz vibrated under the General's skin, matching Ben's.

The skill!

Zoltar's skill and Ben's skill. They were one, passed down from one generation to the next, but fundamentally the same.

Ben wished he knew how to release Zoltar from the Quratis' mental bonds, but he didn't. They were both trapped inside a cage, bordered by the same force field as his jail cell. He rolled onto his side and froze.

Tuli stood there, on the other side of the force field, her piercing blue eyes set on him.

"Tuli," he whispered, his voice hoarse. He tried to get up but was too weak. *"Help us!"*

She got down on one knee and stared at him with some curiosity. She glanced at the Quratis, then back at him. She shook her head.

"Please!" Ben begged.

She cocked her head. *"We cannot,"* she said. *"We are not strong enough. The Quratis is too powerful."*

Ben tried to lean on his arm, but black spots swam before his eyes. He dropped his head back down to the floor, wanting to convince her to help but also knowing that it was too dangerous. If the Quratis awoke...

Tuli pulled something up from behind her and placed it between them. The object slid over the ground, passed through the force field, and slithered over Ben's chest.

Echis!

Benjamin! I sso happy to ssee you! I sso sscared! Big, big bird there! It want to eat me, for ssure! I hide in hoodie now.

The venomous snake slithered into Ben's hoodie, the way it had done many times before.

I never leave here. I sstay. Nicce and warm. You protect me from bad bird, yess?

Ben's eyes welled.

Tuli was still staring at him. *"We cannot help you."* She smiled sadly. *"But perhaps, when the time comes, you will do what is needed."*

Ben opened his mouth, his painful brain filling with questions, but she had already tiptoed across the room and disappeared into the shadows.

That was it, then. No help would come. It was Zoltar and him against the most powerful creature in the universe.

CHAPTER 30 *Face-Off*

"What just happened?" Kaani asked, frowning at the empty screen where Captain Olin had been a moment ago.

Mesmo sat back, his mouth open in shock. He lifted both hands to his head.

"Mesmo!" Kaani insisted. *"What happened to Captain Olin?"*

Mesmo turned and stared at Hao and Adhira, who glanced back at him with pale faces. He finally said to Kaani, *"Get the others on board; we need to leave at once. Tell the commander that his captain is dead and that he is now under my orders. Tell him to follow us."*

Kaani caught his breath and nodded.

Mesmo turned to the humans. "Hao, Adhira,

Jeremy; you're coming with us."

The three humans glanced at each other.

"Wh... where are we going?" Adhira stuttered, eyeing the spaceship nervously.

Mesmo looked at her grimly. "Secretary-General, you are going to have to speak for the human race. You're our best shot."

Adhira paled but nodded.

Mesmo glanced at Hao and Jeremy. "And we are going to need those pictures."

No sooner were Qu'ira and Panaï on board than the spaceship accelerated to ultrasonic speed, leaving the Earth's atmosphere behind.

"Dang! This is something to behold!" Hao exclaimed, glancing at the planet below him.

Adhira gazed out the window, speechless.

Jeremy retched.

Hao patted him sympathetically on the back. "Hey, Busybody, why don't you head on back and talk to Liana. I bet she's got some alien tonic to patch you up."

Jeremy nodded and rushed to the back of the spaceship with his hands on his stomach.

Adhira turned to Hao. "Inspector, look!" she breathed.

Toreq and humans closed in around Mesmo. He had pulled up a three-dimensional screen showing the warships—or what was left of them.

Farther up from their location, the nuclear blast had deactivated the camouflage shield, leaving the warships exposed as they drifted away from the Moon. Remnants from a powerful light as bright as the sun glowed from where the center of the Qu'Tué had been before being ripped apart. Pieces of it still flew through space, while half of the flank had hurled into the warship Codo, leaving a gaping hole in its side as if a giant shark had bitten into it.

Mesmo glanced at Adhira and Hao. "The Toreq are going to blame you for this," he said.

Adhira gasped. "But we didn't..."

"I know," Mesmo said. "It was a setup."

Panaï exclaimed, *"Are you suggesting we blew ourselves up? Are you crazy?"*

Qu'ira said, *"Mesmo, it's time you let us in on your secrets."*

Mesmo glanced at her sadly. *"There are no secrets. Captain Daria and Einar stole a powerful weapon from the humans and used it to blow up the Qu'Tué. Now they can blame humans and reignite the war."* He glanced at Kaani. *"Get my father and the remaining warship captains on screen. I'm going to have to do some tough convincing to change Earth's fate."*

Kaani sprang into action, but his calls remained unanswered. *"Our calls are being jammed!"* he said.

They waited, tense, for a signal.

Qu'ira shouted, *"Look! Over there!"* She pointed at one of the warships on the 3D screen. Hundreds of pinpoints of lights shot out of its belly.

"It's the Zul!" Mesmo exclaimed. *"Daria's warship. She's sending out an attack!"*

"On who?" Hao wanted to know.

They watched as hundreds of speeders headed their way.

"Kaani!" Mesmo yelled. *"Get me General Zoltar, Captain Anaris... anyone!"*

"I can't!" Kaani said, his fingers moving feverishly over the commands.

The speeders descended towards the Earth at an incredible speed but came to a standstill as they reached Mesmo's ship. Communications remained down.

Mesmo opened all frequencies. *"This is the Observer. Do not attack!"*

"Wait!" Kaani gasped, lifting his hands off the commands. *"Someone is hailing us on a broad frequency! The whole fleet can hear us!"*

The screen flickered, and Captain Daria appeared. *"Observer,"* she said. *"What a surprise."*

Mesmo clenched his teeth. *"Surprise, indeed. Were you expecting me to be on the Qu'Tué?"*

A small smile appeared at the corner of her mouth. *"That is what I had been told. Instead, I find you here, returning from a secret trip to Earth where you saved an A'hmun woman—a woman you have been living with for quite some time, so Einar tells me..."* She paused.

Mesmo fumed. He typed a quick message on his computer and sent the message to Kaani. His friend jumped to his feet and whispered to the humans.

"Do not get me wrong, Observer," Daria said. *"I am relieved to find you alive and well, and I am certain there is a misunderstanding regarding this woman. I look forward to seeing you rally to the Toreq cause. The A'hmun have launched a deadly attack on the Qu'Tué. We will take revenge for the poor souls we have lost. Your water skill will be of great value in our attack on Earth. The whole fleet, here, looks forward to seeing you take the lead in our war against the enemy."* She paused again. *"What say you?"*

Mesmo kept his eyes on Captain Daria. *"You know as well as I do that the treachery is on you. You stole the A'hmun weapon. You detonated it and blew up the Qu'Tué! You have Captain Olin's death on your conscience!"*

Captain Daria's smile vanished. *"How dare you! You are the one scheming with the enemy— even adopting one as your own! You tarnish your daughter's legacy!"*

Mesmo was about to roar into the speaker when Qu'ira placed her hand on his shoulder to calm him. Out of the corner of his eye, Mesmo saw Kaani give a small nod.

Mesmo said, *"There is no shame in what I have done. You, on the other hand, will have to explain the theft of this A'hmun weapon..."* He typed a couple of commands and the pictures incriminating Daria and Einar appeared on his screen.

"Is the whole fleet seeing this?" Mesmo whispered under his breath.

Kaani said, *"Yes, but..."*

The screen vanished.

"Whoa!" Kaani exclaimed. *"She jammed us again!"*

By now, Daria's legion of speeders had reached their position and aimed their weapons straight at them.

"Mesmo!" Qu'ira breathed, her hand digging into his shoulder.

CHAPTER 31 *Downward*

Ben leaned on his arm, trying to get into a sitting position, but lacking the strength to do so. A hovering screen flickered on beside the Quratis. Zoltar sprang into action beside Ben. The cage disintegrated long enough to let him step out. He accepted the call, the Quratis eyeing him with beady eyes.

"You told me he was on the Qu'Tué!" Captain Daria shrieked over the screen. *"Now he has some kind of proof to incriminate us!"* Her face contorted in anger. *"What are we supposed to do now? He keeps rallying the fleet to his cause. He's creating a rift among us."*

Ben's heart skipped a beat. Was she talking about Mesmo?

Zoltar let her have her moment while Einar remained behind Daria with his arms crossed.

"Are you done?" Zoltar said after a while.

"No, I'm not done! I'm the captain of the Zul, for goodness sake! I'm taking my warship, and I'll fight the A'hmun on my own if I have to!"

"You will do no such thing," Zoltar demanded.

"Then, what?" Daria yelled. *"Will you not speak? My speeders have him cornered. Give the order, and I will blast him to bits."*

Zoltar must have given her a deathly look because she stopped pacing and added, *"General?"*

Ben held his breath.

Zoltar placed his hands behind his back. *"No,"* he said. *"Leave him. We don't want half the fleet turning against us. We will go to The Great Gathering instead, as planned. When Earth's creatures confirm their repulsion of the A'hmun, we will have full permission to eliminate our enemy."*

"But, what if these creatures side with the A'hmun?"

To Ben's horror, Zoltar turned and glanced at him with fire in his eyes. *"Leave that to me."*

Einar noticed Ben and straightened. *"Why is he still here? He can hear everything we're saying.*

I don't trust him! Get rid of him already!"

"Tsk, tsk. All in good time," Zoltar said. *"Go, now! We meet at The Gathering. You know what to do."*

Daria seemed to want to say more, but she held back, saluted, and shut down communications.

Zoltar wound down like the puppet of a ventriloquist. The Quratis curled its wings around the man, giving him silent orders.

Ben cringed at the sight. He had a small idea of the pain Zoltar was experiencing at the bird's touch. A cold sweat broke on his back, and his heart beat faster. Something was brewing. Something that involved *him*!

Sure enough, Zoltar turned and headed straight for Ben's cage. He activated an opening switch, and the cage evaporated.

Ben scrambled backwards on his hands and feet, only to bump into the wall.

Zoltar grabbed his wrists and bound them with some kind of string that looked like static electricity. Zoltar pulled him to his feet.

"Where are we going?" Ben asked fearfully.

It was scary how strong and distant Zoltar became under the influence of the Quratis. Ben had a flash of memory of Zoltar standing in the middle of his garden, looking relaxed and humming contentedly. Was that the real Zoltar?

There was no time to ponder.

Zoltar pressed his hand against the back of Ben's neck and pushed him across the room. As they headed out, the Quratis became the size of a small owl. It looked quite harmless.

They hurried down a corridor and reached an elevator. Just then, lights within indicated someone was coming down. At lightning speed, Zoltar clamped his hand over Ben's mouth and pulled him behind a wall of hissing pipes.

The elevator door opened, and out stepped a small group of soldiers led by Torka.

Zoltar's grip tightened. "One squeak, and they're dead," he breathed into Ben's ear. The Quratis' feathers crackled like static on Zoltar's shoulder. Its tail feathers rattled menacingly.

Torka advanced into the corridor. He pulled up a screen from his wristband. "Nothing here," he said, before speaking to the soldiers. "Spread out and check the rest of the area." The group moved away, with Torka muttering something about unsanitary warships.

Zoltar removed his hand from Ben's mouth, and Ben breathed again. In a few steps, they were inside the elevator and heading for the spaceship hangar, where they rushed to a separate area where a single, large spaceship awaited.

Zoltar shoved Ben inside and dropped him into a seat. The Quratis hopped onto Ben's knee, spread its wings and stared at him intensely. The bird stayed there, digging its claws into his skin every time he tried to move.

Thrusters roared to life, and they were out, speeding across space, heading for Earth.

* * *

As Daria's speeders closed in on them, preparing to fire, Mesmo yelled, *"Kaani! Where is my father? Why is he not answering?"*

"I... I can't get anyone to answer..." Kaani's fingers sped over the controls, sweat pearling on his forehead. *"Oh... wait!"* A frequency opened suddenly, making him jump back in surprise. *"Someone is hailing us. And it's not Captain Daria."*

Static appeared on the screen, but a muffled voice came through. *"Observer,"* a man said. *"Hold your ground."*

Kaani warned, *"Whoever it is, is heading right towards us, and he's not alone!"*

Mesmo peered out the window, watching a whole new group of speeders heading their way, led by an unidentified pilot. The pilot flew under Daria's threatening fleet and glided up in front of Mesmo's ship to protect it. *"Identify yourself!"* Mesmo ordered.

The pilot opened a broad frequency to the Toreq fleet, his face breaking through the static, and said, *"This is Captain Olin from the Qu'Tué. Put away your weapons and stand down!"*

Mesmo gasped. Behind him, Toreq and humans cheered in relief.

The speeders that had followed Captain Olin circled the threatening ships. Captain Olin continued. *"This is my crew. We are all accounted for. We are alive thanks to the Observer's quick action. He warned us beforehand about the attack on the Qu'Tué, giving us time to escape and hide out on the Moon. We owe him our life. You will back down and listen to the Observer until General Zoltar provides us with further orders."*

A tense silence followed.

Another screen flickered on. *"This is Torka from the warship Ob."* He made a little cough. *"We believe General Zoltar has taken his private ship and is heading down to Earth. He is not responding to our calls."*

A chill travelled up Mesmo's back.

Captain Olin spoke again. *"Let us hope*

General Zoltar is safe. Until then, the Observer must take his place. Captain Anaris, Captain Yigis, are you in agreement?"

Captain Anaris spoke. *"Observer, I have the greatest respect for you. But I am confused. When I agreed to come here, my orders were clear: to attack and destroy the A'hmun. Now you seem to question that order, which came from the Arch Council. Worse, you are accusing one of our people of sabotage. Things were clear when I arrived. Now, they are not."*

Captain Yigis added, *"I tend to agree with Captain Anaris, Observer. Since our arrival to this galaxy, deeper and deeper factions have developed among us—factions that were not there before. You have made some severe accusations against Captain Daria, yet do not speak openly about this A'hmun woman you travel with. There are many inconsistencies I would like to see cleared up..."* There was a pause. *"Nevertheless, until General Zoltar sends us his orders, you are next in line to command. Warship Codo is in a bad state and will require my full attention, but it is ready at your orders, Observer."*

"So is warship Maq," Captain Anaris agreed.

Mesmo let out a breath of relief as Daria's speeders pulled in their weapons.

"*Observer,*" Captain Olin said. "*What are your orders?*"

Mesmo turned in his seat and faced the rest of his crew, then said, "*Captain Olin, Captain Yigis, Captain Anaris, I will speak with you in private now.*" When this was done, he said, "*I want a full status report.*"

Captain Olin spoke. "*There are two hundred and forty-nine injured on the Codo, twenty of them, severely. We are relocating the whole crew of the Qu'Tué among the other warships. We are still dealing with an energy imbalance on the Ob. The Zul and the Maq are fully operational.*"

Mesmo's eyes narrowed in concentration. "*Take your wounded to the warship Ob and have them treated. Place Captain Daria under arrest. She will have to answer for her attack on the Qu'Tué. Captains, use all means to keep the warship Zul in check. I believe my father is heading to The Great Gathering. That is where I am headed with one who will speak for the A'hmun. You three, meet us there as well. Perhaps the things you will hear at The Gathering will set your minds at rest.*"

Once the captains had accepted, Mesmo spoke on a private line with Torka. "*Torka, have you found my son?*"

"*I am sorry, Mesmo. I have sent search teams*"

throughout the Ob. He is not on board. All I found was his wristband..."

Mesmo's jaw tensed. *"Then he is with my father,"* he said, convincing himself. *"I need you at The Gathering as well, Torka. Meet us down there. But before you go, there is something else that you must do for me..."*

Mesmo gave Torka his orders. When his friend took his leave, Mesmo sat back and stared at the group of Toreq and humans that surrounded him.

"Mister Mesmo," Adhira said, stepping forward. "You wish to take us to this *Great Gathering* you speak of. The child, Benjamin Archer, mentioned it, as well. What is it we can expect from it?"

"Secretary-General," Mesmo said gravely. "Benjamin and I worked hard to make the *Gathering* a reality. My people accuse you of mishandling your planet."

"And they're kind of right..." Jeremy mumbled, joining them again and looking much better.

Hao dug his elbow into the reporter's side.

"What?" Jeremy mouthed at him.

Mesmo continued. "*The Great Gathering* was meant to bring animals and humans together, to find common ground for the first time and restore balance to the planet. Only, we did not know then that the Toreq would be part of it. I asked my father for a truce until the time of the *Gathering*. What will unfold there will determine your survival as a species. Whatever it is you can think of to convince my people that humans still deserve to live must be brought up at this meeting."

"No pressure..." Hao said under his breath. "Especially when part of your fleet wants to shoot you out of the sky, Mesmo!"

"Captain Yigis is right," Mesmo said. "Since the arrival of the Toreq, factions have appeared among my people. It is unusual for this to happen to such a degree. I strongly suspect Captain Daria and Einar of stoking extremist thoughts among the fleet. The success of the *Gathering* will depend on which side pulls the most weight. My father is the only one who can maintain the balance. It worries me that he is not making himself heard, considering the severity of the attack on the Qu'Tué."

Qu'ira added, *"That's the part I don't understand, Mesmo. How did you know what the nuclear warhead would be used for?"*

Feeling drained, Mesmo shook his head. *"I didn't know,"* he said, glancing at them each in turn.

"But Benjamin did."

CHAPTER 32 *Canopy*

The blue sky of Earth startled Ben. He squinted at the bright light coming in through the window, surprised that he had gotten unaccustomed to it after weeks spent in the darkness of space. Even the artificial, alien sunlight on the warship didn't do justice to Earth's young sun.

The spaceship descended to ground level, flying over an endless sea of green.

The Amazon rainforest!

Ben couldn't believe it. After months away, he hadn't dared dream of making it to *The Great Gathering.*

It wasn't long before the Amazon River came into view, its brown, nutrient-rich water spilling into the Atlantic Ocean. Zoltar skimmed its entrance and found a small opening between towering trees to land the spaceship. It seemed as though time slowed as they moved into the gloom of the forest, its canopy closing in on them from above. Strong vines dropped down several feet from the treetops, droplets and mist mingling with the deep green foliage.

The humming spaceship came to a standstill, and silence filled the cockpit.

Then Zoltar turned slowly and stared at Ben. His face was expressionless, but a fire lit in his eyes.

Ben's blood went cold. "Zoltar?" His voice trembled.

The Quratis opened its flaming wings and landed on the controls behind Zoltar, blocking out the view as it grew in size. Thin, fiery tentacles unfurled from Zoltar's mind, retracting back into the bird's tail feathers. The General let out a heart-wrenching groan and collapsed to the ground.

"Zoltar!" Ben cried, throwing himself beside the General.

Zoltar moaned and clamped his arms over his head.

"Zoltar! Please!" Ben repeated, pulling at the man's arm, terrifyingly conscious of the Quratis towering above them. When the General didn't react, Ben knew he was alone to face the monstrous creature. The hairs on the back of his neck rose. The bird's tail feather slid before his face and lashed around his neck.

"Argh!" Ben choked, pulling at the noose.

It is your time to shine, Ben Archer. The thousand voices of the Quratis echoed within him.

Through the searing pain, Ben saw the General's eye peek at him from under his arm. Zoltar mouthed the word, *"Run!"*

Ben gagged.

A tentacle slid into his ear, making it feel like his head was going to explode. At the same time, his hands were freed. He blinked away tears and, just in time, caught Zoltar removing his bonds and picking himself up from the ground.

It happened in a fraction of a second.

Zoltar stood to his full height, his back towards Ben. He roared, then threw himself head-on at the Quratis. Man and creature crashed to the ground. The tentacles slipped out of Ben's mind, leaving a burning trail in their path.

"Run, child! RUN!"

Ben rolled towards the door, a rattling tail feather snapping inches from his head. He pressed the opening mechanism, threw himself out, and fell to the ground with a thud. Animals of the forest hooted and screeched around him, disturbed by the mayhem.

Inside the spaceship, Zoltar howled in pain.

There was no time to think. Ben picked himself up and dove into the foliage, his pant leg tearing as something left a gash in his knee. He crashed through the forest, thrusting his arms before him to push away leaves that slapped his face. His foot caught on a vine, sending him sprawling and smacking into the ground. He bit his tongue to fend off stinging tears, and it took all he had to pick himself up again and keep running.

Unable to ignore the strange crackling sounds and dull thuds behind him, he ran, heart aching for Zoltar. When silence returned over the forest, that feeling of despair only worsened. The heat and humidity didn't help. Even his Toreq outfit felt clamped to his body. Breathing became hard. Still, he kept running, ignoring the nagging thought in his head that he had no idea where he was going and that Mesmo's father could be dead. Since he couldn't see any end to trees, he worried that he was heading deeper and deeper into the world's biggest rainforest.

That was when a branch snapped not far behind him.

He dove behind a tree root as tall as he was and made himself as small as possible. He tried to contain his rasping breath but couldn't.

It started to rain. Thick, warm drops drummed on the leaves and the ground, soaking him from head to toe.

Echis stirred in his hoodie. The snake's voice sounded terrified. *Ben Archer! What iss happening? I am afraid...*

Shhh! Don't speak, don't move, or the bird will find you.

Echis tensed like a dead branch.

The forest made strange sounds. Ben glanced left, then right. Things moved. Shadows. It was probably the rain, but fear tricked him into seeing things. A frog croaked. Something crawled over his hand. A bird hooted from above. The sounds became voices—a million voices, of all sizes and shapes, of all colours and types.

Ben's heart slowed, his ears hummed to the skill. He heard them, the animals, millions of them, everywhere, digging their way into the soil, crawling on tree trunks, swinging between trees: jaguars, sloths, macaws, tamarins, capybaras... There were so many Ben had to tone down on the skill. And, not far off, a near-silent zone was being overflown by the mightiest creature of all...

Ben cringed.

The Quratis glided nearby, hunting for its

prey, silent and deadly.

As quickly as it had started, the rain stopped. Humidity rose from the rich soil. Ben dug his hands into the wet earth, grounding himself, hiding their glow. A centipede crawled near his head. He felt the hard bark of the kapok tree digging into his shoulder. Ben became one with the tree. He could hear the flow of vital sap trickling within its trunk. He was its roots, embedded in the soil, and its canopy high above his head. He was one with the forest, and the forest became him. There was a balance here that few places he'd visited had ever conveyed. There was no cancerous illness spreading among its creatures, caused by pollution and human interference. His mind spread out, diffusing over the land, until he became completely concealed from the Quratis.

The beast flew by, leaving a trail of icy silence behind it.

Ben connected with a blue and red macaw resting on the tallest branch, which showed him the direction of the river—to his left and not too far off.

Ben let out a long breath, returning to his body hunched in on itself on the forest floor. He opened his eyes and was Ben again, a thirteen-year-old boy running for his life. He stood shakily, wiping his sweaty forehead and leaving a trail of dirt from the earth he had been grasping. Then he was off, his sneakers sloshing through mud and rivulets left by the rain.

He could hear it, the river. It wasn't far now, but he had to backtrack three times because the way had become impenetrable from towering reeds and knee-deep mud. Mosquitoes swarmed around him, stinging his neck even though he pleaded for them to leave him alone. Finally, he found an area less impacted by the recent rain, making it easier for him to run again. He crashed through the shrubbery and skidded to a halt.

He found himself out in the open, facing the Amazon River, where half-a-dozen motorized canoes each long, enough to fit six people, were stationed at the river's edge.

Ben must have been facing thirty pairs of eyes. Men wearing trousers, short-sleeved shirts unbuttoned at the front, large-brimmed hats to fend off the sun. Some had machetes hanging from their belts; others had arm-length knives, used to cut a path through the forest. All of them carried heavy-looking orange cans, from which emanated a strong, distinctive smell.

Ben's mind did a double-flip.

I know that smell!

They stopped in their tracks and stared at

him. Ben realized he must look like a crazy person wearing alien garments torn at the knee and dirt-marks covering his face, but he also had the eerie feeling that he had caught them doing something illegal.

A couple of the men raised their machetes.

Ben took a step back, then another. He bumped into someone.

"What are you doing here?" Captain Daria asked, grabbing a handful of Ben's hair and pulling back so hard he had no choice but to look up at her.

"Ouch!"

"Answer me! Where is General Zoltar?"

"He's in danger!" Ben winced, grimacing as he squirmed to release himself from her grasp. *"The Quratis is killing him! You have to help him! Please!"*

Daria snorted. *"I'm not in the mood for your lies, vermin!"*

"What's he doing here?" Einar yelled, running up to them, his face livid.

"That's what I'm trying to find out," Daria said, pulling harder at Ben's hair.

"We'll get to the bottom of this. Wait here," Einar said. He turned towards the men and yelled in Portuguese, *"Vamos, rapido! Pegue aqueles*

tanques de gás e queime a floresta. Vá em frente![1] The men took off into the forest.

Ben had understood every word and reeled at their revelation. "What?" he yelled. "You want to burn the forest?" His stomach lurched. That smell! It was gasoline!

Einar turned on his heels, death written all over his face. He took three swift steps Ben's way, then halted. His eyes lifted to something behind Daria. His jaw dropped, the blood draining from his face.

Daria whirled, taking Ben with her. They faced the forest wall. Only, the trees no longer looked natural. Something huge slipped between the trunks, casting fiery shadows and making crackling sounds as it approached.

"The Quratis," Daria exclaimed, letting go of Ben's hair and staggering back. She hunkered down on one knee and bowed as deeply as she could.

Einar dropped beside her, looking aghast.

The creature stayed within the cover of the foliage, each wing as wide as four trees, its piercing blue eyes instilling a primal fear in the onlookers

---

[1] Hurry up! Get those gas tanks and burn the forest. Get on with it!

that none could withstand.

Ben stood frozen to the spot. There was no time to think of an escape plan. The bird's tail feathers lashed out like a whip, coiled around his ankles and pulled. Ben crashed to the ground.

"Argh!" he yelled.

The Quratis tugged, dragging him over the earth. Ben rolled over, frantically grabbing on to anything in his path, only finding slippery moss and sharp stones that cut into his palms.

"Help!" he cried at a gawking Daria and Einar, who became smaller and smaller until he was in the gloom of the forest. He turned onto his back. The Quratis descended on him, its sizzling tentacles ready to strike, and there was nothing Ben could do but brace himself.

CHAPTER 33 ...*And Then They Came*

Mesmo leaned against the wall, his hand covering his face. He had asked Panaï to fly the spaceship towards the Amazon River. He felt a hand on his arm, and Qu'ira appeared at his side.

She glanced at Laura, who remained unconscious on the horizontal energy field that Liana had set up for her at the back of the spaceship. *"I admit we are having a hard time over you being with this A'hmun woman,"* she said. *"Fate dealt you a cruel hand when you lost your Toreq life companion at such an early age. It is something we would wish on no-one, and so we are trying to understand."*

Mesmo smiled sadly. *"Then, that is a start."*

Liana entered the room and approached Laura. She looked up in a hurry. *"Mesmo!"*

Mesmo straightened, but Qu'ira held him back. *"Just be careful, Mesmo. Daria isn't going to let this relationship go lightly. Make sure you don't get yourself banished and hunted by her followers for this."*

Mesmo held her gaze and said, *"I'll take my chances."*

Qu'ira gave him a sad smile and left.

Mesmo hurried to Laura's side.

Liana looked at him. *"She'll be waking up soon. She should be able to hear us already."* She was about to leave when she touched his arm and added, *"Also, I have dealt with that asthma problem you were telling me about."*

Mesmo halted, then placed his hands on her shoulders and his front on her front. *"Thank you!"* he exclaimed. *"I owe you!"*

She smiled at him. *"Be happy, Mesmo,"* she said. *"You deserve it."* She left him alone with Laura.

He bent to stroke her hair, seeing the colour return to her face. "Laura?" he gasped.

She opened her eyes. She looked around and frowned a little.

Mesmo smiled. "You're going to be fine. Just

rest for a bit."

She relaxed and smiled back. "You came back for me!"

Mesmo cast his eyes down. "I should never have left you. I thought I was protecting you by leaving you on Earth. It turned out that was a mistake."

She shook her head. "Don't blame yourself. I told you to get Ben first. I wouldn't have had it any other way."

Mesmo nodded.

"Mesmo?" she added, making him lift his eyes again. "Did you find Ben?"

"Laura," Mesmo squeezed her hand. "You're going to have to listen very carefully to everything I'm about to tell you..."

* * *

Spaceships descended over the Amazon forest. Some were pointy and silver in colour, like the speeder Ben had flown in; others were large and black, like the spaceship Mesmo had lost. However, one was as massive as a ten-story building. It was formidable and intimidating as it hung over the coast.

Mesmo landed his spaceship near a clearing

that had been prepared for the Gathering. He exited, wearing a wine-coloured cape held by a golden pin. Qu'ira, Panaï, Kaani, Hao, Adhira, and Jeremy followed. He'd insisted Liana and Laura stay behind; he couldn't afford to have Captain Daria lash out at Laura. The two women had accepted, though reluctantly.

Spaceships darted overhead, landing next to Mesmo's craft. Toreq men and women bustled about, making last-minute preparations. Seats for onlookers were laid out in a semi-circle with an open area in the middle where the ground had been cleared and beaten flat. A Toreq added a handful of logs to a small fire in its center. Negotiators would sit on the ground around the fire, the Toreq way.

Some of the warship captains were already sitting cross-legged, speaking heatedly about the attack on the Qu'Tué. Mesmo was quick to notice Daria arriving among them.

"Shall I arrest her?" Qu'ira seethed.

"No," Mesmo said. *"My father was right: we don't want a revolt before the Gathering. She still has too many followers. Just keep an eye on her from the outskirts, will you?"*

Qu'ira nodded and slipped away.

"Mesmo," Hao said, approaching him and

speaking in a low voice. "I don't see Einar anywhere."

"Indeed," Mesmo grimaced. "There are a lot of things about this Gathering that worry me. But we are here, and we must proceed. Keep your eyes peeled, Inspector."

Hao nodded.

A Toreq man approached. *"Observer, welcome,"* he said. *"We are ready to start. Except, it is not clear to me who the other participants in this gathering are, besides the Toreq?"*

Mesmo's heart sank. *"Are my father and my son not here, then?"*

The man shook his head.

Mesmo insisted, *"I am convinced my father's spaceship landed here several hours ago. How is it that it has not yet been located?"*

The man shook his head again. *"I am sorry, Observer. Either he never came here, or his spaceship is cloaked, and we cannot detect it."*

Mesmo set his jaw, then turned to Adhira and Hao. "Secretary-General, Inspector, in terms of human representation, I'm afraid you're it, for now."

"No, they're not," a voice said.

Mesmo whirled and found a crowd of youngsters exiting three large helicopters. One of them was Kimi. His eyes widened. "Kimi? What are you doing here? And... who have you brought with you?"

The dark-haired girl approached Mesmo with a big smile on her face. "Meet Ben's followers," she said, showing off the teenage girls and boys behind her. "I figured Ben would need a little backup. These are volunteers who have been contacting me through our website, asking us how they could help Ben's mission. So I took their word for it and brought them over from around the globe. All expenses were covered by one of Ben's benefactors. We have travelled a long way, so this had better be good!"

Mesmo gave a satisfied nod. "Excellent! You are the future of your species. Your word will bear weight in this matter. I suggest you join me in the circle."

"What about Ben?" Kimi asked, searching the clearing.

Mesmo's face fell. "The truth is, I'm extremely worried. I don't know where he is, though I have high hopes we will find him here."

Kimi gasped. "But, without him, this won't work!"

Mesmo placed his hands on her shoulders. "Until he is found, we'll have to do the best we can.

I'm sure he will step forward as soon as he realizes his best friend is here!"

Kimi blushed, her eyes clouding up, but she nodded and followed him to the group sitting around the low-burning fire, where she sat cross-legged next to Adhira and Jeremy, opposite the warship captains. The teenagers were given translation devices as a crowd took a seat in the semi-circle around them, most being Toreq men and women. Humidity rose from the trees, the branches providing some form of shade in the stifling tropical heat.

Mesmo glanced around, stomach twisting. There was no sign of his father or Ben. He noted no sign of any animals, either—something that only added to his worries. He glanced at Daria, convinced she must know something. To his surprise, she avoided eye contact. She looked shaken.

Captain Anaris pulled him out of his thoughts. *"Observer, we cannot wait around all day. Whatever was supposed to happen at this Great Gathering, I see nothing great about it. I would like to get this over and done with."*

There were nods of agreement from the Toreq.

Mesmo glanced at Qu'ira, who was pacing

behind the crowds. Qu'ira shook her head at him. Still no news of Zoltar or Ben. Mesmo held his breath. He looked at Adhira, Hao and Kimi. They were going to have to do this on their own.

He was about to nod at Captain Anaris when the last spaceship made its way to the landing area. Mesmo's heart quickened. *"Wait,"* he said, holding up his hand.

Everyone turned to discover who else might be attending the Gathering. A group of humans, led by Torka, spilled out of the spaceship.

Mesmo glanced at Daria and saw her face pale.

Torka reached the circle and spoke. *"I apologize for the delay. The Wise Ones were hard to locate."* He stepped aside, and two men and three women entered the circle.

Mesmo stood, greeting one of the men who wore a colourful hat with ear flaps. "Amaru," he gasped. "Thank you for coming out of hiding. More than anything, your presence is required today." He turned to the crowds and spoke in Toreq. *"Behold, the Wise Ones, who, generation after generation, have provided the Toreq with valuable observations of the A'hmun. Their words will weigh heavily in this debate. Sadly, we are missing Akeya from Kenya, Einar from Norway, and Su Tai from China."* He glanced at Daria as he said this.

She looked away.

"Amaru is from Bolivia. Please, Amaru, have a seat." He then turned to a short woman with two long, black braids flowing from both sides of her neck to her waist. Mesmo bowed and said, *"Yakut, from the polar regions of Canada."* The woman took a seat beside Amaru.

"Wonomanga, from Australia. Welcome," Mesmo said to a round-faced man whose dark face and eyes were topped by thick, curly hair and a dense, graying beard.

"Welcome, Kahalu from the South Pacific Ocean," he added, greeting a woman with parallel lines tattooed on her front.

The last woman, younger than the others, had straight, black hair that fell down her back in a ponytail. Her dark eyes fell like daggers on Daria. She spoke in Chinese. *"I am Ling Jun Tai. My father was Su Tai, a most honourable man whose life was cut short by the hand of this murderous woman and her accomplice!"* She stabbed a finger in Daria's direction.

Daria sprang to her feet.

Captain Olin spoke. *"Captain Daria, I find there are mounting accusations against you: you recklessly sent your speeders to attack the*

Observer, you are accused of bombing one of our own warships, and now this woman comes forth alleging you killed a Wise One. I do not know what truth lies within all of this, but I will request a full investigation after this Gathering."

Daria's eyes glided towards Mesmo and smirked. *"Fools!"* she said. *"I am a soldier. The best soldier out of all of you, by far. Why? Because I obey orders, no questions asked. And I answer to one, and one alone. I answer to General Zoltar. So go on, investigate all you want. But you will see, in the end, it is General Zoltar's word that will prevail."* Her mouth curled into a smile as her eyes glued on Mesmo.

"Your treachery ends here, Daria," Mesmo said, returning her gaze. *"You know what you have done. I only hope, for your sake, that my father and my son are alive."* He let his words hang before addressing the Toreq and humans. *"Let the Great Gathering begin."*

Customary to Toreq tradition, Mesmo began the meeting by invoking the wisdom of his ancestors. He asked for foresight as clear as the stars and patience as deep as the universe. He asked to borrow the guidance and insights of his father and forefathers. He took a sharp knife that was handed to him and sliced off a piece of a solid, leafless branch that was handed to him. He stood, placed the piece in the embers of the fire, then handed the remaining branch to his neighbour when he returned to his place. Captain Olin completed the same ritual, and this continued around the group of negotiators.

Hao glanced at Mesmo, brows knitted. They were thinking the same thing: how were they going to convince the Toreq to leave humans alone if the *Gathering* did not fulfil its full purpose?

Several Toreq took the stand, voicing their points-of-view with conviction, followed by the Wise Ones. Hao and Adhira did their best, naming all the good things humans had achieved.

Kimi's turn came, and Mesmo wondered if this would be too much of a burden on her, but relaxed when he saw the same kind of determination in her eyes as he would have in Ben's.

Kimi stood and turned to face the semi-circle, wringing her hands together as she looked at the audience. She cleared her throat. "I don't know anything about the A'hmun, the Toreq, or *The Great War of the Kins*," she began timidly. "These are just big words that I've heard you throwing around." She paused. When she spoke again, her voice strengthened. "But I would like to know: why should I be punished for something I know nothing about? Why should they be punished?" She pointed at the teenagers watching her from the sides. "Do you punish children for something their forefathers did?" She waited for a reaction, but when none came, continued, her voice rising with conviction. "There are some among the Toreq and the Wise Ones who would wish to help us, who would teach us to protect this forest, this ocean, this river. So why do you choose war when you could choose knowledge?

"Please, invade us! But invade us with your teachers, your philosophers, your artists. Invade us with hope and optimism. Be our beacon of light, one that we can look up to and admire. Look! I am here. These young people are here. We are the future of our planet. We are ready to learn. So show us, right now, that you are a civilization that we can look up to."

She took a step back, pausing for a long time, then shook her head. "But, no," she said, balling her fists. "You won't do that."

The Toreq looked at each other, frowning.

"You won't do that..." Kimi continued, "...because you're afraid."

Mumbling rose from the Toreq crowd.

"That's right," she said, louder. "You're afraid

of your past. You're afraid of us! That's why you come to taunt us with your heavy war machinery and your powerful skills—things we are defenceless against..."

"That's not true!" someone yelled. *"We saw what your weapons are capable of—just one of them destroyed an entire warship and damaged another!"*

Others yelled in agreement.

Arguments broke out. People stood, shouted over each other, waved their fists in the air.

"Enough!" Mesmo yelled, his voice getting lost in the clamour.

Kimi stepped aside, her face pale.

Mesmo stood, trying to calm the crowd, and as he did so, a soft, warm breeze blew across his cheek, bringing an ocean smell with it. He stopped and listened. There was something in the air; something new, and it didn't come from the arguing crowd; it came from around them, from within the forest and beyond.

A Toreq woman came running from the parked spaceships and tried to shout over the conundrum.

"Enough!" Mesmo yelled again, trying to hear what she was saying. *"I SAID, ENOUGH!"*

People turned towards him, eyes wide. Fists

stopped punching at the air; silence fell over the gathering. They kept their eyes on him, but at the same time, Mesmo knew they sensed the same thing as he did: something was drawing near.

There was a faint sound in the trees, a fluttering, a squawk—then chattering sounds. Tamarin monkeys made their appearance, swinging among the branches. A flock of scarlet macaws swooped across them. Something ruffled the branches of the trees, revealing a family of ant-eaters.

"Over there!" the Toreq woman shouted, pointing towards the ocean. *"Look!"*

A speeder flew across the sea, sending an image on a hovering screen in the midst of those gathered. It showed turmoil on the surface, caused by a stampede of dolphins. Flocks of seagulls and cormorants congregated chaotically above them. Whales breached the water.

Screeches and howls and hooting echoed back-and-forth around them as hundreds of different birds gathered within the trees.

The Toreq and humans looked on in awe, not knowing which way to turn, trying to grasp what was happening.

The birds settled on the branches and quietened down. Sea creatures swam calmly along the border where the fresh Amazon River water met the salty ocean. Piranhas, caimans, catfish and other Amazon River animals remained within the river's boundaries, gathering at its edges.

With his heart beating fast, Mesmo took in the multitude of silent creatures that had suddenly joined them.

"There!" Kimi breathed, pointing into the misty forest. Out of the shadows, hundreds of creatures appeared: black panthers, tapirs, armadillos, lemurs... there were too many to count. And in the middle of them...

Mesmo gasped. "Benjamin!"

CHAPTER 34 *The Great Gathering*

Ben stepped into the clearing, the Quratis weighing down on his shoulder. Filaments from the monstrous creature lay embedded deep within him, intertwined with his skill, running through his veins. The Quratis could have made him do an Irish dance right there, had it wanted to.

The Quratis had told him to call forth the animals of the forest and the water, and Ben had called on the animals of the forest and the water. The Quratis had told him to walk into the clearing, so Ben walked into the clearing. The monster controlled his limbs, muscles and speech, making him look normal on the outside. But inside... inside, his feelings collided against each other like frantic birds searching for an escape.

How had Zoltar done it? How had he survived that long under the bird's control? Ben couldn't handle it, this invasion of his mind.

And then he remembered Counsel Okra, the old man from the bird's memories: a Toreq who had had the translation skill at the time of *The Great War of the Kins*. That war had lasted for years. And the whole time, the Quratis had been with the old man, feeding him incendiary information to fuel the war against the old man's wishes. Ben shuddered inside. How long could the Quratis keep him alive in this state?

Now the Quratis made him walk before the semi-circle, and there—Ben's heart leapt—*Kimi!* He barely had time to glance at her as he passed.

His best friend's dark eyes widened in hope and recognition.

He didn't give her a word of greeting. Not even a nod.

Shock and disappointment replaced her smile, and he thought his heart would shatter. Then the fleeting moment was gone, and he couldn't turn around to explain. His feet stopped, and the animals of the forest surrounded him. He turned to face *The Great Gathering*.

Had the Quratis not been holding him up, he would have collapsed right there. But he was a puppet, doing his master's will.

Thousands of tropical birds decorated the trees, the Amazon River spilled into the sea nearby and, out there, sea creatures had gathered. Whale songs carried over the surface.

Ben took in the unusual mingle of people, ranging from Toreq, to humans, to teenagers, even. And in the middle of the clearing stood Mesmo. His father stared at him with a cautious smile of hope, mixed with awe.

They had all come for him.

Because I asked them to...

Two women ran from one of the spaceships up to the clearing. One was Liana, and the other— Ben's knees almost buckled—*Mom!*

She appeared from beside the semi-circle, running towards him, her eyes bright, her smile melting his heart. Mesmo saw her and held her back with one hand. "Wait!" Ben saw him say. She grabbed on to his arm, never taking her eyes off Ben.

Ben longed to go to her, but he could not. This was not a time for a happy reunion.

The Quratis snapped him to attention, turning his head away from his parents, for it sensed a powerful emotion that it despised. It sensed love.

Focus, now! Its rasping voice seeped into Ben's mind. *See this masterpiece! A masterpiece of your own making. Do you see, now, the extent of our power? We will do great things across the galaxy, you and I.*

Ben trembled inside. He did not want to think about what those great things could be.

Echis stirred inside his hoodie. The venomous snake slid out, taking advantage that the bird had its focus elsewhere to slide down Ben's arm and leg. Only, once it reached the ground, it found itself facing the multitude of forest animals that barred its way.

Ben glanced down, his hands glowing blue, and the Quratis made him reach out to pet a black panther that had taken place beside him.

The panther purred and spoke. *We are here, Benjamin Archer. Your call was heard far and wide, across the oceans, the skies and the land, and we have come. This one time, we come to The Great Gathering to attempt to find peace with the humans.* The panther turned and surveilled the other animals, then spoke to Ben again. *On this hour of the solstice, at the mouth of the greatest river in the world, all creatures of Earth have agreed to grant humans another chance to restore the balance. If humans agree to listen to our terms, we will accept a peace treaty.*

Ben's heart bulged. It had happened! The animals were siding with humans—in spite of decades of mistreatment. He turned to the crowd.

Not one person sat. They stretched their necks, wanting to get a good look at Ben and his strange following, mesmerized by a spectacle they had never seen before and would never see again.

At Ben's feet, Echis slithered nervously at the proximity of the Quratis, its body rolling in on itself in S-shapes.

"What say you, skilled one?" a voice rose from the audience. *"What is the will of these creatures? What do they say? Translate for us!"*

"Yes! What do they say?" other voices rose.

"The Quratis! We want to hear the will of the Quratis! Let it guide us!"

The feathers of the Quratis crackled so only Ben could hear. Its thousand voices echoed in his mind: *And this is where you step in, Ben Archer. This is where you tell them that the animals DO NOT accept peace with humans. That is all you have to do. The simplicity of it! Do you see? Forever will you remember this moment, and forever will they remember you.*

No! Horror gripped Ben. The Quratis wanted him to go against the animal's wishes. He struggled inwardly, trying in vain to make a movement, to utter a moan—something, anything, to catch Mesmo's attention. But nothing came out. He was trapped inside himself.

His eyes scanned the audience, desperately looking for an escape. Mesmo stood so close, looking worried and expectant. And to his left, there stood... *Tuli?* The girl caught him off guard. Well, of course she would be here, enjoying the grand finale. She set her blue eyes on him, her emotions unreadable, her long, white braid ending in a kind of peacock feather. There was something odd about that braid...

A small clicking sound caught his attention and, out of the corner of his eye, another surprise awaited him. Was that really Jeremy Michaels, the Provincial Times reporter, taking pictures of him and the entire gathering?

Ssave me, Ben Archer! Ssave me from the bird! Make it go away! Poor, innocent Echis, oblivious to what was happening on a grander scale, slithered anxiously below him.

The Quratis spread its wings, drawing admiration from the crowd. It basked in its success. *Say it, Ben Archer! Say the words! Unleash the Second War of the Kins!*

Ben resisted. *No! I won't lie! I won't...*

The filaments tightened in his veins, searing hot within him, preventing him from crying out.

Say it!

Ben thought frantically. Mesmo… Tuli… Echis…

Snippets of conversations came together.

A lifetime ago, Mesmo had told him, "If you don't learn to disconnect yourself from the creatures you communicate with, your body may not recognize the difference between you and them anymore, and it will keep the symptoms. And, yes, then you truly will be sick."

It had been one of Ben's first lessons: to create a mental barrier between himself and the sick animals he connected with, so he would not experience the full load of their emotions or illnesses.

And not long ago, Tuli had spoken to him on the warship. *"Perhaps, when the time comes, you will do what is needed…"*

His eyes fell on Echis.

Sstop sstaring at me. It makess me edgy. I bitess when I edgy. Evil bird sso close! I very, very edgy…

Ben's heart skipped a beat.

That was it! That's what he was supposed to do! But that meant… that meant… His eyes fell on his mother and father with great sadness.

"Well, go on!" someone yelled angrily from the audience. *"Have you lost your tongue?"*

The tension in the clearing was unbearable.

The Quratis cackled in a thousand reverberating voices in Ben's head. *I love it! See them die from impatience. Say it, Ben Archer: 'The animals do not accept peace with humans.' SAY IT!"*

Words spilled out of Ben's mouth. "The animals..." he began, glancing frantically from Mesmo to Echis.

The viper hissed, *Sstop sstaring, Ben Archer! I not hurt family and friends. I promissed. But I edgy! I very, very edgy!*

Ben ignored the snake's plea. He kept his eyes on the deadly snake. He called forth the skill, the one he had promised never to use again, and spoke gently to Echis, not knowing whether his thoughts were getting through but knowing his stare would be enough. *You promised not to hurt family and friends, but you never promised not to hurt me.*

Then Echis struck.

CHAPTER 35 *Sacrifice*

Faster than lighting, Mesmo saw the snake strike Ben. He blinked, not understanding. But then Ben stiffened strangely, the colour drained from his face, and their eyes locked in a moment of agony and terror.

Silence fell over the audience. Everyone could tell something had happened, but they weren't sure what it was.

Still focused on Mesmo, Ben's eyes hardened. His hands began to glow a dark red.

The Quratis made little, nervous hops on Ben's shoulder, a sound like static electricity came from its wings, and its long tail feathers wrapped around Ben's throat.

And Mesmo understood. His cry carried out

over the clearing. "BENJAMIN! NO!"

The alien skill burst out of Ben, exploding up into the sky in a fiery red.

The Quratis screeched, its millions of voices tearing through the crowds, making them scream and thrust their hands to their ears.

Ben's skill locked onto the bird, pouring into it. The Quratis spread its wings, growing into a formidable creature.

"BEN!" Laura screamed, bolting forward. Terrified people scampered in all directions, blocking her way.

Ben gave his parents one last, sad look, then his eyes rolled back into his head, and he crumpled to the ground.

The Quratis took flight, its feathers crackling like fireworks, a red glow imprisoning its body. It flew in jerking movements, screeching in pain. Behind it, huge flames burst from the forest.

"FIRE!" someone screamed.

As if on cue, a wall of flames ignited around the *Gathering*, sending thousands of birds flying in all directions. Toreq, humans and animals trampled each other, screaming in terror, as Mesmo and Laura tried to reach Ben.

Someone grabbed Mesmo by the arm. "I'll get him!" Hao yelled. "You put that fire out!" He pointed at the river.

Numb with dread, Mesmo shook his head, throwing himself forward.

"Mesmo!" Hao insisted. "We'll burn to a crisp if you don't do something now!"

But Mesmo had stopped listening because something new was happening. He, Laura, and Hao watched, mesmerized, as a girl with a long white braid walked before the animals that surrounded Ben, her body shining a brilliant blue. She lifted both hands before her, palms up, and as she did so, her braid lifted. The end of it shimmered, growing bigger and bigger. The whole braid blurred and transformed, detaching from her completely. Blue wings unfurled from it, revealing the sharp features of a phoenix-like creature beneath.

"There's two of them!" someone screamed.

Identical to the Quratis, except for its colour, the creature used the girl's shoulder to push itself into the air. The girl gasped under the weight, crashing to the ground as the blue bird took flight. It was smaller than the first but just as terrifying.

The girl rubbed her shoulder, watching the sky as the blue creature dashed through the air towards the other. It lifted its dagger-like claws before it, throwing its full weight at the Quratis, attacking it in a violent frenzy.

A terrible battle ensued. Red and blue wings mingled, beaks clashed, claws tore at flesh.

Speechless, Mesmo remembered what he was supposed to do. He nudged a gawking Hao. "Laura, Inspector! Get Benjamin! Take him to my ship!" He darted away from them. He'd seen Torka not far off, desperately trying to lead people and animals to safety.

"Torka!" he yelled. His friend whirled, eyes aghast. *"To the river!"* They both dashed to the embankment, animals darting away from them, some of them plunging into the rushing water in a vain attempt to save themselves from the blaze.

The fire grew at an unnatural speed, sending black smoke billowing into the sky.

Mesmo and Torka glanced at each other.

Torka grinned viciously. *"Just like in the old days?"* he shouted.

Mesmo nodded. *"Just like in the old days."*

Both dove into the wild waters of the Amazon River.

* * *

Hao and Laura headed towards where Ben lay—and froze. A dozen of the animals that had accompanied Ben prowled and growled, watching over the boy and blocking their passage. The black panther bared its teeth at Hao.

Cold sweat draped his back. "Nice kitty," he muttered, waving his hand at it. "Move over, will you?"

The panther moved aside.

"Ben!" Laura cried, her voice breaking.

She and Hao made their way through the animals and found Kimi next to Ben with his head on her lap. Her cheeks were wet with tears.

Laura threw herself to the ground, taking Ben's face in her hands. "Oh, Ben! What did you do?" she sobbed.

"I'm here to help," Hao told Kimi. "We've got to get him away from here!"

Kimi shook her head, her eyes wide. "We can't," she said, pointing at Ben's chest.

A red-and-black snake coiled there, making sizzling sounds.

"Oh boy," Hao muttered. "It had to be a snake." He realized he needed to take the snake with him if they were going to find Ben an antivenom drug. "Move over!" he warned Kimi and Laura, taking off his jacket.

Both backed away, holding on to each other.

Hao set his jaw, then dropped the jacket over the viper, snatching it up as fast as he could and wrapping it tightly into the fabric. He nodded to himself. "There! Caught my first real criminal in a while." He handed the wrapped-up jacket carefully to Laura. "Guard this with your life," he said.

Laura stared at him numbly but nodded.

Hao picked up Ben in his arms and raced off, the animals dispersing in all directions. Burning leaves and smoke billowed into the air around them. Coughing, they kept running towards the spaceships.

The girl with the long, white braid followed them. Only, her braid had disappeared. She had pixie hair now. Hao saw her stare at Kimi, her face expressionless.

"Who are you?" Kimi yelled as they ran.

"We go where he goes," she said, glancing at Ben in Hao's arms.

"Look!" Laura interrupted, staring at the river. Water gushed out of the Amazon River, cascading skyward like an upside-down waterfall. The wall of water rose, then came crashing down on the other side, smothering part of the fire, creating a protective bubble over the clearing. Toreq and humans used this welcome cover to dash for the spaceships and helicopters.

Adhira ran up to them. "Is he all right?" she gasped, glancing at Ben.

"No time to check!" Hao panted. They were almost at the spaceship.

Jeremy appeared out of the smoke, coughing raucously but also aiming his camera everywhere, taking as many pictures as he could.

Just then, a woman stepped in front of them, blocking their way. Her long, white hair and cape billowed in the smoke; her hands glowed blue. *"Give him to me!"* Daria yelled, her face contorted with hate. *"Don't you see? He's killing the Quratis!"*

Hao tightened his grip on Ben. Laura, Kimi, Tuli, Adhira and Jeremy rushed to stand before him.

"Then die by my hand!" the Toreq woman yelled, lifting her glowing hands.

An invisible gust of wind knocked her aside. Kaani, Panaï, Liana and Qu'ira rushed to their aid. *"What are you waiting for?"* Panaï yelled. *"Get out of here, humans!"* He thrust his glowing hands forward, knocking the woman over with his skill, but she fought back.

Hao kept running, almost tripping over a frantic family of anteaters. Parrots swooped over his head, screeching in terror.

Spaceships took off on all sides, escaping the inferno that was engulfing the tropical forest behind them. They were just about at the ship when a heartstopping crack froze Hao in his tracks.

"Watch out!" Jeremy yelled, just as a massive, burning tree crashed on top of the spaceship.

CHAPTER 36 *A Fight for Supremacy*

Mesmo saw the tree crash onto the spaceship from the river. His heart sank. *"Torka!"* he shouted.

His friend turned, and his eyes widened as he understood the situation.

They rushed to join the humans by the spaceship, the water bubble they had created over the clearing quickly evaporating.

Kaani, Panaï, Liana and Qu'ira appeared through the smoke, coughing and rasping.

"She got away," Kaani said, referring to Daria.

New flames shot up into the sky in the forest behind them, trapping them.

"This fire's not natural!" Liana said. *"Someone's stoking it!"*

"What do we do?" Qu'ira yelled above the crackling sound. They glanced at the empty area where the other spaceships had been.

"We must turn back and get to your father's ship," a voice said.

They all whirled and faced a girl with white, pixie hair. Her hands glowed blue. Mesmo recognized her: she was the one the blue creature had detached from.

The girl glanced up suddenly and yelled, *"Get down!"*

They threw themselves to the ground just in time to avoid the two battling monsters that emerged from the billowing smoke in a mingle of blue and red feathers. Their claws slashed. Ferocious, ear-splitting cries erupted between them. Their wings untied from each other long enough to send them barreling back up into the sky, their screeches piercing the brains of those on the ground.

When the survivors got on their feet again, Mesmo took Ben from Hao's arms. Laura rushed to his side. *"Who are you?"* Mesmo yelled at the girl over the racket made by the fighting monsters.

"You may call us, Tuli," the mysterious girl said, seeming unfazed by the chaos around her.

"Tuli?" Mesmo repeated, remembering

something Ben had said about having met a girl in the warship. *"Do you know where my father is?"*

"We do."

He glanced at her bright blue eyes. *"You are not Toreq!"* he noted.

"We are not," she agreed.

Hao jumped in. "Can we do introductions later?" he yelled.

Mesmo nodded. *"Lead the way,"* he told Tuli.

The girl whirled and led them back across the clearing, beyond the semi-circle, and into the thickness of the fire.

"Panaï!" Mesmo yelled. *"Work your magic!"*

Panaï rushed before them, glowing hands outstretched, and sent billowing wind through the fire, opening a path for them. Then they were on the other side of the blaze, entering the thick tropical forest, chased by stifling smoke.

The girl slowed down, and suddenly they were standing before General Zoltar's spaceship.

Mesmo rushed inside. *"Father!"* he cried, finding the man lying in a heap.

Kaani took Ben from Mesmo's arms so he could rush to his father's side. Liana followed. They bent down and rolled the General onto his back.

Liana scanned his body hurriedly. After a pause, she looked up and said, *"He breathes!"*

Everyone jumped into action, carrying the wounded to a back room of the spaceship. There, Liana called up two horizontal energy fields where they placed Zoltar and Ben.

"The boy first!" Liana said, scanning Ben from head to foot.

Mesmo caught Laura glancing at him in anguish as they saw the extent of Ben's wounds: the reddish glow around his body, the tear in one knee, the gash and swelling in his ankle, the twitching movements in his fingers.

"A snake bit him!" Laura said. "We have to give him an antivenom injection." She held up Hao's jacket with the snake in it.

"No," Tuli spoke behind her.

They turned to the pixie-haired girl. She blinked at them with her crystal-blue eyes.

"You must not cure him," she said. *"If you cure him, all will be lost."* She took the jacket from Laura and released the snake.

"Hey! Watch out with that!" Hao warned.

Taking no notice, the girl let the snake curl around her arm. She stroked its back with her glowing hand, then stared at them again. *"We, too, have the translation skill,"* she explained.

Mesmo stared at her in wonder. *"But, how? Who are you?"*

She stared at them in turn. *"Our name is* ꞁƆYƀƎ5G,*"* she said, her voice making a clicking sound. *"It is an unpronounceable name to you. Therefore, you may call us Tuli. We come from a distant planet within this galaxy. Not long ago, a celestial creature we call a Lifegiver presented itself to us. Lifegivers are born within the black holes of galaxies, feeding and growing on the matter that gets sucked into them. When they are strong enough, they leave the nest and wander their galaxy, distributing their energy to create new stars and nebulae. This blue Lifegiver, however, came to us because it had sensed the arrival of another, more powerful celestial creature within its boundaries.*

"We came to investigate and found the trespassing creature and its victim." She glanced at Zoltar. *"It became clear that we were not dealing with another Lifegiver."* She glanced at them. *"Instead, we were dealing with a Lifetaker. You call it the Quratis."*

"Why are you calling my father a victim?" Mesmo interrupted. *"My father is no victim! He is honoured to have been chosen by the Quratis!"*

"You are mistaken," Tuli said. *"Your Quratis has chosen darkness over light. It will choose extinction over life. It imprisons the minds of its*

victims and makes them act according to its will. On the outside, your father seemed normal to you; but on the inside, he was submitted to the will of the Quratis.

"Just think: your people came armed with weapons and warships. That is the doing of a Lifetaker. A Lifegiver would never come to wage war. It would never imprison the mind of its ally. We stand before you, an ally of a celestial creature, yet we come alone and in peace. Our mind is free." She pointed at Zoltar and Ben. *"Theirs is not."*

Anger and fear built within Mesmo. *"Are you saying my father and my son have both been imprisoned by the Quratis?"*

Tuli nodded. *"We believe the Quratis attacked your father, leaving him for dead, choosing instead to live within a younger body."* She glanced at Ben.

Laura swayed, having to hold on to Mesmo's arm.

Mesmo rubbed his face, trying to bring the blood back to his cheeks. He shook his head. Images of his father came back to him, their long evenings talking and catching up... And then, Ben, who had accused Zoltar of terrible deeds. It hadn't made sense. He stared from the alien girl—who looked strangely like Kaia—to Ben, whose body made jerking movements on the energy field. He looked deathly. *"So, you are saying the Quratis took Ben, and my father tried to stop it?"*

Tuli nodded. *"We told Ben not to remain on your warship. We told him he was in danger because he had the translation skill. But he wouldn't leave. We believe he was trying to understand what was happening to your father. Perhaps Ben thought he could save him."*

Mesmo wiped his brow.

Laura sounded frantic. "Well, we can't leave him like this! We've got to get snake's venom out—and the Quratis."

"No," Tuli insisted. *"Ben would not want you to do that. Curiously, it is the venom that is keeping him safe from the Quratis. He took it upon himself to get bitten by a deadly snake, so through him, the venom would be transmitted to the Quratis. He knew he could not escape the grip of the Lifetaker, so he decided to take the Quratis down with him."*

They watched the angry glow around Ben's body.

Mesmo spoke in wonder. *"He is using the skill to take over the will of the Quratis..."*

Tuli nodded again. *"Their wills are battling. Ben is attempting to control the Quratis while fighting for his own life. He now rides the Lifetaker, transmitting the venom from his own body into it. We believe the Quratis has never experienced such deep pain in its life. It believes it was struck by the snake itself. It has not yet caught on that it is Ben who is infusing this idea into its mind. If it realizes it has been tricked, then Ben is lost, for the Quratis will raise a mental barrier to fend off Ben's attack, and it will turn against him. And then it will turn against us."*

She broke off, then spoke in a tired voice. *"When Ben asked the snake to bite him, we knew we had a chance. You see, our Lifegiver is not as strong as your Quratis. But when Ben attacked the Quratis, he gave our Lifegiver a chance to attack, as well."*

They could hear the angry screams of the two birds somewhere high above them.

Tuli's voice lowered in awe. *"These creatures are extremely jealous of their territory. They do not share. The Lifegiver and Lifetaker battle for supremacy over this galaxy, as we speak."*

Mesmo stared at her, a cold ripple running down his back. *"So, if we remove the venom from my son..."* he began.

"...we remove the only weapon he has to fight the Quratis," Tuli finished.

Laura thrust her hands to her cheeks. *"But,*

the venom will kill him, anyway!"

Tuli looked at her. *"Yes,"* she said. *"But Ben knew that."*

* * *

Mesmo and Laura sat on each side of Ben, watching Liana monitor his condition.

Secretary-General Adhira arrived and glanced at Ben, then at Zoltar. "How is your father?" she asked.

Mesmo shook his head. "Stable, for now," he said.

"Go on, then," Adhira told him. "You have things to do. Laura, Liana and I will keep watch." She glanced at Laura, then went over to sit by Zoltar's side.

Mesmo looked at his son, then at his unconscious father, and lastly at Laura, who, he realized, was so shocked the tears wouldn't even come to her eyes. He set his jaw. "I have lost one family," he said in a grim voice. "I will not lose another!"

Laura looked up at him, her eyes drawn, her cheeks pale.

"I left Ben alone, Laura," Mesmo said. "I shouldn't have. But I'll make it right, I promise. I'll bring him back to you."

She reached over Ben and clasped his hand.

Mesmo bent closer and whispered something in Ben's ear. Straightening, he said, *"Liana, can you remove the venom from my son?"*

Liana was bending over the boy's ankle, cleaning out the wound. Her face looked troubled. *"Yes, but I thought..."*

"Don't do anything, yet, not until I tell you to," he said.

Liana frowned at him.

"Keep him as comfortable as possible. Just..." His voice broke. *"...just don't let him die."*

Liana's face darkened. *"Then whatever it is you're going to do, Mesmo, do it quickly."*

CHAPTER 37 *Mutiny*

Mesmo found a single speeder below the deck of his father's spaceship. He had barely put on a spacesuit and taken off when Torka hailed him.

"Mesmo! Is that you?"

"It is."

"WHAT are you doing?"

"I can't leave Benjamin out there on his own. He needs help!"

Torka muttered under his breath, then said, *"How come you get to do all the fun stuff?"*

Mesmo grinned. *"Don't worry. I suspect you'll get your fair share of the action. Head to the Ob, but watch your back. Daria's bound to be up to something. And contact the warships to gather a team skilled in fire—humans are going to need all the help they can get to put out that forest blaze and save the animals."*

"Yes, Observer," Torka grumbled, signing off.

Mesmo smiled, then called up Captain Olin. *"Captain Olin, what is your situation?"*

"Reporting, safe and sound. All Toreq, humans and Wise Ones that were on the ground are accounted for. I have dropped off the young humans in a safe location."

"Good," Mesmo said, speeding through space. He could see the Quratis and the Lifegiver rising from the Earth's atmosphere, leaving the scorching forest behind. *"I want you to take full control of the Zul."*

There was a pause. *"I don't think so, Observer. Captain Daria is already on the Zul. She took a speeder. My going is slow. I have a heavier ship and too many passengers."*

Mesmo tensed. He looked up and saw the four remaining warships in plain view. Hundreds of pinpoints of lights spilled out of the Zul.

Gasping, he opened a communication channel with the whole fleet. *"This is the Observer!"* he spoke. *"Do not engage in any attack! I repeat, do not engage—on Earth or otherwise!"*

The speeders continued to advance.

Mesmo's blood went cold. *"Captain Anaris,*

Captain Olin, Captain Yigis! Torka is flying my father's spaceship. Daria is going to try and destroy it. I order you to protect it and its crew at all costs!"

"At your orders, Observer!" Captain Anaris barked. A split second later, a cluster of new speeders shot out of the Maq, flying head-on to intercept Daria's squadron.

In response, half-a-dozen balls of fire shot out of the Zul and travelled across space.

"Captain Anaris! Watch out!" Mesmo warned.

The Maq destroyed five shots mid-way, but the sixth one crashed into it.

Captain Anaris bellowed, *"Captain Daria! Have you gone mad?"*

The speeders met head-on in a chaotic mass of shots and explosions.

"This is mutiny!" Mesmo yelled. *"Fight back! Disarm the Zul! Torka, can you make it to the Ob?"*

"Who do you take me for, Mesmo?"

"Just... get there safely."

There was a silence.

"That goes for you, too," Torka said finally, signing off again.

Mesmo tightened his grip on the controls, fighting the urge to oversee the battle. But he needed to save Ben. He dove towards the curious ball of red-and-blue light that was rising faster and faster through space. The Quratis and the Lifegiver were locked in battle—their wings, tails and heads mingled—as one tried to overcome the other. The Quratis glowed in the same angry red as Ben, indicating the boy and the monster were connected. The birds had grown to a massive size—at least half as big as the warships. At this rate, Mesmo noted in alarm, they'd end up in the middle of the cross-fire...

* * *

Kimi entered the room-turned-infirmary and stood beside Laura. Her stomach twisted as she watched Ben's deathly pale cheeks. His eyeballs darted behind his closed eyelids, and an unhealthy red halo enveloped his body.

"He is your friend, yes?"

Kimi whirled and found Tuli sitting cross-legged against the wall, a faint halo of blue light shining around her body. Kimi nodded.

Tuli looked at Ben. *"You are lucky,"* she said.

Kimi took Ben's cold hand. "Don't you have friends back home?" she asked.

"Friends..." Tuli mulled. *"It is a strange concept to us. Where we come from, we are one. There is no place for friendship."*

Kimi wasn't sure she understood. *"Are you, like, a common consciousness?"*

"You could say that, yes. Therefore, friendship is irrelevant to us, though it is interesting to think we could become friends with another species. To be friends, you must be different from each other."

Kimi frowned, wondering if her words made sense.

Tuli jerked. Her eyes shut tight, and she groaned.

"Tuli?" Laura gasped, rushing to her side. "You're bleeding!"

Tuli looked at her arm.

"Liana!" Laura yelled, standing up from Ben's side.

The Toreq woman rushed in and saw the dark-bluish liquid dripping from Tuli's arm. *"What happened?"* She dashed forward to heal the wound with her skill.

"It's nothing," Tuli said. *"We are connected to the Lifegiver, just as Ben is connected to the Quratis. We can see and feel it fighting the Quratis when we close our eyes. We try to place a protective barrier in our mind to fend off the onslaughts of the Quratis on the Lifegiver, but sometimes we lose our concentration and..."* she

pointed at her arm, *"this happens."*

Liana froze with her hand over Tuli's arm. *"Are you saying that when you lower your guard, you feel everything the Lifegiver is feeling, and you are hurt the way the Lifegiver is hurt?"*

Tuli nodded.

Liana locked eyes with Laura, and Kimi's stomach squeezed. The three of them turned their attention to Ben.

Liana rushed over and gently lifted Ben's shirt. Then she lifted it higher.

Laura shrieked and thrust her hands to her mouth.

"Oh, Ben!" Kimi gasped.

They stared at the wounds: ugly bruises, torn skin, gashes.

"Tuli!" Laura wailed. "Tell the Lifegiver to stop attacking the Quratis! It's killing Ben!"

CHAPTER 38 *The Second War of the Kins*

Slashing. Tearing. Beak hammering. Tail feathers whipping.

I am the Quratis.

Ben spoke in a thousand voices, feeling pride and domination. He clawed at the vile Lifegiver, inflicting a deep wound in its blue wing.

No! A tiny faraway voice pleaded—*his* voice.

His mind wavered. The skill gushed from his every cell, mighty and unstoppable, trapping the Quratis in its grasp. He was one with the creature, living its million lives, embracing a universe of knowledge, conscious of all the living things within its galaxy.

I am the most powerful creature in the

universe!

The vile Lifegiver lashed at his back with its beak. Ben screeched, then caught himself when he heard his terrifying voice.

What am I doing here?

Some part of him sobbed in agony. He didn't want to be here. It hurt too much. Venom spread through his veins, swift and deadly. He wanted to let go.

If I let go, I will belong to the Quratis...

That faraway thought gave him new strength. He latched on harder to the Quratis, pouring every sensation of pain from the venom into the Quratis and steering it straight towards the vile Lifegiver so the Lifegiver could attack.

I have to hang on... Keep hanging on... Until the end...

Because, now, he was powerful. More powerful than the Quratis. The skill gushed out of him, intoxicating, hungry for control.

No! That tiny voice again. He had unleashed the full power of the skill; he could no longer rein it in. *It's okay,* he thought, trying to reassure himself. *It will weaken as I weaken...*

The Quratis flipped over itself, losing direction. It flapped its mighty wings, the vile Lifegiver dashing after it in pursuit.

There were dark masses in the sky, spewing flashes of light at each other. Ben was supposed to know what they were, but trying to figure it out cost too much effort.

The vile Lifegiver came at him at full speed, hitting him in the stomach like a bullet. He jolted back, wings folding over, then crashed into one of the huge, black things... *Warships!* His back... no, the *bird's* back... cracked, and for a moment, his vision went dark. Excruciating pain travelled up his spine.

"Ben! Hang on!" A ghostly voice spoke.

Kimi's voice.

But how?

The vile Lifegiver pulled back and watched him from a distance. Had it given up?

He tumbled, falling in a mass of whizzing wasp-like things that shot at him.

Anger welled.

How DARE they? How dare they hurt me? I will smother them! They will know my wrath for eternity! I...

No! That tiny voice again. Always bringing him back. Agony seared through his every limb. He wanted to rest, give up, yet he kept holding on because that was the only thing he knew for certain was part of his fate. If he let go, everything would be lost: life on Earth, his family, his friends... His brain became foggy, his hold on the Quratis loosened. He glanced at the battle unfolding around him: warship against warship, speeders against speeders, Toreq against Toreq, and despair grasped his mind. How had it come to this? Had he failed and begun *The Second War of the Kins*?

One tiny spot of light shone among the chaos, speeding in a straight line towards him. Ben eyed it warily.

"Exit race."

Ben lurched. A voice had spoken to him not long ago, whispering in his ear. He had not understood the meaning of the words then.

"Son," the voice had said. "Exit race. Follow me."

Hope rose in his chest. Exit race. Follow the speeder. Follow Mesmo.

With superhuman effort, Ben thrust his skill once more into the Quratis, holding on to it with all his might, bending the creature to his will. He followed Mesmo towards the Ob, rose over it, glided at full-speed along the flank of the warship, dodged left-and-right and speeded after the cumbersome wasp-like speeder. Eager to catch it, the Quratis sped after Mesmo, reaching the front of the Ob.

And then... *And then what?*

Ben felt hope fading. They had reached the end of the warship. What now?

Mesmo's speeder didn't waver. It raced on through space, straight ahead. Straight towards the Earth. Down and down it went, the Quratis tearing after it, Ben sobbing inwardly from the effort of having to hang on, but hanging on anyway. Into the atmosphere they went. Air friction caused heat to rise through the beast's feathers. It burned within, from fury, reaching out to smother Mesmo's speeder, while Ben desperately ordered it to pull back. The Quratis plunged through the sky in a ball of fire, heading straight for the ocean.

The ocean!

The faint part of him that was still Ben leapt with recognition. Mesmo was heading for the vast expanse of water! With every last ounce he still had in him, Ben clung on to the Quratis, riding it in a direct line towards the sea.

The Quratis screeched in terror, realizing where they were headed, yet unable to stop itself as its trajectory was set—to fly straight to its doom. It implored him to stop. Ben reeled under its plea but wouldn't let go. It resisted, trying to pull back.

A large shadow darkened the sky. Ben turned, just in time to see the vile Lifegiver crash into him, shoving him closer to the ocean's surface. The

Quratis plummeted through the air, Ben clinging on to it as a dull numbness spread through his body. The Quratis slashed at the vile Lifegiver with its tail feather, and, to Ben's dismay, the blue creature retracted.

Exhausted, Ben let go for a fraction of a second...

...and the Quratis sensed his weakness. *You tricked me!* Its thousands of ice-cold voices resounded in his mind, raging in surprise, baffled that such an insignificant human could have deceived it.

Ben almost lost his grip.

"Ben," a woman spoke. It was a kind, gentle voice. It filled his heart, making it burst with joy. "Ben! Stay with me. I love you!"

Mom!

Ben's mind flooded with recognition and warmth, his feelings of utter happiness pouring straight into the Quratis who had never known love.

It howled, wanting to thrust Ben aside. Too late: it smashed into the ocean, taking Ben with it. Its brilliant, flaming body reeled at the contact with water. It rolled over itself, struggling to get back up to the surface. Only, Mesmo had dived out of the speeder after it, blocking its way.

Mesmo faced the mighty Quratis, looking at it straight in the eye—no, looking at *Ben*. "I'll take over now, son," Mesmo's voice said through the ocean.

So Ben let go.

* * *

"He's having a seizure!" a voice shouted.

A hand grasped his. "Ben!" That was his mom. "Stay with me!"

A girl's voice spoke from a distance. *Tuli... "They did it! They trapped the Quratis under the ocean!"*

"That's it!" Kimi's voice burst through his thoughts. "This is his escape! You have to heal him *NOW!*"

"Extracting the venom..." Liana spoke beside him, her voice strained. *"Kimi, go and inform Torka!"*

Their voices faded. The grip of the Quratis faded. The monster's filaments tried to grasp whatever they could as they slowly let go. Ben was tired, he wanted to sleep, and a deep void awaited him, welcoming him in its arms. The void would make him forget the scathing marks that the Quratis was leaving behind.

"I'm losing him!" Liana's voice came from far away.

"Ben!" Laura cried. "Don't you dare die on me! Fight back!"

Ben was tired of fighting. The emptiness embraced him, silent and undemanding, sending him deeper and deeper away from the voices. He floated in it, enjoying the calmness and lack of consciousness. There were no monsters with unattainable demands here; no violent births and deaths of star systems; no clashing of atoms or hungry black holes. There was only peace and the pitter-patter of tiny paws. A dog reached his side and lay down beside him. It licked his hand.

Tike, Ben said. *I missed you.*

I missed you, too.

There was a sudden jolt and a loud, rasping sound of metal against metal somewhere far away. People screamed. His mother screamed.

They need you, Tike said.

And I need you! The grinding metal and shouting voices scared him. Ben was safe here, with his terrier.

One day, many years from now, we will be together, Tike said. *But not today.*

I want to stay with you. Nothing will ever replace you.

Tike nudged him. *And nothing will replace me. I will always have a special place in your heart. But now you have made new friends: Mesmo, Kimi, Tuli... And they need you. They are in danger. You must help them.*

Ben's stomach twisted with worry. *But, who will take care of you?*

Someone whistled.

Tike's ears pricked. He got up from Ben's side.

Tike? Ben called, sensing a last burning filament unfurling from his mind.

His dog answered with a bark, then sprinted towards a man. Ben's grandfather gave the dog a good rub.

Ben watched his grandfather and his beloved dog stroll away from him while he remained in this limbo where nothing was expected of him. But now, he felt empty—like something had been ripped from his soul; like he had lost more than his grandfather and his dog.

He hung on to the last shreds of his being. It was not his time yet. He was needed. Resilience washed over him. *Mom! Kimi! They're in danger!* And so he turned and let himself rise towards the terrifying sounds, towards consciousness—and pain.

"He's breathing again!" Liana shouted. A warm, healing sensation crept up Ben's ankle where the snake had bitten him. *"Kimi! What's going on out there?"*

"They've latched on to us!" Kimi shouted.

"Who?"

"Torka says it's the Zul." A sharp noise came to Ben's right. "They're towing us in!"

Ben opened his eyes a crack. It was as if his physical self had been thrown under a bus. Liana's face swam before his eyes.

She stood over him, staring down at him with big, terrified eyes. *"Hang in there!"* she breathed.

"Ben!" Another face came into view.

His heart bulged. He tried to speak but couldn't.

His mother's face was pale, her brow knitted over her green eyes. "Focus on getting better," she said. "We'll protect you."

Protect me? From what?

He glanced out the door.

Hao came running and glanced into the infirmary. "We're being boarded!" he yelled. "Quick! Give me something to defend us with!"

Liana searched desperately around her. *"I... There's nothing..."*

Hao blinked and puffed out his cheeks. "Fine,

then. Lock the door."

"What about you?" Laura cried.

Hao stepped back and glanced from Laura to Ben. "They're coming for him," he warned. "Keep him safe. Just... lock the door."

Ben lurched. "Inspect...!" he croaked, but the man was already gone.

CHAPTER 39 *A Trade*

Ben listened to the chilling sounds coming from the cockpit: grating metal, pounding, fighting. Laura squeezed his arm too hard.

Liana, Kimi and Tuli stood before him, staring at the door, breathing fast.

Ben struggled off the hovering bed, but he was too weak to stand. He tumbled into a sitting position, held up by his mother.

The sounds neared. Dull thuds and cries came from the other side of the door, then silence. The others closed in around Ben.

The doors groaned open, revealing the dark corridor beyond... and Einar. The Norseman stepped into the doorway, staring at them, eyes dark, his pose foreboding. Then he glanced down the corridor, made a gesture, and Toreq soldiers swarmed into the room. A quick and desperate struggle followed, but Ben and his friends were no match. Soon they were overpowered and dragged out of the infirmary, where Ben caught a glimpse of the Inspector's body lying on the floor.

Toreq and humans spilled out into the empty hangar of the warship Zul. Ben could see Daria's multiple speeders whizzing outside the force field that protected them from space, fighting the war that raged beyond. Warships launched strikes at each other; speeders zoomed around at hair-rising speed to avoid being hit. *The Second War of the Kins* was not a war between humans and Toreq— the Toreq had turned against each other!

Then Ben noticed Mesmo's friends: Torka, Panaï, Kaani and Qu'ira. The four were held in place by Daria's soldiers. Kaani had a deep gash on his head.

Daria advanced towards them, followed by a group of Toreq soldiers. The rogue captain stopped and set bitter eyes on them.

Without warning, Einar came up behind Ben and brought him to Daria.

"*You!*" Daria spat. "*You have committed the ultimate crime! You have killed the Quratis! You will pay for this!*"

"It still lives," Tuli spoke from the side, surprising Daria. Tuli's hands glowed, and her eyes were closed. *"It is fighting its last battle against the one you call Mesmo. It does not have long to live."*

Daria jabbed her finger at Ben. *"You will save the Quratis! I order you! Do it now, or I will kick your repugnant friends off the Zul myself!"*

"You will do no such thing." The voice came from behind Ben.

Daria's eyes widened in utter shock. She thrust her three middle fingers to her forehead and bowed deeply. *"General Zoltar!"* she exclaimed. *"You are alive! I feared the worst!"*

Ben strained his neck and gasped.

Zoltar stood in the doorway of the spaceship, leaning heavily on Secretary-General Adhira Prabhakar.

Daria's soldiers hurried to salute their General in the same form.

Zoltar took in the group of Toreq and humans. *"You will release the prisoners,"* he ordered.

The soldiers did so immediately, but Einar backed away, pulling Ben with him.

Daria's jaw dropped. *"General?"* she exclaimed. *"What are you doing? I have everything under control! The Toreq who have sided with*

Mesmo and the boy will soon surrender to me. The core of Mesmo's filthy rebellion lies here at your feet! All that remains is for us to save the Quratis!"

General Zoltar let go of Adhira and made an effort to stand on his own. *"No, Daria. This stops now. You have been misled. Your judgment has been clouded to a level of depravity and wickedness that will put shame on the Toreq for generations to come. I order you to stand down at once!"*

Daria looked utterly perplexed. *"But... General... You are mistaken. I have not been misled... Misled by whom?"*

Zoltar held her gaze. *"By me,"* he said.

Her face clueless, Daria had trouble focusing her eyes on any one person.

General Zoltar spoke to a soldier. *"Grant me access to the fleet. They must hear what I have to say."*

The soldier pulled up a screen from his wrist, typed in some commands, and nodded.

Zoltar spoke. *"This is General Zoltar. I call for a truce. I order you to drop your weapons and listen to what I have to say."* He swayed, and Adhira had to help him straighten up again. *"I have not been able to speak freely in many, many star-rises."* His voice faltered with emotion. *"Since long before our departure from Torequ'ai, I have not been myself. I have been a prisoner, in mind and body, of a terrible monster. A vile creature infiltrated us under the false promise of friendship and wisdom."* He glanced at them. *"Yes, my friends. I have been under the domination of the Quratis."*

Soldiers glanced at each other, frowning.

Zoltar's eyes fell on Ben. *"I would still be a prisoner of the Quratis were it not for the bravery of this one child, my grandson."* He smiled sadly, then placed three fingers to his forehead and bowed at Ben.

"What are you doing?" Daria's voice was thick with horror. *"General Zoltar, what are you saying?"*

Zoltar straightened. *"I am saying, Captain Daria, that every single order I have given you since we travelled through the wormhole was not my own. The Quratis used my skill; spoke and acted through me, and I was powerless to resist."*

His voice turned to ice. *"How could you have believed that I would ever send an assassin after my only son, my granddaughter, or this child? I committed an unforgivable offence every time I did so, and it tore me apart that you would believe and obey my orders."*

Daria's face had gone white. She glanced left-and-right, searching for a way out of her nightmare. *"You... you are not yourself, General,"* she said, taking a step back, followed by Einar. Ben had no choice but to step back, as well. Her hands crackled. *"You... you have fallen under the spell of the A'hmun! There is trickery!"*

"Yes," Zoltar agreed. *"There is trickery. But the trickery comes from the Quratis. It has toyed with us for millennia, from the time when it first appeared to us before The Great War of the Kins. It has whispered words of deceit and stoked hatred and fear through the mouths of the skilled ones. It has used the translation skill to stoke the fires of war. It has set kin against kin for the sole purpose of its evil enjoyment. But no longer will we bow to its depravity!"*

"Stop!" Daria spat. *"You... you lie! I... I believed in you! In your vision! We came to destroy the A'hmun. That is our purpose! That is why the Arch Council sent us here!"*

"No, Daria," Zoltar said quietly. *"You don't understand."* His chin shook. *"The Arch Council did not order us through the wormhole to destroy the A'hmun."* He swallowed and spoke with difficulty. *"It was I who did that."*

It was as if Zoltar had just punched them all in the gut. Not a single person, Toreq or human, moved, floored by his revelation. All eyes were set on Zoltar.

"It's true," Zoltar said sadly. *"When the Quratis arrived on the Mother Planet and found me, it was but a shadow. Yet, through me, it convinced the Arch Council to send my grand-daughter Kaia to Earth. It did not want another translation skill in its vicinity that could have uncovered its treachery. The Quratis placed words in my mouth that sent my grand-daughter to her death. Then, as the Quratis strengthened its grip on me and realized that the assassin I had sent after my son and my grand-daughter was dead, it knew it had to come itself... The Arch Council never ordered me to invade the A'hmun. I did that myself, under the constraint of the Quratis. I was weak. I am sorry."*

Daria wailed. She took another step back. *"But you... you made me do all these things! You... you made me turn against my kind!"*

Zoltar looked at her with pity. *"I did not have to convince you. Your mind was already set. You have always been the most dutiful, obedient soldier I have ever known, unconditionally following the orders from your superiors. And the Quratis knew that. That is why it chose to use you."*

Daria roared and flung a massive blow of electricity at Zoltar. Panaï flung himself forward, thrusting the deadly blow aside with his power.

"Seize him!" Daria yelled, pointing at Zoltar.

Zoltar cried, *"Stand down, Daria! As your General, I order you to obey!"*

Soldiers glanced around, baffled, not knowing who to follow. A few detached themselves from the group and ran to protect Daria.

Einar pulled Ben away with him towards the elevator.

"Ben!" Laura cried in alarm.

Ben struggled, but the Norseman was too strong, and he, too weakened by his ordeal.

"You leave me no choice!" Daria cried, lashing out at Zoltar's soldiers. Then she ran behind her men to dive into the elevator behind Einar. The doors slid shut, and the elevator rose.

Spots swam before Ben's eyes, and he almost lost consciousness. Einar had to hold on to him and half-carry, half-drag him to the warship's main bridge, where Daria sent the remaining crew scrambling in all directions.

"Seal the bridge!" she ordered the few soldiers who had followed her. She hurried to the main controls and began steering the warship away from the other ships.

"Where are you going?" Einar demanded.

"To save the Quratis," she said, sending

goosebumps up Ben's arms. *"My people will hail me as a hero if I save our sacred creature."*

"But... what about what Zoltar just said about the Quratis?" Einar wanted to know.

Daria snorted. *"You don't really believe that foolishness, do you?"*

"It's true!" Ben said weakly, feeling sick to the stomach. *"The Quratis only wants to cast death and destruction around it. You can't let it get away with this!"*

"Silence, boy," Daria snarled. She glanced at Einar. *"We head for Earth."*

"Daria!" Einar warned. *"The ship won't hold during an entrance into the Earth's atmosphere. It's too damaged!"*

"It will hold." Daria had become incredibly calm. There was a pause, then she glanced out of the corner of her eyes and spoke words that turned Ben's blood cold. *"We're going to make a little trade."*

CHAPTER 40 *Letting Go*

The Zul lurched and nosed down, taking Laura and the others by surprise. Something must have destabilized the warship's gravity because instead of levelling out, the whole floor of the hangar tipped.

"Let me go!" Laura yelled at Torka, who was holding her back so she couldn't go after Ben.

"Ben!" Kimi wailed, struggling in Qu'ira and Liana's grasp.

They were beginning to slide across the slanted floor, the spaceship grinding behind them.

"We have to go!" Zoltar yelled. *"Get back on the ship, quickly!"*

"No!" Laura sobbed.

A speeder crashed into the side of the

warship, sliding over the hangar in a ball of fire. The force field protecting them from space flickered.

"Into the spaceship, NOW!" Zoltar bellowed.

Half-aided, half-pulled by Torka, Laura found herself in the spaceship once more, heat from the burning speeder hot against her cheeks.

Kimi threw herself into Laura's arms, and they watched, helpless, as the door to the spaceship slid shut, cutting them off from Ben.

"Torka!" Zoltar cried. *"The Zul is falling apart. Get us out of here!"*

"Yes, General," Torka said, sweat rolling down his face.

* * *

Deep in the ocean, the Quratis slammed into a wall of ice, sending a shockwave through Mesmo's arms as he tried to hold the solid barrier before him. The Quratis retracted, preparing for another onslaught, desperately trying to find a way out of Mesmo's icy prison under the ocean—one Mesmo kept having to rebuild every time the bird smashed into it and cracked it.

Mesmo's water skill gushed out of him, taking

every ounce of energy he had left in him, for, even after Ben and the Lifegiver's attack, the Quratis still had enough strength to do some damage.

The Quratis knew it was fighting its last battle, and that gave it a desperate, dangerous strength that sent it into a frenzied dance within the ice that closed in around it.

Mesmo held his ground, and after some time, the Quratis began to lose its sheen; its golden, fire-coloured feathers withered, its size diminished, until, finally, the celestial monster gave up and retracted into itself, whimpering.

Mesmo watched for a moment, floating in the depths of the ocean, as the light from the Quratis faded.

Mesmo cast aside the ice and gathered up the afflicted creature, which was now the size of a cat, and sped towards the surface. In a last-ditch effort, he created a platform of ice close to his speeder so that he could drag himself up. He rolled onto his back, breathing heavily, then opened his eyes to see a darkening sky.

Above him, fire descended upon the ocean. The Zul entered the Earth's atmosphere at full speed, oblivious to the damage it could incur, yet, by some miracle, coming to an unsteady standstill four storeys above Mesmo. It covered half the sky.

It was severely damaged: the blast from the bomb, the dent from something large crashing into it, the fires burning in random places and holes like open wounds, spitting out precious fuels that kept the warship in the air.

Mesmo quickly rolled over and struggled to his feet. A wide door slid open in the warship, revealing a barely visible Daria, Einar and—Mesmo's heart skipped a beat—the Norseman held Ben in his grasp, dangerously close to the edge...

Daria's hair and cape billowed in the wind. She did not speak until she was sure he understood the situation. *"The Quratis..."* she yelled, *"in exchange for the boy."*

Mesmo stared, horrified at the height of the warship. Ben would not survive such a fall.

No sooner had she spoken than Daria sent down a hollow drone, big enough to contain the Quratis.

Mesmo glanced at the warship, gritting his teeth. He knew that once he handed over the Quratis, Ben would be at their mercy.

Einar stepped closer to the edge, his arm wrapped around Ben's neck.

"All right," Mesmo yelled. He bent to pick up the Quratis, breathing fast. He lifted the creature in his arms and raised it, then froze in utter terror.

Ben had grabbed Einar's arm. He bit into it, hard. Einar howled, letting go, and Ben tumbled over the edge.

* * *

Air smashed against Ben's body, sending him spinning towards the ocean. It only lasted a few seconds—enough to make his stomach reel—then he slammed into the Lifegiver.

The stunning blue creature swooped under him, catching him on its back and enveloping him in a layer of soft feathers.

Ben humphed, having barely enough strength in his muscles to pull himself up into a safer position on the bird's back. Trembling, he realized what he had just accomplished. He'd seen the Lifegiver swooping through the clouds, staying out of sight so Daria and Einar wouldn't notice it. He'd waited for a chance to act, confident that Tuli had been watching through the eyes of the Lifegiver.

Now he crouched atop the bird, hanging on tightly. Blue filaments from the Lifegiver unfurled around him and held him in place so he wouldn't fall off.

He wasn't afraid. Contrary to the Quratis, the

Lifegiver spread a sense of protection around him, making him feel secure.

The massive bird turned back and headed straight for the warship.

Ben grasped tightly.

It spread its wings vertically, hurling itself with its full weight into the front of the warship, tearing with its mighty claws at the main bridge. It backed away and struck again and again, with Ben hanging on for dear life.

Agonizing sounds ripped through the warship. Explosions detonated across its hull, catapulting loose pieces and smoke into the sky. Ben yelled, shutting his eyes and leaning down as flat as he could, while flames burst over his head.

Then the Lifegiver broke through the chaos and rose into the sky, watching the result of its onslaught.

The Zul fell towards its doom, crashing into the ocean in a mixture of skyrocketing smoke and water. Huge waves sped away from the drowning ship.

Ben scanned the surface of the water worriedly, searching for Mesmo. He found his father clinging on to a large slab of ice, drifting away from his hovering speeder.

The Lifegiver swooped down and landed on

the ice, which swayed heavily up-and-down with each wave. Ben lay there with his eyes shut, concentrating on remaining conscious until the waves settled.

"Benjamin!"

Ben opened his eyes and found Mesmo peeking over the Lifegiver's wing at him. He couldn't move. A deep feeling of being broken inside—that he had lost something of himself within the void—overwhelmed him. He unfurled his grasp, finding torn pieces of blue feathers stuck to his palms from having gripped so hard.

"Son," Mesmo said gently, reaching out for him. He pulled Ben by the arm, letting the boy slide down the bird's wing. Then, Mesmo wrapped him in his arms.

Ben swung between consciousness and darkness. He grasped the edge of Mesmo's cape, letting the soft material guide him back to awareness. When his sight stabilized, he whispered, "Wanna do that again?"—he asked this without a trace of humour.

Mesmo's eyes widened. "You..." he said, jabbing a finger at him. "You..." He shook his head, unable to find the words, and Ben knew they were both too stunned by awareness of all that could have gone wrong. Instead, Mesmo said, "I'm sorry

I didn't listen to you, son. I will never doubt you again, I promise."

Ben shut his eyes for a moment, then managed to say, "I like the sound of that."

* * *

Torka's spaceship descended from the sky, coming to a hovering standstill beside the ice. A whole group of people spilled out of it: Laura, Zoltar, Kimi, Jeremy, Adhira, Torka, Panaï, Kaani, Qu'ira, Liana and Tuli. Hao was not among them.

"Ben!" Laura rushed to his side and hugged him. "I'm never letting you out of my sight, ever again!" she said, making Ben smile in agreement.

He glanced at Mesmo, who wrapped his arms around both of them.

Humans and Toreq shook hands; some hugged, others slapped each other on the back.

By the time Mesmo released Ben and Laura, Tuli had retrieved the Quratis—or what remained of it. It looked like an ugly, deformed duckling with closed eyelids over bulging eyeballs. Wrinkled feathers dropped out of its skin. Tuli held it out before her.

Zoltar's eyes became hard as he stared at the sad sight. *"We looked up to you and admired you, but you abused our trust. Never again will you cause harm.”* He picked up the limp body from Tuli's hand, intent on dumping it into the sea.

"Wait!" Ben said.

Zoltar looked at him.

"Let it go."

Zoltar's mouth dropped.

Ben pressed on. "At *The Great Gathering*, the animals told me they were willing to give humans a second chance." He pointed at the Quratis. "I want to give the Quratis a second chance, too."

Zoltar shook his head. "But, child, it's too dangerous. After everything we've been through, you, more than anyone, should know that!"

Ben thought about the bird's feelings of loneliness, out in the depths of space, watching others love and hate, laugh and cry, live and die, being together, while it always remained alone. He struggled to stand and held out a hand, where Zoltar placed the ugly creature. It rolled into a ball, trembling.

Ben held it up towards the blue Lifegiver. He spoke out loud. "How about it, Lifegiver? Will you teach it?"

The Lifegiver bent down and peered at the Quratis.

Tuli stepped forward with her hands glowing.

She seemed taller, somehow. Older, too. Ben wondered why he had thought she resembled Kaia when this was clearly not the case. She smiled. *"Yes, the Lifegiver will nurture the Quratis. We will take it with us. It will be cared for until it is time for it to return to its galaxy."* She took the Quratis from Ben, her body expanding and towering over him.

The blue Lifegiver spread its wings, and as it took flight, it lessened in size so it could land on her shoulder. The beautiful blue wings folded and the creature wrapped around Tuli's back, turning into a long, white braid with a brilliant peacock feather at its end.

"You have made a wise choice, Ben Archer," Tuli said, her voice sounding like the wind. Tiny, bright sparks travelled around her body, as the planets would around the Sun. *"The Quratis is connected to the black hole from whence it came. Had you destroyed it, it would have caused the black hole to rupture, incurring catastrophic damage within its galaxy. We doubt the planet of the Toreq would have survived."*

Ben's jaw dropped. "And you hadn't thought of telling me this before?"

Tuli smiled. *"Had we told you before, would you have risked overpowering the Quratis the way you did?"*

Ben fell silent.

Tuli bent down and kissed the top of his head. *"Thank you for having been our friend, for a short time."* She turned to Kimi. *"Take good care of him."*

"I would like to be your friend, too," Kimi said. "You can take friendship with you, wherever you go."

Tuli made a little bow. *"Friends, then."* More and more sparks whirled around her body, and she began to fade.

"Will we see you again?" Ben asked.

"We are not sure our people would allow it." She smiled. *"But in a Universe where anything is possible, perhaps rules are meant to be broken."* She raised her hand in farewell, her body bursting into a million spots of stardust that rose into the sky.

* * *

They laid High Inspector James Hao to rest on the ice. Mesmo and Torka created a dazzling coffin of frozen water that caught the sunlight. They let the slab drift off with the currents, and Ben and Laura followed it with their eyes until they could no longer see it.

Captain Olin arrived with the Wise Ones, and

it was decided that the Toreq would return to their remaining warships, which were the Ob and the Maq. The Zul and the Qu'Tué had been destroyed, whereas the Codo was beyond repair and would be left to crash on the Moon. The Toreq would heal their wounded and set up a base on Saturn's moon, Enceladus. There, they would deliberate what to do next: wait to return home, observe humans from a distance, or be more daring and reveal themselves, to help humans better themselves. But first, they would need time to get over the shock of having fought among each other.

The Wise Ones would return home but were willing to hear from Mesmo about how they could help.

Zoltar took off his General's cape, saying he could no longer lead the fleet. Even if he had not been in charge of his actions for a long time, he could not forgive himself for what he had done. He vowed to go back to his roots: to heal Earth's animals and protect them. He gave his cape to Captain Olin.

Mesmo took off his own cape and gave it to Torka. His friend accepted it, his eyes becoming grave and proud under the weight of responsibility.

"I cannot return to the fleet, either," Mesmo said. *"I can no longer be the neutral Observer. That*

title no longer belongs to me." He smiled at Laura and Ben, then added, *"I have to take care of my family now."* He glanced at his Toreq friends and said, *"It would be best if you declared me and my father dead. The rest of the fleet is not yet ready to accept a mingling of species. Let us hope that one day that will change."*

Mesmo bid farewell to his friends, then he, Ben, Laura, Adhira, Kimi, Jeremy and Zoltar took their place in the spaceship, which Torka had left them, along with Mesmo's speeder. *"...so you can practice your exit race,"* Torka had said.

They flew off in silence, hovering for a moment above the remains of the Zul that hadn't yet sunk into the ocean.

"Do you think Daria and Einar survived?" Laura asked Mesmo, making Ben jolt upright.

"No, I don't," Mesmo answered, wrapping his arm around her shoulders.

Ben relaxed and leaned against Kimi, sitting at the back of the spaceship, and watched his mother and father embrace while Echis appeared and slid into his hoodie.

A clicking sound made Mesmo and Laura turn around.

Jeremy had his camera pointed at them. "Don't mind me," he said, fidgeting awkwardly.

Adhira joined them. "You know you won't be able to publish a single one of those pictures, don't you?"

Jeremy gawked at her.

Adhira took the camera from his hands. "The Earth is not yet ready for an alien encounter. Countries will be too busy surviving the climate catastrophes that hit them. I'm not even sure they will have had time to look up at the stars and notice the battle that took place there. Many conspiracy theories will circulate, no doubt, but humans will focus on rebuilding first, and I, for one, will do everything I can to make sure that happens in a balanced way."

She patted Jeremy on the arm. "You may accompany me on my mission, if you wish, as my appointed aid. I will give you exclusivity in all my meetings with world leaders."

Jeremy's mouth opened and closed like that of a fish. "Uh... Thank you... I think," he said, looking longingly at his camera.

Adhira turned to Zoltar. "I could use your help too, Zoltar. World leaders will need to prepare to receive your people one day. It will be to everyone's advantage for things to run smoothly next time."

Zoltar paused to think. "Only if you promise

to show me your planet's most beautiful gardens along the way," he said.

Ben smiled to himself, then dropped his head on his friend's shoulder.

"Kimi?" he said.

"Hmm?"

"I have no idea how you got here, but I'm glad you did," he mumbled, before falling into a deep sleep.

EPILOGUE

Ben woke in his bed, tucked under a thick, warm duvet. He stretched and blinked. There was something in the air, a faint smell that he knew well. He jumped out of bed, ignoring the cold morning, and threw his drapes open. Snowflakes drifted before his face. A thick layer of snow blanketed the cornfields.

"C'mon, Echis!" he burst with glee, dressing in a hurry and taking the viper out of its warm box. He rushed down the stairs with the snake in his hands, then clumsily put on his winter jacket.

"Up you go," he told Echis, sending the snake into the jacket hoodie. He rushed past the kitchen. "Morning, Mom," he called as he passed. He reached to grab a steaming waffle from a plate filled with the dessert.

Laura slapped him on the back of the hand. "Hey!" she scolded. "Breakfast isn't ready yet. Call your dad, would you? He's out by the maple tree."

"'kay," he said, snatching a waffle from the plate as soon as his mom had her back turned again.

"And don't forget your scarf and glo..." she shouted after him, but Ben was already out the back door, stuffing the waffle in his mouth in three big bites. He went to greet Nutmeg in her new stable like he did every morning since he'd come home. He made sure the horse was fed, then he took his dog, Buddy, for a run in the fields, enjoying the crunching sound of fresh snow on the ground.

He found Mesmo under the large maple tree, just as his mother had said he would. Mesmo had used his skill to melt the snow around him and was now sitting on a patch of dry grass.

Ben sat beside him and found himself in a transparent bubble that the snowflakes could not reach. Echis slithered out of his hoodie.

"You wanted to see snow," Ben told the snake. "Take a look around, but stay close. You're not made for this weather." He paused. "And remember we're taking you home after breakfast."

The snake didn't answer.

Ben sighed and lay down with his arms crossed behind his head, watching the snowflakes dance down from the sky. Mesmo lay beside him, munching on a long piece of dry grass.

They stayed like that for quite some time, then Mesmo reached out his glowing hand, capturing snowflakes. He winced, pulled back, and handed something to Ben. "It's not perfect," he said, dropping a snow crystal in Ben's hand. "And it's a bit late, but happy fourteenth birthday, son."

"Thanks!" Ben breathed, turning the ice crystal over in his hand and noticing it was twisted and uneven. He smiled sadly, glancing at his dad's hands. "Do you think they will ever fully heal?"

Mesmo stroked the palms of his hand with his fingers. "They'll be fine," he said. "Liana said to give it some time."

Ben needed to believe this was true. Buddy came to lie down beside him and placed his head on his chest. Ben stroked the dog's ears.

"Dad?" he said.

"Hmm?"

"What are we going to do now?"

Still looking at the sky, Mesmo spoke with the blade of grass stuck to the corner of his mouth. "We start from the beginning," he answered. "Our mission hasn't changed. We'll take it one step at a time, one change at a time..." He paused, glancing at Ben. "If you still feel up to it, that is."

Ben offered him a half-smile, still patting Buddy.

When he didn't answer, Mesmo frowned. "What?" he said. "Is something the matter?"

Ben felt a hole open up in the pit of his stomach, and he remembered the feeling of loss when he cast the Quratis from his mind. "It's just that..."—he bit his lip—"I've been meaning to tell you..."

"What?"

He could barely get the words out. "I think I might be losing the skill."

The blade of grass fell from Mesmo's mouth.

Ben looked at Buddy. "It's true," he said sadly, lifting his hands before his face. A faint blue glow appeared around his fingers, then vanished. "I think the Quratis damaged it." He sighed. "And maybe that's a good thing. It had become too powerful."

Mesmo kept staring at him. "Benjamin..." he whispered, his voice laden with concern. "I think you're mistaken. I mean, I saw you use the skill to speak in the Toreq language after the Zul crashed."

Ben shook his head. "That's the thing. I wasn't using the skill, then." He reached behind his ear and pulled off a small black dot from his skin to show Mesmo.

"A Toreq translation device!" Mesmo exclaimed, taking it from Ben. "How long have you had this?"

Ben sat up and crossed his arms over his knees. "Since before the Toreq trial," he said. "I was afraid of what I could do with the skill, so I asked my attorney to give me a translation device so I wouldn't need to rely on the skill as much. I still used the skill to speak with animals, of course; in your father's garden on the Ob, at *The Great Gathering*... But when the Quratis let me go, I felt the skill weaken within me. And since then, I've struggled to talk to Echis, Buddy and Nutmeg."

Mesmo sat up. "What about Tuli and the Lifegiver? You communicated with them before they left, didn't you?"

Ben shook his head. "I never used the skill to communicate with Tuli or the Lifegiver. I simply spoke to them the way I speak to you now."

Mesmo stared at him. "Why didn't you tell me before?"

Ben shrugged. "I wasn't sure. I thought maybe I was still recovering." He pressed his cheek against his knee. "Let's hope I'm wrong, and both our skills are on the mend."

Mesmo reached out and clasped Ben's hand.

"Anyway," Ben continued, looking at the damage on his dad's skin. "I came to realize something."

"What's that?"

Ben glanced up. "Skill or no skill, the mission remains the same, just like you said. We take it one step at a time, one change at a time. Kimi is rallying young people together around our cause; your father and Adhira are addressing world leaders. The Wise Ones have offered their knowledge; organizations like the one we donated money to are trying to save the rainforest... There are many others out there who are doing their part." Ben smiled. "You see, Dad, skill or no skill, we are no longer alone."

THE LOST SPACE TREASURE SERIES. BOOK 1
EXOSTAR
FROM BESTSELLING AUTHOR
RAE KNIGHTLY

K E P R A - 2
INDEPENDENT PLANET
MAGNUS STAR CLUSTER
MILKY WAY GALAXY
INTEREST: NONE.

CHAPTER 1 *The Identity Problem*

Trinket came into existence when she was six years old. There weren't many other ways to put it. One minute she didn't exist; the next, her eyes flew open, and there she lay on a hard table, the Old Scientist peering down his long nose at her with his thick eyebrows drawn together. It was as if a switch had been activated.

Six years later, she still didn't know who or *what* she was. *A piece of scrap.* That's what a rude cyborg in the town of Axiopolis had yelled at her a little over an hour ago.

I'm not *a piece of scrap,* she thought

vehemently for probably the hundredth time. She kicked at a pebble and watched it roll down the barren hillside toward the town.

Piece of scrap, piece of scrap...

"I'm *not* a piece of scrap," she snapped, as if saying it out loud would silence the taunting voice in her head. "I don't care what they say. I'm *not* a botched machine created by a mad scientist! I'm... I'm... er... Trin... *Moonrise*." She kicked stubbornly at another pebble, then listened.

Her inner voice didn't respond.

"All right, then." She spoke with renewed determination, turning her back on Axiopolis and limping up the steep hill towards the Old Scientist's shack. "So, how about it? I'm Trin Moonrise, fourteen years old." She repeated the name, testing its sound. Moonrise was a common family name in Axiopolis. She might get away with it.

Whether a sophisticated android or a mortal being, Trinket guessed that she was the equivalent of a twelve-year-old girl. But twelve wasn't old enough to fulfill her plan. Twelve was too young to get her off-world.

She thought up some more names. "How about Trin *Astera*, thirteen years old?" Loose gravel rolled under her right foot, and she stumbled forward, catching herself from falling just in time by stretching out her hands. She straightened, then wiped her fingerless gloves together to remove the ochre-colored dust that clung to them. She leaned over to check on her prosthetic leg. "Hey, Champ, don't you dare give up on me today." She eyed the carbon fiber frame, which clung to her left leg stump, tapping the sturdy material for good measure, and found it intact.

Oblivious to her situation, a muffled voice—a *real* voice this time—spoke close to her ear. "What is Champ? Please define *Champ*."

"Forget it, Empty. It's not important." Trinket adjusted her Mass Transfer Device around her ear before placing it snuggly under her scarf headband. Aside from her prosthetic leg, the articulate device was the one other thing she couldn't afford to lose. It was an old-fashioned adult model that didn't have the malleable option to adapt to the wearer's ear. It was a bit too big for her.

Trinket had found the Mass Transfer Device in a junk pile two years ago after it had no doubt been cast away in favor of a more modern version. Or perhaps the previous owner—most likely on the run from the Interstellar Alliance Law Enforcement—had wanted to get rid of the last thing tying them to their identity.

People called these mini information devices

MTs for short. Trinket hadn't expected this old model to contain much information, so she had nicknamed it **EM**p**T**y.

At first, the name Empty had been a bit of a joke. Only, over the years, Empty had become the closest thing she'd had to a friend, and the name had become more than just a silly word. She knew it was a fancy computer devoid of feelings, but the fact that it didn't have personality modes like the newer models suited her. Empty never got angry, never judged her, and was always there when she needed it.

"Please repeat," the device insisted, the male voice now loud and clear in her ear. "Define *Champ.*"

"Give me a break, Empty," Trinket grunted, plowing forward despite her near-fall. "It's just a nickname I came up with for my prosthetic leg. It's short for *champion.*"

Empty disagreed. "*Champ* is not an appropriate name for your prosthetic leg. *Champ* is deteriorating fast and must be replaced on the planet Kepra-1 as soon as possible. Your Shuttle to Kepra-1 leaves Space Central in sixty-three-point-two local planetary hours. You must input your final identification details into my core memory prior to that."

Trinket rolled her eyes. "As if I didn't know."

Travelers had to be older than twelve and own an ear device linked to their name before they were allowed off-world without adult supervision, whether it be an official MT Device or a mediocre, unofficial copy that Non-Alliance aliens nicknamed *plugs*. Empty was the real deal, however—a device manufactured by the Interstellar Alliance mega-corporation MADAT Inc. itself!

Trinket had cracked Empty's core memory and removed the previous owner's details—something she would never have achieved in a newer model. Now she just had to input a new identity—if only she could decide which name would provide her the safest passage.

As if reminding her of the urgency of her task, a distant roar made the ground rumble under her feet. She gazed at the horizon to the East and watched as the daily Shuttle to Kepra-1 left Space Central. It shot up from the ground, its powerful thrusters pushing it through the heavy atmosphere in a wide arc. It would soon join Kepra-1, which was rising in the distance, the planet's outline warped by the heat.

Trinket sighed. Within two days, she would be on that Shuttle, heading for a better life. It was the only way she could save her prosthetic leg—and the little orphan boy.

She just needed to pick up one last thing from the Old Scientist's home.

She glanced up the hill. She still had a fifteen-minute climb before reaching the rundown shack. *Might as well make the most of it.* "All right, Empty. Let's try that again. Initiate Shuttle Security questions." She grimaced, resuming her hike and trying to ignore the tiny but persistent creaking sound of the rusting screw in her metal leg.

"Very well," Empty said. "State your name."

Piece of scra— "Trin Moonrise!" she blurted out, then held her breath. Her inner voice quietened, but she could almost sense it lurking in the back of her mind, waiting for an opportunity to provoke her. "I'd better avoid the name *Astera*," she told Empty, trying to steer away from her inner struggles and focus on her identity problem. "It's the name of a local mobster family. It could get me into trouble."

"Indeed," Empty replied, never missing a beat. "Trin Moonrise, then, state your age."

"Fou… Oh, *quarks!* Thirteen." She was taller than most children her age, but fourteen was probably stretching it a bit, and could lead to questions.

"State your city and planet of residency."

"Axiopolis. Kepra-2."

"State your city and planet of destination."

"Omopolis. Kepra-1."

"What is the nature of your visit to Omopolis?"

Trinket had to think about that one. "Great question, Empty!" she praised the device.

"Thank you, Trin. What is the nature of your visit to Omopolis?"

Trinket grinned. Empty was playing the part of Shuttle Security very well. She hesitated for a second and declared the first thing that came to mind. "I have been sent to Omopolis to buy clothing and medical supplies for the orphans of Axiopolis." Then, she caught herself.

What am I doing, using the orphans like that? She was about to abandon them. Who would shield them from Stinge, their caretaker? Who would keep them out of the mines? Who would tell them bedtime stories? She knew they were old enough to fend for themselves, but still—

"Remnant military spacecraft approaching," Empty spoke in her ear.

—it didn't feel right. She had just used the orphans to— "Hold it! *WHAT?*"

Empty repeated patiently, "Remnant military

spacecraft approaching. It is coming in from a south-easterly direction. Estimated flyover time: ten seconds."

Trinket reeled. *A Remnant aircraft? Here?*

She glanced around hurriedly. The hillside was dry and sun-beaten, except for some distant boulders beyond, which followed a precipice that fell into the sea. There was also a single dead tree a short distance away. Forgetting to be careful, she leaped toward it and plunged into its shadow. This time, her prosthetic leg twisted from under her, and she landed hard on her side. "Ouch!" Her metal leg had loosened from her stump and now lay at an angle. Heart thumping, she pulled it in quickly, so it would be out of sight.

Just in time.

A dark cylindrical spacecraft emerged from over the south-eastern mountains, lifting a trail of dust as it swooped past her and disappeared behind the top of the hill she had been trying to reach.

Trinket coughed into the end of her scarf headband, blinking against the swirling particles. "The Remnants!" she gasped. "What are they doing here?"

"I don't know the answer to that question," Empty stated. "But that's a Class One Remnant spacecraft. And the only Class One Remnant spacecraft on Kepra-2 belongs to—"

"—Count Solomon Drakir!" she finished, tensing. "That can't be good." What could have attracted these cruel invaders to the area?

She glanced up the remainder of the hill, blinking rapidly. "Let me get my leg back on properly. Then we're going to find out what the Remnants are doing in my house, Empty!"

"That's no longer your house, Trin. The Old Scientist is dead. And proceeding is not recommended," Empty advised. "The probability that you will get caught by the Remnants and sent to the mines is high. And the probability that they will kill you is even higher."

"Right," Trinket agreed, gritting her teeth. "And when did that ever stop me?"

CONTINUE READING:
Exostar
(The Lost Space Treasure Series, Book 1)

PREQUEL:
Read the prequel to The Alien Skill Series,
The Great War of the Kins:
www.raeknightly.com

Visit www.raeknightly.com

Get discounted bundles.

Subscribe to 'Rae Knightly's Stellar Newsletter'

https://www.amazon.com/dp/1989605311

Discover other books.

Get an autograph from the author.

About the Author

Rae Knightly invites the young reader on a journey into the imagination, where science fiction and fantasy blend into the real world. Young heroes are taken on gripping adventures full of discovery and story twists.

Rae Knightly lives in Vancouver with her husband and two children. The breathtaking landscapes of British Columbia have inspired her to write *The Alien Skill Series*.

Follow Rae Knightly on social media:
Facebook/Instagram/TikTok/YouTube/Substack
E-mail: rae@raeknightly.com

Acknowledgments

Special thanks to author Cristy Watson for being a guiding star throughout *The Alien Skill Series*. Special thanks to Giselle Schneider and Paul Hill for their in-depth comments of the story. To D'artagnan Maciel for providing cultural feedback.

The Alien Skill Series is a team effort. As a self-published author, I could not have produced a quality story without the help of a professional book cover designer (thank you, Roger Despi), beta readers, ARC-readers, and a supportive writing community.

And finally, a special thank you to you, Ben Archer fans, for taking the time to read *Ben Archer and the Toreq Son*.

Thank you!
Rae Knightly